ISLAND PURSUIT

THE ISLAND ESCAPE SERIES, BOOK 2

R. T. WOLFE

ePublishingWorks!
love what you read.

Book and cover design by eBook Prep
www.ebookprep.com

August, 2019
ISBN: 978-1-64457-087-6

ePublishing Works!
644 Shrewsbury Commons Ave
Ste 249
Shrewsbury PA 17361
United States of America

www.epublishingworks.com
Phone: 866-846-5123

Special thanks to Suzi Fox and Kathy Doddridge of Anna Maria Island Turtle Watch & Shorebird Monitoring, EMT, Matt Cummings, and Jim & Val Winkler for their expertise with diving.

ONE

Willow faced the Gulf as an orange-tinted sky ignited the
horizon. The long, lazy waves of her hair whipped over her
bare shoulders and down her back. Like magic, the water transformed from pitch black to deep, serene blue.

Warm waves caressed her ankles, immersing her feet deep into
the sand. It reminded her of the strong draw she had to this island
she loved, and how impossible it would be for her to pull anchor and
leave the land, the sea, her friends and her family. Closing her eyes,
she lifted her chin and filled her lungs with the coastal air. This. This
was her peace, her life energy. The water left her ankles in a rush,
much like the danger that had faced her family.

Her arms hung still at her sides as daybreak coaxed Ibis Island
alive. Nearly all the human inhabitants remained behind the closed
doors of their homes or rented condos. Most of the winged and
four-legged inhabitants, however, did not. Shore birds dodged in
and out with the waves. Ghost crabs and coons scurried to their
burrows after a long night of hunting.

"Mom, you're falling behind," Willow's daughter yelled from
down the beach. "Again!"

The corners of Willow's mouth curled. She turned in the direction of Chloe's six-year-old annoyed voice. Grabbing her grandma with one hand, Chloe pointed inland with the other. Harmony Clearwater wouldn't allow just anyone to pull her around. Chloe's blonde locks bounced as she dragged her grandmother toward a row of dunes. Turtle tracks. It was time for Willow's other peace. Protecting the sea turtles.

She pulled her shoulder bag higher and made her way toward the two of them. As she walked along the edge of the water, Willow noticed her mother gesture to a spot near a cluster of sea oats. Chloe leaped and ran, keeping her distance from the potential nest of between eighty and a hundred and fifty ping-pong ball-sized eggs. Would her daughter ever tire of this? Willow hadn't.

Before Willow made it to where they stood, her mother lifted the tablet used for logging Turtle Watch data and announced, "False crawl." Regardless, it needed to be recorded.

Yes, Willow nodded as she stepped closer. No bowl or oval-shaped markings. No scattered sand the turtle would have thrown to conceal the nest. Chloe dragged her small feet, destroying the long line of flipper tracks leading inland and back so other Turtle Watch volunteers wouldn't stop to investigate. Her daughter's knowledge and young expertise added yet another slice to Willow's peace pie.

Her mother slid a hand through Willow's arm.

"You only snuggle up to me when you want something," Willow said, glancing at her from the corner of her eye.

Her mother dipped her head. "I think you and Raine should go see Detective Osborne and ask why we haven't gotten Seth's remains back yet."

So much for peace. Air filled Willow's lungs, but this time, the deep inhale was followed by a heavy sigh. Seth. Her brother. Her murdered brother.

She turned toward a spot in the sand that seemed to move. It was most likely another ghost crab.

"The arson burns aren't even healed yet on Zoe's arms."

"Chief Roberts was caught red-handed," her mother added, wiping her hand down the long gray-blonde ponytail she always wore.

It was useless to argue, yet Willow did. "Dane's home has yet to be razed."

"There is no need for them to keep Seth's remains from us any longer." Her mother rotated toward the water and yelled to Chloe, "Now, stop that, dear."

Chloe ran, ignoring her grandmother, and scattered a group of Ibis.

"Don't disturb their feeding," she added. "You should know better than that."

Willow placed her hand on her mother's shoulder. "Mom, wait. She does know better." Together, they watched as Chloe snatched a discarded bag of bread from the sand before continuing her job of wiping away turtle tracks.

Through the proudest of grins, Willow said, "She also knows that human food like bread keeps the birds from the true nourishment they need. I have a beach yoga class at 7 a.m. and Pilates at 8 a.m. I can drop Chloe off at your place and head to the St. Pete's Police Department after that. Since Zoe actually mentioned something about her camera locked up in the evidence room as well, I'll ask her first."

"You've got yourself so busy." Her mother paused, then shook her head. "Sometimes what you're missing is right under your nose."

The movement from the sand erupted. It was no ghost crab. "Chloe! Mom!" Willow yelled as she spotted the first tiny flipper, then the sun as it lifted from the horizon. "Chloe, go to the car and get the bucket. Run! Mom, call Raine."

Her mother eyed a nearby flock of gulls. "We don't need Raine. We can handle this on our own."

The sand bubbled like boiling water. Willow's heart both cringed with fear and swelled with excitement. Daylight was upon them.

Hatchlings, each about the size of a silver dollar, scurried out of the sand like ants scattering from a sudden rainfall. This was a surprise nest, unmarked and tucked between the sea oats. A gull landed nearby, eyeing the hatchlings, then Willow. "Don't even think about it," Willow growled.

3

She spotted Chloe as she sprinted from the beach access where Willow had parked the four-wheeler. Sheesh, her little legs were quick. Baby turtles scampered around Willow's feet and over her toes as they raced to the water. The first bird swooped as Willow's mother ran, tiptoeing around hatchlings, yet waving her arms and yelling obscenities like a madwoman. Willow would have taken out her phone and videotaped if tiny lives weren't in danger.

Chloe came with the bucket, dropped to her knees by the babies, and hesitated. She looked to Willow with the biggest of blue eyes.

Willow answered Chloe's unspoken question. "To hell with regulation." State law may allow only certified volunteers permission to handle hatchlings, but this was life and death. As her mother waved off the growing number of birds, Willow and Chloe gently tossed hatchlings into the bucket.

The sound of opening patio doors and curious voices came from the other side of the sea grass-covered dunes. Willow's mother likely woke the families with her shouting. The first few hatchlings made it to the water as Willow and Chloe gathered and pitched the toddling brothers and sisters into the bucket. She couldn't help but count as she tossed. Fifty-six, Fifty-seven. Occupational habit.

From the corner of her eye, something large and blue flapped in the wind. Her mother had graduated from waving hands to waving a large piece of cloth to swat away the birds. After a double-take, Willow winced and noted the piece of cloth was her mother's shirt. At least she'd worn a bra that day.

Two curious families came running from their rentals to find a six-year-old and a Turtle Watch volunteer chucking sea turtle hatchlings into a bucket as a topless, middle-aged woman waved her shirt and cussed like a sailor at swarming, hungry gulls.

One of them dodged Willow's mother and got ahold of a flipper, flying away with its breakfast as the first of the families arrived on the scene. "Can we help?" the dad panted.

"Yes, please!" Willow yelled. "They shouldn't emerge from their nest in this daylight. The predators in and out of the water can see them too easily. I think a few got lost in the sea oats over there," she said as she pointed to the side of the path. It was also against the law to step on sea oats. She was going to Turtle Watch hell for this.

As they gathered the last few hatchlings that were in the open, her mother let out one more crazy-person scream and swatted her shirt to the cloud of gulls over her head. "Six made it to the water," she said. Her mother, too, would have the occupational habit of counting hatchlings. She strolled toward the group of tourists as if she hadn't just been battling a group of birds and wasn't walking shirtless toward complete strangers.

"Forty-two," Chloe added, making Willow smile from ear-to-ear.

"I found one! I found one!" the father said as he came from the sea oats cupping a hatchling.

"And I counted sixty-one," Willow said. "That makes one hundred and ten. Well done, team. We'll cover the one hundred-four with a towel and let them get back to sleep until dark."

That was, after she scoured the area for any other hatchlings and did a less hectic recount. "Would you like to join us this evening when we release them?" she asked the families. "We will come back to this location at dusk."

As Liam Morrison wrote the day's lesson on his classroom interactive board, he noted a special disinterest coming from the boys. Sam and Aiden didn't want to be there and, frankly, neither did he. But, since his students needed to pass physics that fall, here they all were.

"Your parents are paying me. It's easier to be tutored if your eyes are open."

"I don't have parents." Aiden emphasized the 's' as his cheek rested in the palm of his hand.

Liam sighed. He wanted to bark a sarcastic comeback about how Sam's mom and dad plus Aiden's single dad equaled parents plural, but it was sunny and eighty-five on Ibis Island and living without a mother sucks. So instead, he erased his lesson plans and wrote three words on the board.

Hydrochloric acid

Aluminum

The boys didn't budge, which was one of the reasons they needed to be tutored in physics instead of out on the Gulf or better yet, diving in it.

He opened the cabinet above one of his sinks and took out a beaker. Changing his mind, he put it back and chose a bigger one. He considered setting it between the boys on their table, but with what he had planned, that might not be safe. So, he placed it on the counter and paused.

Sam lifted his chin from the palm of his hand and turned his head toward the beaker. Progress.

Liam opened the drawer neatly labeled Foil, and thought of how Willow ribbed him for his organization. Willow. Distraction.

He shook his head clear. Ah. There it was. After pulling out about a half foot, he ripped the foil from the box before shoving it back in the drawer. As he shut the drawer with his hip, he wadded the foil into a ball.

"Most people do this using sealed two-liter bottles, but that's not safe. It can explode, the toxic liquid burning plants and animals. We will be responsible and not blow anything up. Today."

Aiden sat up at the sound of the words 'blow up,' exposing the faded red tongue of his Rolling Stones t-shirt. Boys were easy. "While I go down the hall for the last ingredient, you two discuss what I might be doing that involves a beaker, aluminum foil, and something that will definitely *not* make a bomb. No using your phones."

They definitely would use their phones, which would pique their interest more, so win-win. He left them to their wits as he made his way to the custodial closet. Two men in suits walked along the end of the hall. Their backs were turned, but he could tell who they were, the principal and the super. He found the hydrochloric acid he needed and tiptoed back to his room before the men remembered he used his classroom for summer tutoring.

The toilet bowl cleaner bottle was half full. Or was that half empty? Shrugging, he read the list of ingredients. This one had 20 percent hydrochloric acid. That would work.

As he entered the room, he noted the boys had abandoned their upright beds and stood by the beaker. "You're making a Works bomb," Sam said with the appropriate amount of enthusiasm.

"Let me repeat. I am unequivocally not making a bomb." Liam held out his arm, then shooed the boys away from the beaker. "What did you find out while I was gone?"

Without trying to hide it, Aiden held up his phone and read, "Hydrochloric acid. A strong mineral acid with many industrial uses."

Liam rolled his eyes at Aiden's lack of attempt to hide his phone. "Examples of said uses, please," he said as he wrestled with the childproof lid. Push and turn or squeeze and turn? All lid manufacturers of the world should make a pact and use one or the other.

"Hydrochloric acid uses," Sam interrupted.

Aiden wasn't having it. "Hey, I've got this. Give me a minute. There. Batteries, fireworks." His eyes grew and he pulled his phone closer to his face. "Used to process sugar and make gelatin? Damn." He said the last word in two syllables.

"Language," Liam said, reminding himself of something Harmony Clearwater would say.

"Sorry, Mr. Morrison."

"Pretty cool, huh?" Liam asked. "Sam? You got aluminum?"

"What is this, chemistry class?"

"We can go back to the lesson plan for the day if you prefer."

"Aluminum," Sam said, and pecked his phone with his thumbs. "Used to make cans and foil. Thrilling. Low density and nontoxic." He turned his eyes to the beaker and squinted.

Liam stepped closer and held up the toilet cleaner in his hand. "First one to write the periodic symbol on the Smartboard for both gets to pour the acid."

He leaned his backside against the counter and folded his arms as the boys shoved each other, juggling the forbidden phones. He had the best jobs he could think of. Physics teacher during the school year and diving instructor/tour guide during the summer. Along with some construction side jobs and tutoring, he made a living doing the things he loved. Life was good, and it was complete.

Through the window, a burgundy-colored smart car caught his eye as it drove over Pelican Bridge. Willow. She had a passenger he couldn't make out from the distance, but he knew the car. So, maybe life was good and almost complete.

The boys were out of breath, HCl and Al were written on the board, and they stood staring at him. He nearly let both of them pour the hydrochloric acid when a voice came from the doorway.

"Good day, Mr. Morrison. Thank you for helping out our young citizens in need." Dr. Hart, the school superintendent. Liam may have never seen the man out of a suit or minus the extremely straight side part in his hair, but at least he did show his face now and then, and that said something. But *young citizens in need?*

Liam scratched his head. "You're welcome, although these boys are in need of very little." He slipped the bottle away from them. "They outsmart me every time I turn around."

"Very well, then. Carry on." Hart hadn't said a word to the boys.

"With the looming boss of my boss on the premises," Liam whispered, "it looks like you two sit, and I pour."

He poured just enough of the clear liquid to cover the foil, then stepped back and sat. They waited. And waited.

"Low density. Nontoxic," Sam drawled. "Is that the point of the lesson, 'cause if it is—"

The toilet bowl cleaner began to bubble, then smoke. Sam grabbed the sides of the table and pulled his chin back. Aiden did the same but scooted his stool closer. It fizzled and bubbled like a rising volcano, then turned a dark gray color. The reaction caused the mixture to nearly boil over, but Liam knew it wouldn't. He'd used this experiment dozens of times with classes that needed a pick-me-up.

"Get out your journals and write up what we did today. You can nix the reference list, but I want the title block, abstract, body, and figure. Include a hypothesis on what would have happened if the beaker had a sealed lid, and you're free to go."

He glanced out the window toward the bridge as they clicked their pencils and opened their books. Distraction.

TWO

W illow stepped through the front doors of the St. Petersburg
Police Department and paused. A U.S. flag stood on one
side of the entrance and a Florida state flag on the other. People in
uniforms with polished, black shoes marched through the long hall-
ways and open areas. She knew they were police uniforms, but her
imagination saw casualty notification officers wearing military dress
greens.

Her head spun enough to make her reach out and place a hand
on her sister. As she wrapped her fingers around the part of her
baby sister's arm that wasn't bandaged, Willow took a deep,
cleansing breath. She used the meditation tools her mother taught
her and her siblings since childhood, and imagined she was kicking
her fins along the floor of the Gulf rather than walking into a
government building with a Volkswagen-sized bronze plaque at her
feet that read, "To Serve and Protect."

Glancing over, she found her sister grinning the warmest of
grins through strands of straight blonde hair. Zoe always
understood.

Willow spoke low. "You're not even fully healed from Chief

Roberts trying to kill you," Willow said, lifting Zoe's bandaged arm. "I should be holding you up. Not the other way around."

As she rotated her wrist so that her engagement ring was inches from Willow's nose, Zoe smiled. "There are flowers in the weeds, Willow. We caught our brother's killer. That's what matters. And, we're sisters. I can't imagine what it must be like for you to enter a government building, even if it is police rather than military." Zoe pulled her toward reception. "We'll hold each other up."

They approached the large desk in the center of the area. Offering no greeting, the short woman with a jet-black bob lifted her brows at them. Willow saw both a challenge and a lovely distraction. Since a plethora of extenuating circumstances may have put the woman in her obvious mood, Willow offered a "Good morning." Looking at her name badge, she smiled her warmest smile. "Your name badge is backward."

The woman stared at Willow before glancing down, then flipped the name tag around.

"Officer Lorenzo," Willow said. "How lovely. How is your morning going so far?"

The muscles in the woman's face melted. "Could be better." She pulled her chin back. "Thank you for asking."

Zoe said, "We're here to see Detective Osborne, please."

"What can I say you are here to see him about?"

"We're personal friends," Zoe interrupted. "Zoe and Willow. He'll know."

The woman lifted a landline receiver and ran her finger down a list of extension numbers.

Zoe leaned her head toward Willow's ear. "You are the Zen master."

Willow thought Zoe deserved that title this morning, but decided that arguing the point would be ungrateful.

"Detective Osborne," the receptionist said into the receiver. "There is a Willow and a Zoe here to see you. They say they—yes, of course." The officer hung up. "He told me to send you up. Have a nice day."

"Good to meet you, Officer." Willow lifted her hand in a wave as they headed for the elevators.

Zoe pressed the elevator button. The soft music helped soothe Willow's nerves. In a building like this, she assumed it was purposeful.

Stepping into the upstairs hall, Zoe said, "I half expected Matt to be waiting when the elevator doors opened."

The area smelled of a mixture of bleach and freshly vacuumed carpet. Willow nodded to a cluster of men in dress pants and buttoned-down shirts who glanced in their direction.

"His office is this way," Zoe said, pulling Willow along.

"Good morning, ladies," Matt said as Willow stepped into his office, followed by Zoe. He wore the same type of clothes as the cluster of men in the hallway. Dress pants, these were charcoal gray, and a buttoned-down shirt, this one an earthy purple. Must be the uniform, except he also wore a black gun holster over his shoulder and a set of handcuffs at his side.

He didn't stop arranging his boxes as he spoke, which wasn't nearly as disconcerting as the fact that he had boxes to arrange.

"Good morning, Matt," Zoe said. "Thank you for taking your time to see us."

Willow sat in the farthest guest chair. "How does this moment find you?"

Folding a side of a box into itself, he answered, "Good. What can I do for two of my favorite Ibis Island girls?"

"Did you get fired?" Zoe blurted.

Matt grinned a toothy smile but didn't stop what he was doing. He had a lovely smile. Smart and warm. She could see why Zoe was such good friends with him.

He ran a hand over his military-tight haircut and answered, "Transferred, not fired, but thanks again," he said with a hint of sarcasm.

Willow noted his box packing was as neat and tidy as his haircut. And, his office, for that matter. Everything was labeled and piled in straight, equal stacks. She made a mental note to refrain from ever inviting him to her home for a welcome-to-the-island tea since it was rarely neat or tidy.

That didn't seem to be a good enough answer for Zoe. "Where to?"

"Funny you should ask," he said and sat in his chair. "I've been assigned to serve as the Ibis Island interim chief of police."

Zoe grasped her neck like she was choking. Willow understood the reaction, but Matt might not. "Forgive my sister, Matt. She, um, likes you is all."

Zoe's wide open emerald green eyes turned to glare at Willow.

"Ah," Willow said. "Let me rephrase. Zoe thinks highly of you, as a friend, of course, and the precarious situation you've been placed in."

Matt folded his hands on his desk and leaned in. "I've worked as a detective in Reno, Chicago, and here at St. Pete's. I hope you will have confidence in my ability to serve as chief for however long."

Willow explained. "Zoe, and frankly myself, don't doubt your chiefing abilities. We simply feel for any chief of police who has to work with our sister. And, since Raine is the primary permit holder of Ibis Island, that means she pretty much runs the place."

"Ah, yes. I'm not sure what a primary permit holder is. I'll have to check that out, but I do remember Raine's issue with authority. I think I can handle her."

Willow's shoulders fell at the visual.

"I do have a long list to finish by this afternoon. What can I help you with?"

"We want our skull," Zoe said, then dropped her chin and added, "And, my camera."

Nodding, Matt said, "Ah, yes, I should have known. I am sorry for your loss and realize your desire to have your brother's remains returned to you."

"And, my camera," Zoe repeated.

"However," he continued as if she hadn't spoken. "Until the case is over—

"Over," Zoe interrupted. "The murderer is in prison—"

"Jail," Matt corrected. "And awaiting trial. Now, until the potential sentencing—"

Zoe's face reddened. "Potential." She held up her bandaged arms, palms up.

This wasn't going quite as Willow had planned. In this scenario, Zoe was meant to be the easier sister.

Matt continued, "I know you wouldn't want to do anything to jeopardize the trial."

"He was caught red-handed," Zoe argued.

Willow stood, causing both of them to pause. "We understand, Matt." She looked him straight in the eye. "And we trust you." Mostly. "Thank you for all you've done. You are a good friend. Please let us know as soon as we can allow our mother to make arrangements for cremation."

Matt rubbed a single hand across the back of his neck. "I am guessing it will be months, maybe several of them, before you get your brother's remains back. I am deeply sorry."

Nodding, Willow forced a smile and held out her hand. As they shook, she placed the palm of her other hand over their joined fingers and looked him in the eye once again. "Trust," she repeated. "Best wishes on your move, and welcome to Ibis Island."

Liam's knees pressed against the dash, almost crushing the dozen orange carnations he bought for Willow's mother. "Are you sure this is okay?" he asked as Willow turned onto Riley Road. "This seems more like a family thing."

"You are family," she said. "And Chloe insisted," she added as she bumped her smart car over the entrance to her parents' drive.

He squinted in her direction. The long blonde hair covered part of her face, but he could still see her cheeks. "I know that grin. It's not even a grin. It's a smirk. You're smirking. I want to know why."

"I don't know what you're talking about," she said as her nose grew before his eyes.

Movement from the roof of the single-story home had him

craning his head under the visor to see if it was one of the four female goats that spent their days grazing on the thatch on the roof. No stilts for the Clearwater home. It had been grandfather claused in when the city voted that all new construction homes be set on stilts. The thatch Henry grew up there bent over in the island breeze, but no goats were to be found. Henry had already ushered them down the ramp for the evening, or they were lying in the grasses and couldn't be seen from the ground.

The bright yellow stucco walls of the home had begun to chip at the edges, exposing the bright orange paint from last year. "The hollyhocks and honeysuckle are still in full bloom," he said, mostly thinking out loud.

Willow tapped the brakes, bringing the car to a stop. She craned her neck, exposing her beautiful blue eyes, and smiled. "A man who knows his flowers."

Without telling them to, his shoulders fell and he wished he'd brought Harmony a nice bottle of wine or a plant as a dinner gift. Maybe a drill or a sander. "What? Nah. It's just that it's late in the season, and they look pretty, I mean nice, I mean good, damn it." He tried to swing an ankle on his knee and cock an elbow on the windowsill, but the car was so damned small and he was so tall and skinny, the juggling made the whole situation worse. Yet, it made Willow's smile change from up-to-something into the kind that reached her eyes. Since that didn't generally happen with Willow, the embarrassment was well worth it.

She pulled her car around the pickup that belonged to her older sister, Raine, and parked in the spot in the yard next to the palm tree where only a smart car would fit.

"Dane's here," he said as he spotted his friend's ostentatious Jeep. "Glad I won't be the only non-family member. Unless engaged counts as family."

Her smile turned into a frown. "You *are* family," she said. "And, I could sort of use you as a buffer for when I tell my mother it will be months, maybe several of them, before we get Seth's remains back."

"Glad to help." His voice was sarcastic, but he mostly meant it.

Chloe stood on the front porch, rocking on the balls of her feet with her little hands cupped in front of her. Her long hair swung back and forth as she rocked. She was by far the cutest kid he'd ever known and absolutely had to be what Willow was like as a child. Smart, grounded, and full of life.

"The shrimp is waiting for you," Liam said from the passenger seat.

"She is so not waiting for me," Willow said as she reached for the flowers. "Here. Let me get those for you."

Confused at his suddenly empty arms, he climbed out of the torture chamber of a car. Chloe walked a straight line toward him, carrying something as if it were a miniature wedding cake.

"Liam. Liam," Chloe squealed, ignoring Willow. "Look what I found!" She opened her fingers as she made the last few steps to him.

THREE

An egg rested in Chloe's palms. It was the right size for a chicken egg, but it was white, which meant it did not come from Mrs. Clearwater's stash of organic brown ones. He put a knee to the ground and took a better look.

"Awesome?" he said like a question, then glanced to Willow with an expression that he hoped explained he had no idea what was special about this egg. The sight of her standing there. The sun behind her head, lighting the strands of blonde hair in a golden silhouette around her head. That with the bright orange bunch of flowers stirred something inside of him he had banned from his insides long ago. "Um…where'd you find it?" he asked, forcing his eyes to the shrimp.

"Grandma and Grandpa's backyard. Can we keep it?"

Keep it? We? Willow, the traitor, stood and grinned but remained mute.

Liam scratched the back of his head. "Well. I, um. Do we know what it is?"

"Grandpa said it's a Muscovy."

He glanced back to Willow. That damned smile of hers could make him forget his name.

"Of course, of course," Liam stuttered. All he could think about was the rotten egg from Charlotte's Web and what would happen if it broke. "I'm not sure it's okay to eat a Muscovy egg."

In slow motion, Chloe's lips opened and every muscle in her face fell.

Liam recognized the expression of mutiny. "I mean—" he stammered.

"Muscovy duck egg." Finally, Willow spoke. "Probably stolen by a coon or laid away from the nest by a mama Muscovy not quite ready to be a mama yet."

The corners of Chloe's mouth fell.

Willow sighed. "It probably isn't even viable."

Chloe's round little cheeks started to quiver and shake.

"And who knows how long it's been away from the nest," Willow pleaded.

Liam wrapped his fingers around Willow's forearm. "What your mom is trying to say is that this little egg is a, is a potential living creature and that we should not eat it, no, but give it a fighting chance to be born."

Tucking Chloe's long, blonde hair behind her ear, Willow grinned. "I think the two of you have a plan."

What? No. No plan. "But," Liam's voice squeaked like a girl.

Willow spun toward the front door, taking his flowers with her. "I'm going to check on Grandma in the kitchen."

And just like that he was alone in the middle of hollyhocks and honeysuckle, kneeling in front of a beaming six-year-old with a duck egg.

In an attempt to shrug off the image of Liam dropping to his knee, Willow walked up the familiar path, passed her mother's mint and rosemary, and entered her childhood home.

Liam as a Muscovy egg buffer trumped Liam as a buffer between Willow and her mother any day.

The scent of fresh cilantro and basil mixed with cooked tomatoes and lemon balm. She paused and looked around at the kitchen that was void of any other family members, blood or not blood. "What are we having?" she asked as she continued, then stepped to her mother.

Her mother sliced cucumbers. "Cheese rounds with honey, walnut, rocket, and umeboshi, a tossed salad, and breaded eggplant rollatini."

Willow wrapped a single arm around her mother's shoulders, closed her eyes, and inhaled. "It smells amazing. Thank you for taking care of Chloe today. Do we know who is doing the release tonight?"

"Mary Jane. She's been incredible and has Oliver to help her. It will be her first time without a section coordinator. I trust all one hundred and four will make it to the water."

Willow cracked the door to the oven and inhaled. "And maybe one of those will make it to adulthood."

"One in a thousand is a rough statistic, dear."

"I'm still sorry we won't be there to see them off," Willow said, careful not to look her mother in the eye.

"And I'm sorry you don't have better news from Detective Osborne."

How did she always know? Willow sighed. "I tried."

Her mother paused before she nodded, then used the back of her cutting knife to scrape the pile of diced cucumbers from the cutting board on top of the tossed salad.

"Are those from Liam?" she asked. "Chloe has been asking about him all day."

"Yes." Willow turned to look through the glass door to the upper cabinet that held her mother's vases. "She stopped him at the front door." The picture of him down on one knee flashed in her mind again. Warmth in her cheeks grew.

"He feels the same about you, you know."

The muscles in Willow's body tensed. "Jacob's birthday is coming up." After setting the flowers down, she chose a country blue glass vase from the front of the cabinet.

Her mother paused from chopping off the bottoms of the bouquet. "I see. Why don't you take him with you?"

"Who, Liam? To the cemetery?" Willow barked, not intending to be so curt.

"He was Jacob's best friend," her mother said.

Willow shook her head and reached in front of her mother to fill up the vase. "I'll have Chloe. His family will be there."

"How about one of your sisters?"

Willow faced her mother. "How about my mom?"

Her mother's eyes softened. She grinned and nodded, then held the large bowl of salad out to Willow. "Set the table?" her mother asked.

Willow placed the flowers in the vase, adjusted one that fought the tangle and stuck out above the rest, then took the bowl from her mother.

Mom turned away, slipping on a pair of cartoon pig oven mitts and opened the oven door.

With arms full, Willow stepped into the sunroom. Two tables had been set. Seven chairs circled one and the other held a crockpot, two pitchers that held what looked like peach tea and pink lemonade, along with a large plate with an assortment of salsa-covered bruschetta.

"Better late than never," Raine said from the window seat along the far wall. She could have passed as taking a nap if not for her greeting that wasn't a greeting.

The assortment of corner sea shell wind chimes spoke to her in the breeze.

Willow ignored Raine and focused on the windy melody. "Hello, everyone. I'm sorry I'm late."

"Liam with you?" her father asked while keeping his nose in his book, then took a sip from his Thugs Need Hugs mug.

"Chloe stopped him in the drive," she said, pulling her shoulders back. "I was able to successfully dodge one egg plus transfer a science experiment over to him. Points for me." She placed the flowers in the center of the table meant for eating and salad on the other.

"Patting you on the back from here," Raine said without opening her eyes.

Her father nodded as his gaze traveled back and forth over the pages of Catcher in the Rye. "Muscovy egg. The two bottom drawers of Seth's old dresser are empty."

She couldn't focus on the mention of the egg. The reference to her brother made her feet stop, arms full of plates and flatware and all.

He had been her best friend, her rock when her husband was killed in the line of duty. He would have gone with her to the cemetery on Jacob's birthday. And, Willow had only bad news to share about his remains. The holes in her heart would never go away.

"Sis?"

She blinked and glanced in the direction of Zoe's voice.

Everyone looked at Willow. Even her father. She forced a grin. "Have you put the goats away for the night, Dad? Could you use some help?"

Her father glanced at the roof of the sunroom as if he could see through it. "Not yet, and yes," he said, closed his book, and grabbed a paper bag full of goat food from the wicker basket next to him.

"The goats!" Dane shrieked with joy and popped up from his spot next to Zoe.

Willow tilted her head. The next smile was sincere. "A treasure hunter with a barbed wire tattoo and leather bracelets who shrieks like a girl and a physics teacher who knows his flowers," she muttered and followed behind them.

Her father used the back door of the three-seasons room and around the side of the house to get to the goat ramp.

"Whoa!" Dane said and jumped from the stepping stone path as they passed the giant mural of the mermaid with the swimming goldfish. "I forget that's there."

"Be glad it wasn't last year's giant moray eel," Henry said, passing Chloe and Liam on the way to the ramp.

Liam had crossed his long legs in the small patch of grass. Chloe sat next to him. Their foreheads were close together, and they didn't seem to notice adults passing them and instead whispered like they were plotting a trip to the moon.

"The two bottom drawers of Seth's old dresser are empty," her father repeated as they passed.

Both slowly craned their heads toward her father at the same time.

"He cares for her," Dane said.

"Yes." Willow inhaled deeply. "Yes. She loves him, too. Speaking of love, how are wedding plans?"

"Oh. Uh. You might have to ask her about that."

Typical guy.

"I know I have a flower thing to show up to, and a try different cakes thing. And, that we, or she, is making invitations."

She mentally retracted her typical guy judgement. "What a guy."

"I am so coming out ahead on this one."

"Handheld shop light's in the shed," her father said to Liam and Chloe as he reached for the latch on the gate. "It's the one with the fire safe cage."

Her plan to escape people and spend some time with the goats was backfiring.

"How will you get them down?" Dane asked as her father opened the gate and stepped in front.

The horizontal wooden slats helped both goats and humans from sliding down the steep incline.

"They know." Henry shrugged.

The ramp was narrow, wound around the edge of the roof, and she was in the middle. "Dad, your belt is about to be goat dinner."

As he tucked the loose end in a belt loop, he unlatched the gate at the top of the ramp. "Whoa, ladies," her father said and opened the gate a few inches. "We go through this every day," he added, as if they understood human. "I can't open the gate when you're standing in front of it."

"Have good manners," he said. "We have a visitor."

A chorus of baas and goat cries were accompanied with a melody of several hooves clomping on the wooden floor.

"We've upset their routine," Willow explained.

"So, this is it." Henry gestured his free arm around like a tour guide as the three of them crowded in. "They have shade over there and snacks over here." He pointed to the low roof, then the thatch.

"How big is this?" Dane asked, holding his arms out around him.

Henry ran his fingers along his 5 o'clock shadow. "Ten foot by fifteen."

"It's genius. Eli made it?"

"He did, indeed." Henry nodded. "Didn't think it would help put the neighbors' minds to ease if I made it myself. Eli made it unofficially official." Her father winked and warmed her heart.

The two of them spoke back and forth about the area as if there weren't four, hundred-fifty-pound goats nipping his clothes and shoving into him. "Fences are six foot. Goats like to jump. Four foot is minimum, but I didn't want to take any chances, them being on the roof and all."

Willow was thankful for the break from life. Taking the broom and dustpan from the corner, she began sweeping up goat pellets.

Her father scratched the side of Grateful's gray and white cheek as if she were a golden retriever. "Sleeping quarters are down the ramp, on the other side of the house."

"Sleeping quarters," she repeated and laughed to herself.

One pushed against Dane's thigh. "Look at the size of them."

"That would be Bertha, for obvious reasons."

Dane reached, then ran his hand along her back. "The hair is coarse like a terrier."

Bertha's big butt shivered.

"How do you get them down the ramp?"

"They just do."

Tails flicked and the girls bumped into her father. Impatiently, they called out to him as the hair on their backs twitched and shook.

Dane whistled. "Damnedest thing I ever did see."

That said a lot for someone who traveled the world in search of buried treasure.

He scratched the top of Happy, the oldest and calmest of the girls on the top of her head with two of his fingers. "They're bigger than they look from the street."

Henry handed Dane the bag of dry goat food.

He opened it and took out a small handful. Bertha pushed her way in and devoured it like she hadn't eaten in a week, shoving and pushing and rubbing her lips over Dane's hand like a vacuum.

"Sheesh, girl. Are you starving?"

"Nah," her father said. "Just goats."

"They don't even smell bad," Dane said.

"I'll finish up with the sweeping, Dane," Willow said with the straightest face she could keep. "So, you can take care of the milking when we get down the ramp."

Every muscle in Dane's face fell. Bertha knocked the food out of his hand.

Willow laughed as the goats moved around the bag like football players in a huddle. It was good to laugh. "I'm joking."

He looked at his empty hands. "Sorry, man. Now, what do we do?"

"Follow me," her father said.

Willow took caboose behind Dane. She hooked the gate open, so it would be ready for the morning and wouldn't bang in the wind through the night.

With the empty bag in Grateful's mouth, the goats marched down the narrow ramp, behind Dane and her father.

FOUR

Dinner was ready. Willow headed down the hallway in search of Liam and Chloe. The ancient hardwood floor creaked as she passed framed sea shell sculpture shadow boxes and family photos. The one of the four of them walking away made her stop. Seth was twice as tall as the three sisters. She wasn't sure if it was her father or mother who took the shot but thought Seth would approve. The lighting. The color. The moment.

She heard Liam and Chloe whispering. It filled her heart more than it should've. Without announcing her presence, she stepped into the doorway and leaned against the frame. She was spying, but the joy in Chloe's young voice made it worth it.

Liam squatted like a catcher at the plate in front of one of the dressers her parents had saved from Seth's apartment. With his long legs, he looked like a frog from the back, and Willow had to cover her mouth to keep from laughing. Chloe sat on the backs of her feet next to him, and together they huddled much like they had in the grass not long before.

The bottom drawer of the dresser they chose was pulled out about halfway. In it was what she recognized as her father's shop light. It was the worn yellow one with a safety cage encasing the bulb.

The drawer above was pulled out enough for her to spot a gathering of garage rags with a single white egg in the center. The scene sent such an odd sensation through her body, she nearly forgot why she was there.

Liam adjusted the rags closer to the egg as Chloe wrapped her arms around his neck. Warmth filled Willow's heart just before a memory flashed in front of her eyes. It was Chloe shortly after she had learned to walk. She clung to her father's neck with her feet in the sand as they watched the sunset. It was the last sunset they'd shared.

Blinking, she shook her head clear of the guilt that poked at the back of her skull. "So, this is what all of the drawer-and-portable-light business is all about," she said, announcing her presence.

Chloe jumped and ran to her. She wrapped her small arms around Willow's waist and squeezed. "The rags are the nest," she said into Willow's shirt. "The light will keep the egg warm like her mommy would."

"It's a girl, is it?" Willow asked, tilting Chloe's head back so she could see her big blue eyes.

Chloe shrugged and ran back to Liam. "Mom," she said like an irritated teenager. "We don't even know if it's vibble. I just hate calling it an it."

"Viable," Willow corrected.

As Willow squinted at the drawers, Liam asked, "You okay?"

Her eyes turned to his. "You know me," she said without answering him. "Dinner is ready."

Chloe and Liam turned to face each other. Chloe covered her mouth with both hands, and Liam opened his eyes wide. Willow's shoulders shook with laughter as they stood and rushed toward the kitchen, Liam winking on his way out.

She stood for a moment, staring not at the man-made nest, but at Seth's dresser. Slowly, she lowered herself to the ground and crossed her legs. She knew this piece of Seth's belongings, right down to the scratches on the front. She and her sisters had gone through each box in every drawer. It was here they found the secret love letters from the wife of Seth's murderer. It was here they found the plane tickets he and Miriam would have used to run away together had Miriam's husband not stabbed him in that underwater cave.

Willow and Zoe's trip to see Detective Osborne had been a waste. If she was honest with herself, it wasn't as if his words were a surprise. Realizing the hands on her legs were intended to rest loosely instead of gripping her thighs, she rotated her shoulders and consciously relaxed her body. Scalp, facial muscles, neck. Her baby sister was to have been Seth's diving partner the day he went missing. Zoe placed too much guilt on her shoulders for standing him up that fateful day.

Shoulders, arms, hips. Raine was the oldest now and carried that responsibility with a vengeance. Thighs, calves, feet. Her mother lived in mourning, her father in his pillar of peaceful strength. Willow lived in simple pursuit of memories and nostalgia.

The smells of this room. The feel. Of course, it was no longer the bedroom of her only brother. It had been transformed into a music room long before Seth's death. His murder. The dresser rested in the closet, egg and all.

Banjos, acoustic guitar. Her mother's accordion. Today, it was the scent that called to her. It was one of gulf air and family, of sea shells and love. It could never be replaced with new furnishings.

Lifting her knees, she wrapped her arms around them and cocked her head at the dresser. Something wasn't right. She stared at each worn mark, scratch, and crooked-sitting drawer. Taking a deep breath in and out, she craned her head closer and focused on the top one.

It was crooked. Tilting her chin, she reconciled that the drawer wasn't all that crooked, and she had little room to judge. She was the messiest Clearwater of all, but Seth would want straight drawers. Zoe may have labeled each box in its proper and symmetrical place but didn't seem to have run the drawers properly in their slides.

She decided dinner would have to wait and that she would be

the one to fix the drawer. Pulling, she wiggled and lifted until it was nearly all the way out.

Willow tried to test the success of her wiggling and slid the drawer shut again. It was stubborn and refused to close the last eighth of an inch. Gently banging a few more times, she noted that the feel was not of wood hitting wood, so she took it out completely. As she laid it on the floor, she noticed an envelope attached to the back.

An envelope?

She looked around as if someone might be watching. Filling her lungs, she turned the front of the drawer completely away from her and, without touching it, stared at the discovery. A regular, white business-sized envelope. The tape affixing it to the back of the drawer was dusty, but not yellowed.

Goose bumps erupted on her arms as she slowly reached for it. She drew it away from the wood, careful not to rip it. The best thing to do would be calling a family meeting and opening it together. Her fingers did not listen to such reason, and she turned the envelope over. Her phone buzzed, making her jump.

Ignoring both the text and the heart that nearly beat out of her chest, she slid her finger beneath the flap. It lifted easily from the glue that had once sealed it. Inside was a folded piece of regular copy paper.

Why was this here? A chill ran through her body. Had Seth put this here? She unfolded the paper and recognized, right away, his handwriting. She read.

Her Legacy
The wet uncharted
The cornerstone that is Home
The under under

A Haiku? Tears welled in Willow's eyes. This was just like him. Photographs, legends of treasure, and poems. The biggest of smiles filled her face as she sat alone in the room that used to be his.

The wet uncharted. Her shoulders shook as her smile turned into laughter. The cornerstone that is Home. She covered her mouth with her free hand. The under under. She brought the paper to her chest until tears of laughter turned to cries of loss. Clinging to the paper, she rocked back and forth and let the tears run over her cheeks.

The seat at the table remained empty. Willow hadn't responded to Liam's text. No one questioned eating without her, and he wasn't about to either. The rollatini wasn't bad, but he would have preferred salmon steak or a plate full of crab legs.

"Mrs. Clearwater," he said through what he thought was a sincere grin. "This is the best rollatini I've ever had."

"Liam Morrison," Harmony said in her tone that made him want to crawl in a hole. "Don't you patronize me."

She always knew. His chin pulled toward his neck like a magnet.

"And thank you," she added. "For the stunning flowers and for making the day of the best little granddaughter a grandma could ever have."

Liam glanced next to him at said best little granddaughter, who gazed at him with stars in her eyes. She was also the best kid he'd ever known, but at that moment, he was more interested in the empty seat on the other side of her. Movement came from the backyard. He assumed the others noticed, but his were the only eyes that peered out the window to Willow as she approached the fire pit.

It was custom to give Willow space not awarded others in the family. It had been five years since Jacob's death, but the custom remained firmly intact. Liam understood. High school sweethearts torn apart by loss, by death. By war. Jacob wasn't only a casualty of war. He was a war hero. Willow's type. A humble jock who enlisted not because he had nowhere else to go, but because he wanted to serve his country. He had been the opposite of Liam, yet his best friend anyway. And, the only reason Liam and Willow became friends too.

The tight, black pants things she wore for yoga, Pilates, and anything else were mostly covered by her oversized button-down shirt. He took a bite of something green as he watched her create a teepee in the pit using something he didn't recognize. She picked twigs from a pile of sticks next to the circle of stones and expanded the construction until it was ready for a match. He'd been so engrossed in what she was doing, he hadn't realized the dinner table had been quiet for much longer than was acceptable for the Clearwater family.

Dane broke the silence. "Those damned incredible goats."

Harmony interrupted with one word between bites of something that was not salmon steak or crab legs. "Language."

"Sorry," Dane said unconvincingly. "I swear I've got to get me one."

"Goats?" Zoe squeaked. "Or, we could simply enjoy Dad's and save our home from the mess, cost, noise, and time."

"Our home," Dane repeated and rested his lips on hers.

"I'm eating, for crying out loud," Raine said with her mouth full.

Chloe asked, "Where's Mommy?"

The six-year-old was the only voice of reason, and the only one too short to see Willow making the fire.

"She's out back, honey," Harmony answered. "She needs some time. You understand."

Did she? Chloe had no memory of her father or his death. Yet, she nodded anyway and rested her head on Liam's arm as he ate his last bite, then pushed his plate away. Henry lifted from the table and gathered dishes.

One by one, everyone joined in clearing the table. Liam reached for the silverware and napkins, but Harmony placed a hand on his forearm. "Thank you, Liam, but I think Willow needs you more than we do." Her smile was much like Willow's, warm and honest but didn't reach her eyes.

He chose a spot around the fire pit on one of the log benches Henry had made forever ago. The pit was a circle of stacked retaining wall bricks in the center of the circle of benches that sat far enough away from the fire that no one wanted to feel, but everyone enjoyed watching and hearing.

Willow blew on the fire like he wasn't there. Cracks of sparks licked Willow's creation, making the sticks come alive. Like the rest of her family, he knew something had happened. Unlike the rest of her family, he had no idea what to do or not to do. What could have happened in the past fifteen minutes that made her eyes red and swollen?

Tapping the heel of his foot, he filled his lungs. "What did you use for kindling?" he asked, feeling utterly stupid.

She lifted her gaze and smiled through glossy eyes. "Toilet paper rolls filled with dryer lint." Adding bigger logs to the growing flames, she said, "Thank you."

"For what?"

"For being here. For being you."

Really? That was it? Because, he felt rather worthless right about then.

One by one each of the group joined them. Willow picked a spot on the other side of the fire. Chloe climbed on Liam's left knee.

Zoe scooted to the front of her bench. "Our trip to St. Pete's was a wash."

The elephant in the room.

FIVE

"Matt says they have to keep Seth's remains until the trial is over," Zoe continued.

Henry's shoulders fell. Harmony obviously already knew.

"Are you sure?" Dane asked.

Raine barked, "What the hell?"

Chloe said, "Yeah, what the hell?"

"Language," Harmony said again.

"I have good news," Willow interrupted, causing everyone to go back to silent. She crept a hand around her backside and pulled out a slightly aged white envelope.

"So, I found this. It's...well." Her chest rose and fell. "The top drawer of Seth's dresser was crooked. It bothered me."

"Since when?" Zoe asked.

"Shh," Harmony said.

"I was messing with it, and I found this."

"We've been through those drawers," Zoe interrupted again. "That was not in there."

Willow turned it over. It wasn't sealed. "It was taped to the back," she said.

Harmony's knuckles turned white as she gripped her knees.

"Whoa," Dane mumbled.

"Not really 'whoa,'" Willow said. "It's just a Haiku."

"Read it," Raine said.

Willow gingerly removed the paper from the envelope, and she read, "The title is 'Her Legacy.' The wet uncharted. The cornerstone that is Home. The under under." Holding the paper in one hand and the envelope in the other, the backs of her hands dropped to her thighs and lay there.

Dane wrapped an arm around Zoe as she covered her mouth. A single tear ran over Harmony's cheek.

"Pass it around," Raine ordered.

Willow nodded and handed it to her first.

"This is just like him," Raine said, shaking her head.

Willow nodded. "I thought the same thing."

Was anyone going to address the fact that it was taped to the back of a dresser drawer? Liam wasn't about to.

"Few words that speak volumes," Harmony added. "Seth loved exploring the wet uncharted. He loved his home, both here in this house and his home that was Ibis Island, and he loved to dive."

"Definitely special," Zoe said through her tears.

"And taped to the back of his dresser drawer," Dane added with tight eyes.

At that moment, Liam was thankful for his friend's lack of tact.

Willow opened her eyes to the pastel yellow walls of her childhood bedroom. Blinking, she turned her head toward the window. Still dark. With a sigh of relief, she reached over to the end table and patted the surface for her phone. Instead, she found the envelope.

Why did Seth hide it? How was it that special? That important? They may never know.

Rubbing her face, she grabbed her cell and checked for messages. She might as well get up. Her Tuesday morning section walker would check in any minute.

Next to her, Chloe slept with her little mouth open. Willow

smiled as she lifted the hypoallergenic sheets and scooted to the edge of the futon. She smelled the aroma of raspberry tea. The next, deeper inhale detected toast and eggs. If she didn't have a dozen people waiting for her, she would skip 7 a.m. yoga and spend the time with her parents.

She was able to slip out through the door without waking her daughter. Her feet had barely made it to the hallway before she heard Raine's voice. "I'm going myself."

"This is a busy time for you, dear," her mother said. "Zoe already went."

"Without me. I don't like it."

A few dishes clanked as Willow stepped into the kitchen, making her entrance undetected. Raine stood at the sink, her ponytail much shorter and darker than their mother who stood next to her, cutting the tops from fresh strawberries.

The dishes from the night before had already been put away, each in their special spot behind the glass doors of the white-framed cabinets.

Spots of algae in the shapes of fingerprints clung to the backs of Raine's shorts.

"Where are you going?" Willow asked.

Raine dropped her coffee mug in the sink, making her mother snicker. "Jeez, Willow. You scared me."

"Nothing scares you," Willow said and stepped next to them. Raine already smelled like diesel fuel and fish.

"Raine, dear," their mother said. "Willow and Chloe spent the night."

Raine took a dry towel and dabbed the front of her shirt as she said, "I'm going to St. Pete's to talk to Osborne myself. They can't just keep a person's remains from his family. I'm going to talk to his supervisor if I have to."

Willow opened the door of the cabinet that held her mother's mismatched coffee mugs. "You might not have to travel." She lifted the lid of the pig-shaped cookie jar and took out what was on top. "Oatmeal raisin. Yum."

"What are you talking about?" Raine asked.

Willow smiled, probably much too pleased with sharing the news. "Matt has been asked to take the Ibis Island chief of police position until the council finds a permanent replacement for Chief Roberts."

Raine's mouth opened, then shut. An unrecognizable word began to come from her lips, then nothing. She finally rolled her eyes and said, "Fine. Good. Fine." She wadded up the towel in her hand and tossed it on the counter. "Ibis Island City Hall it is, then."

While pouring hot water over a mango tea bag, Willow smirked at Raine's general dislike, albeit justified, of anything resembling a police officer.

"Should we tell him about the poem?" her mother asked.

Willow's smile vanished. "What for? The case is closed."

Her mother continued as she brushed strawberry greens into her free hand. "A man like that nice Detective Osborne—"

Raine cleared her throat.

"Would surely want to know," her mother finished and threw the greens into the box reserved for the compost bin, then clipped a few leaves from the potted basil on the windowsill that stood to the side of her array of toy-sized animal figurines.

"I'm with Willow on this one, Mother. The murderer is in jail. His trial will be here, hopefully, sooner rather than later."

All but ignoring her mother's suggestion, Willow said, "I'm going to frame it." She wrapped the tea bag around her spoon and pulled, squeezing the last bit of flavor from the tea bag. "I'm going to sign it with Seth's name and frame it, yes. Then, I'm going to hang it somewhere he would have wanted me to."

A few days later, Willow slowed for a bicyclist before turning into Luciana's parking lot. She took the moment to dwell on the gravel. It wasn't pampered asphalt like Show Me's, and she didn't have valet parking, but this was an island, she convinced herself. An island with the feel of an island rather than an amusement park, and those kinds of things didn't come from asphalt and valet parking. Or, at least, that was what she hoped.

The cyclist may have worn a helmet, but between the gray braid that lay down the middle of his back and the brass framed circular glasses, she knew who it was. Rolling down her window, she waved and called out, "Mr. Oberweiss, hello!"

His tires slid to a stop as both shoulders lifted.

She pulled into a side spot and shifted her smart car into park.

"What brings you this way?" she asked as she got out of the car with the warmest smile she could manage. "Did you come to see the progress?" This was, after all, the pub honoring the island's legendary Luciana Bezan, and Glen Oberweiss was the owner of the island's museum.

"Willow. Look at you." Mr. Oberweiss set a single foot to the gravel but didn't dismount from his seat. "I swear you get prettier every time I see you."

"Come on in," she said and waved him over. "I'll show you around."

"And kinder," he said. "I don't have the time at this moment but will be here for the grand reopening. This weekend. Is that right?"

"Next. This Saturday is more of a soft opening for friends and family." Awkward. "But...you're invited, of course. Come anytime, please."

He pointed to the large four- by eight-foot sheets of plywood that covered the back half of the pub.

"Those will be easy enough to take down." Familiar symptoms of feeling in over her head scratched at her. Dutifully ignoring it, she turned to Mr. Oberweiss. "I've had that half turned into an area for dancing. I wanted it open and airy, and tore out the walls, leaving the weight-bearing beams. Liam reinforced and covered them to look like oversized sail masts. We left the existing half as the inside of Luciana's ship."

"Luciana's lover's ship," he corrected.

She smiled the largest of smiles and said, "Yes, of course. The port hole windows in tucked away booths remain. But the dance floor, it will be more like the ship's deck." She hoped. "With the helm platform serving as a stage for live musicians." Or, musician, singular, until she could get some of the construction costs paid down. She inhaled.

"I love it already," he said and placed the palms of his hands together like he was praying. "I always knew you had a sound balance between creativity and business sense." He pressed the nose piece of his glasses closer to his face. "Morrison is doing the work?"

The lines around his eyes had deepened since the last time she'd seen him. When was that? "He is. Sometimes he has help from my father or Dane Corbin. How is the museum? I haven't been to see you…to see it…in far too long."

He nodded as he secured his foot in the strap around his pedal. "Very well, thank you. Very, very well."

The balance between politeness and an awareness of body language had her saying, "I won't keep you. Look forward to having you for the grand reopening."

"And you as well, my child. Come by the museum. We have new posters for the Turtle Watch display. 'Dig the dark,' they read." He waved as he checked for cars before pulling onto the thin two-lane road that circled the island.

She dug around in the oversized bag she used for everything from workout clothes and coloring books, to her Turtle Watch tablet and a toothbrush. Pointing the fob behind her, she locked her car door. The sound of an electric sander reminded her that Liam said he was working on the bar early that day. The grand reopening might not be until the following weekend, but the soft opening was Saturday. A christening of the dance floor. She grabbed the handle of the door and straightened her shoulders.

The corners of her lips turned up. The sound of several voices reminded her that Liam said he was bringing reinforcements.

SIX

As Willow flipped the switch for the neon open sign, she noted that Dane was the other voice. He worked the sander along the bar extension. The large sheet of plastic Visqueen that separated the existing bar tables and booths from the dance floor addition gathered against the wall in a bungee cord. Neither noticed her entrance, so she took a moment to assess the progress. Her breath caught. The backs of her eyes burned.

The new area nearly doubled the size of the pub, her pub. She'd lost her office space, but administrative tasks could be done at home or in the break room.

The muscles in Liam's shoulders, which he always swore weren't there, flexed under his shirt as he used sandpaper to scuff the planks of wood covering the reinforced stilts that would hold up the roof. The new matched the old so well she could hardly tell where one stopped and the other started.

Weathered wood flooring. Metal deck tools that hung from the walls. The inside of Luciana Bezan's legendary lost ship. Mr. Oberweiss would love it. She had to believe that. Liam stood and tilted his head as he looked at his work. At well over six feet, his head nearly hit the heavy braided rope that hung from the ceiling.

He gave Dane a shove in the shoulder, causing him to stop the sander and shove his safety goggles to his forehead.

"You sure this is going to work?" Liam asked him. This was the second time in a week she had eavesdropped on him and had yet to feel guilty about it.

"Nope."

"It has to work." Liam sounded angry and he never sounded angry.

Dane set the sander down, blew the dust from the bar top, and said, "Have faith, man."

Liam scratched the back of his head. "You're the one who said, 'Nope.'"

"You're the one who needs everything to match exactly." Dane used his fingers to make quotation marks in the air around his last word, which was interesting with the sander still in his hand.

"I'm just surprised," she interrupted.

The two of them jumped at the sound of her voice.

"That you tore yourself away from my baby sister for a morning, Dane," she said.

"Willow," Dane said with his smile that could light up any room.

She walked toward him with open arms and counted in her head as she gave him a tight three-second hug. "Not that I'm not grateful for the help, but you should be working on your place before my pub. Since the fire, you've hardly been away from Zoe."

"Can't do anything with my lot until the wreckers are done, and Zoe's taking point as diving class captain today, because until this job gets done, Liam is worthless to me."

"I'm standing right here," Liam said under his breath.

"Oh, Liam," Willow said. "Thank you for taking such good care of this project. I could never have done it without you." She put a single arm around his back. He returned the gesture, patting her twice on the shoulder.

Dane rolled his eyes large enough to go around the moon and back. "Incorrigible," he said, flopped his goggles down over his eyes, and turned on the sander.

The sight of Seth's Haiku caught her eye. Yes. The spot over the bar back had been just the place for it. The wide matte surrounded by the even thicker frame may have been overkill for an 8 ½- by 11-inch piece of copy paper, but she didn't care. It was Seth's poem, and this was Luciana's.

The Legend of Luciana Bezan. Her brother's obsession. If he hadn't been so captivated with the legend of the missing dowry, he might not have rushed to earn his diving certificate. If he hadn't gotten his certificate, he might not have been overly confident enough to dive alone when Zoe stood him up that fateful day. If he hadn't been diving alone, Chief Roberts wouldn't have murdered him in the hidden crevasse. It hurt her brain, and she expanded her lungs.

She noticed the sander had stopped again and turned to Dane, whose eyes were on the poem. Gesturing his chin toward it, he asked, "How long have you had that up there?"

Liam came and stood next to her, crossed his arms, and took a deep breath.

"I don't know," she said. "When did we find it?"

"When did *you* find it," Liam corrected.

Dane shrugged, set down the sander, and leaned a single hip against the bar. "I've been meaning to talk to you about it." He blew the pieces of hair that fell over his eyes. "Everyone knew...knows about Seth's infatuation with the legend of the dowry."

Willow waited for him to finish. It wasn't like Dane to trip over his words. Liam moved close enough that the muscles that weren't supposed to be there flexed where they touched. "Which is why I had it framed and hung it here," she said.

Dane rubbed the side of his nose with his thumb. "The Legend of Luciana Bezan," he said. "The Cuban girl born into poverty, her family coming into wealth from farming sweat and tears. The rich Spaniard who fell in love with her, angering his family enough for them to sink his ship and everything in it, including him and Luciana. The dowry said to be full of solid gold toilet seats, gaudy silver candlesticks, and large costume jewelry minus the costume and plus the diamonds and rubies."

She sighed and looked from him to Liam and back again.

"Listen to him," Liam said. "He knows what he's talking about."

"I can do that." She folded her hands in front of her. "Except he hasn't said anything yet."

"Her Legacy?" Dane said as a question. "The wet uncharted? The cornerstone that is Home? The under under?"

Liam wrapped his fingers around her arm making it nearly impossible to concentrate on what Dane was trying to say. They were warm and gentle and long enough to circle her entire upper arm.

Dane asked, "Have you had any new customers?"

"This is a tourist bar," Willow said without a hint of sarcasm.

"I mean local new, or at least locals who don't usually come here."

"I'm remodeling, Dane. I feel like it is expected to have locals who are as curious as the tourists."

"Okay." Dane's shoulders fell. "Look, Willow. What if this—?"

The front door opened. Her best employee, Paula, was followed by the first customer of the day.

"Hello, Paula," Willow said to her. "We only have a few more days of working around the mess." She would be lost without her best bartender. Paula blew around the counter with a mouthful of bobby pins, using one, then another to secure her mop of curly red hair into a messy bun.

"No worries, boss," Paula said, the freckles on her nose twitching the way they did when she was irritated. "You get the new hires in here yet?"

Paula worked solo, came early, and stayed late for the shifts she shared. She was bossy, arrogant, and Willow adored her. It was going to be hard for her to work with others, but with the expansion, Willow needed more hands. At least, she hoped she would.

"I have indeed," she said, a little disappointed that Liam's fingers slipped away from her arm. "They've been through the ever-growing list of government regulation videos and are coming mid-afternoon for a meet and greet." She stepped to the pile of mail and began thumbing through it. Junk, junk, bill.

Grabbing a pencil and sticking it through the bun, Paula asked, "Meet and greet who?"

Willow's brows lifted as she tossed the junk mail into the recycle bin. "You, my dear." Willow turned to Liam. "Are we on track for a Saturday soft opening?"

He didn't answer. Neither he nor Dane had returned to working. Willow followed Liam's eyes, which followed Dane's, which followed the customer.

Looking up, she noted the man was a sight for sure.

"Could have come," Paula leaned over and whispered to Willow as she clocked into the computer, "right off the cover of a rock star magazine. Yum."

Dreads, rows of hoop earrings, tats, and thick chains around his neck.

"You're not wrong about the magazine cover," Willow agreed as she eyed the exchange. "He's all yours."

"Hello, Dane," the man said, exposing a gold tooth in the front.

Oh, definitely not her type.

As Rock Star swung a leg over a barstool, his eyes lifted to Seth's poem. He added, "New job?"

"I thought you were on your way out of town," Dane said, stepping toward the man with a giant smile that didn't reach his eyes.

Rock Star shrugged. "Since you blew off Australia, I got nothin' pressing."

Dane slid his safety goggles back over his eyes. Liam cleared his throat louder than was reasonable.

It was like watching a tennis match. Liam, then Rock Star, then Dane, who pushed his goggles right back up as if he'd forgotten something. "Willow, Liam. This is Lucky. We've done some treasure hunting together. Lucky, Willow and Liam."

"Yo," Liam said and tipped up his chin.

Willow stopped the tennis match at Liam and mouthed the word, 'Yo,' to him.

"Nice to meet you, Lucky," Willow said, still staring at Liam. "What can we get for you today?" She smiled her best owner-of-the-bar smile and turned to offer a hand.

His were calloused. Each finger held a ring.

"Double Jack." He smiled, and the gold tooth sparkled in the bar lights. "No ice."

Dane released the Visqueen from the bungee cord and turned on the sander as Lucky made his way to a booth beneath one of the porthole windows. It was early for a double shot, but she wasn't here to judge. Island time was just that.

He slid close to the wall. All she could see of him was a tattooed arm that held his cell phone.

The front door flew open and small feet clicked along the weathered wood floor to the back.

"Hello, Chloe," Paula called as the flash of blonde waves ran past her and sped right to Liam.

Her father followed.

"Chloe. Dad. There you are. You headed to the restaurant?" Willow asked.

He nodded. "Are you sure you don't want me to take her with?"

It was hard enough for Willow to juggle a six-year-old while working. She would never ask it of her father. "No, thank you. I'm grateful for the help with yoga."

"Liam, Liam," Chloe yelled from the other side of the plastic loud enough for all to hear. "I was a good egg. Mommy and I took care of her and I turned her every six hours just like Siri said."

Through the plastic, Liam's laugh was contagious and brought her the sense of peace it always did.

"Or, Grandpa turned the egg," her father whispered.

Liam rechecked the anchor as Dane gave the final directions to the group.

"Recall signal is one long, two shorts," Dane said. "I'd use the side of my swim step, here."

Since the three pairs of divers were experienced, Liam was only half listening.

"Current is average today and from the south," Dane continued.

Liam spread his feet for stability, stood tall, and looked out over the water. It was only slightly choppy, and the clouds were a welcome relief from the heat.

"Port side and straight down are the railroad cars courtesy of Uncle Sam. Highly recommended," Dane added. "Starboard and inland you'll find one of the larger crystal springs caves. Upon return remember to take the full three minutes at the fifteen-foot safety stop and when you surface to keep your distance from the ladder as you wait your turn to board. Now get off my boat!" he yelled with a toothy smile.

SEVEN

As Dane directed one diver after another on their roll-off into the water, Liam turned up the song about pina coladas and getting caught in the rain. He prepped the hang bar and poly line. Waves licked the side of the boat, reminding him he had the best summer job there was.

When the last diver dipped out of sight, Liam made note of the time and dropped the hang bar next to the swim step. The divers would appreciate this new one Zoe had bought for their longer fifteen-foot safety stop. Spotting a plastic water bottle at the foot of a seat, he grabbed it and chucked it into the recycle bin.

Tossing the poly line starboard, he checked to make sure it wasn't tangled, then recognized that Dane had been much too quiet. "You're quiet today. Wedding plans on the mind?"

Dane shook his head. "You're stupid." He picked up the boat clipboard.

"What?" Liam stood tall and crossed his arms.

"You don't remember Lucky?"

Who could forget a guy named Lucky Nemo, who looked like a cartoon character? "Yeah. So?"

"So?"

"What? Are you taking off again?" Wouldn't surprise him. Sun Trips Touring had always been a cover for Dane. It paid the bills so Dane could afford to take off for weeks or sometimes months at a time on treasure hunting trips. Or, at least that was before he fell for Zoe Clearwater. Fell hard. Liam understood.

Shrugging, he picked up his water bottle and plopped down on one of the backseats. The view was nothing he would ever get used to. Ever wanted to get used to. Water as far as the eye could see. Spotted with white caps, sailboats, and an occasional dolphin fin. The blue of the sky was insane and broken up with bright white clouds at all the right places.

A firm hand landed on his shoulder. "No. Don't you *remember* him?"

Liam looked at the hand on his shoulder, then at Dane as he collapsed in the seat next to him.

"Lucky Nemo—"

Liam snorted.

"Named before the movie," Dane added. "Dude, he's dangerous."

Regardless of the clouds, Liam pulled the sunglasses from his head over his eyes. "What are you trying to say?"

"Man, the poem!"

Liam glanced at Dane. "Yeah," he said. The poem. "It's a map. I get it. I don't disagree."

"What are you going to do about it?" Dane asked.

Do about it? Liam opened his mouth, then shut it again.

"She's *your* girlfriend," Dane barked.

"Shut the hell up." Liam jerked his head toward him. "I told you to quit saying that."

"You're an idiot."

"You're an asshole."

Dane took a deep breath. "Dude, Lucky," he said slower and little louder.

"I know, I know. What am I supposed to do about it? The author of the poem is dead. Seth is dead." His heart hurt for Willow as it always did when they talked about her brother.

45

"Everyone wants to think this is a poem and go looking for Luciana's dowry."

Dane rubbed his hands over his face, then leaned forward with his forearms on his legs. "You are the stupidest smart person I've ever known."

Liam wasn't qualified for this kind of banter. "And, you're a dick. What are friends for?"

"Treasure map?" Dane said like a question. "Lucky? Willow?"

The muscles in Liam's face fell. His eyes turned to Dane, but he couldn't see his expression behind the sunglasses. "You think Willow could be in danger from Lucky?"

Dane nodded exaggeratedly.

"And, that's why you think Lucky showed up at Luciana's?" Liam looked through Dane to the choppy water beyond him. "In the day. When Willow would be there."

Liam didn't pay attention to his friend's reaction. "It doesn't matter if it's a map or not." He was more thinking out loud than anything. "If Lucky thinks it's a map."

Dane's nod turned from condescending to agreement. "And," he added, "how did he know about it?"

Liam asked, "Do you think we should tell the detective?"

"You hear he got stationed or assigned or whatever—"

"Ibis Island interim Chief of Police, yes," Liam said, staring at nothing. His brain was jumping from tangent to possibility to possibility to tangent. "The Clearwaters have a habit of stuffing things. All is okay. People are good."

Dane cleared his throat. "Except Raine."

"There is that," Liam agreed.

It was too hot for a fire, but Willow sat outside anyway with her blue painted toes propped on the edge of the fire pit. On her lap was a shoe box filled with the photos retrieved from her brother's apartment after he went missing. After he was murdered.

Her phone buzzed in her pocket. It made her jump. That had been happening a lot lately.

I'm in the Luciana's parking lot. I do not see your car.

A grin beckoned at the corners of her mouth. Liam was the only person she knew who used perfect grammar in text messages.

on my way after a bit. dropping chloe off at my parents

Sighing, she added…

everything okay

She stared at her phone longer than comfortable before he answered.

All is well. I am coming to you. If Chloe is with that egg, I should come by.

The right thing to do would be to tell him there wasn't a need for him to do that, but she decided not to.

I mean, that super great egg.

At that, she laughed and set her phone next to her on the bench.

Her mother came out wearing orange and black leopard leggings, an oversized Turtle Watch shirt, and flip-flops with a large fuchsia daisy on each. In her hands were two drinks with ice cubes.

She moved over to give her room. "Is Chloe with the egg?" Willow asked.

"Oh, yes," her mother said and handed her one of the glasses. "She turned it and is currently talking to it. I set out oatmeal raisin cookies and almond milk."

Willow sniffed the contents. Peach tea. They sat in silence for a blissfully long time. "How long do we let this go on?" she finally said as more of a statement than a question.

Expanding her lungs, her mother exhaled loudly before setting her feet next to Willow's on the empty fire pit.

Changing the subject, her mother said, "Your father and I will take care of the Waterfront this evening, dear."

A cringe of guilt touched Willow's heart. She sighed. "I'm sorry, Mom. I've been so wrapped up with the renovation, I haven't been pulling my weight at the restaurant."

"It's never a problem." Her mother set a hand on Willow's leg, making everything okay.

Tapping the box of photos, her mother said, "You must have those memorized by now."

It was true. "Sometimes it feels like browsing through a section of the Ibis Island Museum. The array of colors of the sky at dusk, the greens of the water." Willow flipped through the photos with her free hand, searching for a good example. "Seth could always catch the emerald green of the water. The Ibis Island Museum owner came by Luciana's the other day. I think I should see if he wants copies of any of these."

"Glen Oberweiss?" her mother asked.

Willow began to answer but was interrupted by a voice coming from the side of the house. "Willow?"

"Ah," her mother said. "I should leave you two alone."

"What for?" Willow asked, impressed with how fast Liam had made it there.

His voice became louder. "Are you back here?"

"Yes. Back here," she yelled as her mother walked through the door to the four-seasons room.

He stopped before reaching the fire pit and noted the closing door behind her mother, then to Willow. "Was it something I said?"

Willow shrugged and patted the vacant spot next to her.

"Did I miss Chloe?" he asked as he sat down and picked up the discarded glass of tea. "Is this for me? I need to talk to you about something." He took a long drink before she could answer.

His thigh brushed against hers, and he jerked it away.

It was enough of a distraction that she forgot what he'd asked. "What did you say?"

He looked at her with his dark brown eyes, smiling wide, his white teeth contrasting his boat tan. It didn't help her coherency.

"I asked if I missed Chloe. Is she inside?"

She shifted on the bench. "She's eating cookies and milk."

He looked down at the glass of tea. "I didn't get cookies. Why didn't I get cookies?" Leaning over her shoulder, he said, "You're going through Seth's old photos." After a short pause, he added, "Again."

"Look at this," she said and took out a photo. "Grouper. He's got zillions of them. You know how hard it is to find a grouper?"

"No. All I can think about is the spot you lost where that picture goes."

It made her laugh, and she rested her head on his shoulder. The air around her became safer, peaceful.

"It does make me think of something," he said. "With all the times you've looked through these, I imagine you have them memorized."

"My mother just said that."

He scooted close enough that she could smell the scent of clean gulf air and cologne. Why did he smell good? Didn't he just come from the morning Sun Trips Scuba tour?

She looked at the box and tilted her head. Yes, she said in her mind before repeating it out loud. "Yes. I do. It's true."

"What about what's not here?" he said as if he solved a physics problem. His gaze moved around the yard like he was looking for something, except his eyes never focused on anything.

"Where are the pictures of Chief Robert's wife, Miriam? They were having an affair, right? In love and all that?"

She repeated, "And all that?" She couldn't help but smile. "How romantic."

Liam wagged his head from left to right. "I mean they were running away together. Why are there no pictures of her, of them?"

She looked at the box, then back to him, and rested her cheek on his shoulder again.

"Maybe he has them saved on his computer," Liam suggested. "People do that."

She closed her eyes. "I've been through his computer. I didn't find any saved pictures. No external hard drive. Maybe you could take a look?"

"I am a physics geek, not a computer geek."

"Better than me."

"Point taken."

"Liam!" Chloe's voice came from inside.

Willow straightened to an upright position and tidied her shirt.

Chloe ran out the back door and wiggled her hips from side to side, scooting her little body between them. "The egg is great. I turned it, but you should probably check on it."

Willow sighed with relief knowing Chloe wasn't talking to her.

"You said you wanted to talk to me about something?" Willow asked before he was swept away by a small child and a duck egg.

His eyes went to Willow, then Chloe. They were honest and warm. "I...came to check on the egg."

EIGHT

After toeing off his shoes, Liam plopped down on the beach access bench. He dug his feet in the warm sand as his phone vibrated in the pocket of his khaki shorts. Caller ID said Dane. Since this was definitely not who he was expecting, his answer may have been less than polite. He checked the time on the screen before answering. Nine o'clock.

"What's up?" Liam asked. "Aren't you doing the evening cruise?"

"Docking now. What did Willow say?"

Liam sighed. "I haven't told her yet."

"What the hell?"

"Her head bartender took the day off. I had tutoring. She had a Turtle Talk thing."

"Lucky isn't someone to mess with."

"I know. I know. I'm waiting for her now. Walking the beach for lights after dark."

"Right," Dane said. "It's Saturday. New crop of tourists day."

"I'll tell her tonight."

"Get your head out of the damned clouds and make her understand, or I'm telling her myself."

"Get my head out of the clouds? You're telling her yourself?" Liam rose to his feet. "Don't threaten me."

"Liam?" Willow's voice called from too close.

Dane said barely loud enough for Liam to hear, "She's standing right behind you, isn't she? Good luck, man." And, he disconnected.

"Telling who what? Who is in the clouds?"

The heat growing on his neck traveled over his face. "There's something I have to talk to you about." He forced his legs to turn and face her.

She wore shorts that were more of the legging material thing she wore and a shirt that fell off one of her shoulders. Damn, she had the longest legs.

"I'm here," she said with that bright smile that was contagious. "You're blushing. Why are you blushing?"

Craning his head from her, he flicked his fingers like he was shooing a fly. "It's nothing."

"Turtle Talk was marvelous. I had twenty-four show. I think a few are going to adopt nests." She stood on her toes and turned her gaze down the beach. "Look at all of those lights on after dark. I swear that Richard Beckett isn't even trying to lay out rental instructions regarding lights out at dusk. His properties are almost always the ones that—"

"Willow," Liam said. He took hold of her wrists and pulled her down to the bench.

Her tiny wrists were much like she was—soft and warm, yet strong. Shaking his head, he lifted his gaze to meet hers.

"What is it?" she asked. "You're scaring me."

He looked down at his hands, then jerked his arms back, palms out.

"I don't mean that." She crossed her arms, took one of his hands, and placed it back on a wrist. "It's your expression. Is everything okay? Are you okay?"

Liam shook his head once more. "Yes. No." He bent his head closer to hers. He tried a reassuring smile but wasn't confident of his delivery. "I want you to listen to me. This is going to sound crazy, but please hear me out. It's the poem."

She tried to interrupt. Again. But, he put a finger to her parted lips.

"Please," he said again. "I want you to listen to me. The wet uncharted? The cornerstone that is Home? The under under? Willow, your brother was obsessed with two things. Running away with Miriam Roberts and Luciana Bezan's dowry. Dane and I...we think the poem is——"

"A map," she finished his sentence for him.

Liam squinted his eyes and looked into each of hers, one at a time, as if one might tell him something the other didn't. "You know?"

She shrugged. "I don't know anything," she said, pulling her arms away and standing. With her back to him, she lifted her arms straight above her head, clasped her fingers and stretched before dropping her arms to hug herself. "I figured it out when the six divers who went down with Seth the day he went missing...the day he was murdered...started showing up at Luciana's."

"What? Who?" Standing, he took her shoulders and turned her to face him.

"The original six. Or at least the five who aren't sitting in jail awaiting trial for killing my brother."

"Not just Lucky," he murmured, fear gripping him, and he pulled her into him.

She rested her warm cheek on his chest and seemed to melt against him.

"At first it was Richard Beckett," she said into his shoulder as she wrapped her arms around his back. "It made sense that he would want to see the renovation since he's a real estate agent. He was curious. That's all. Then, it was Blake Eaton. Same thing, you know? He owns the only other establishment, other than the Tiki Bar, that has dancing. I thought he was coming to check out the competition."

He had a hundred questions but was afraid if he stopped her from sharing, she might not start again. Instead, he rested his chin on the top of her head and inhaled. She smelled like peaches and fresh salt water.

"But then, Timothy Hart showed up and even Miriam."

At that, he pulled away and looked in her eyes. "Miriam?"

"I know, right? I am going to make her a copy. Seth was hers. She should have a copy of the poem. I feel awful for not thinking of it before. And then, I thought, so what?" Her shoulders shrugged again.

He pulled away and ran his hands up her arms and rubbed his thumbs over the bare skin of her exposed shoulder. "So, what?"

"Let them think it's a map, or know it's a map, or whatever. Let them look all over the Gulf for the wet uncharted for some imaginary treasure."

"What if people become dangerous? What if it's not imaginary?"

Her gaze bore holes through his, but only lasted a short moment before it dropped to his mouth.

"I still don't care," she said without taking her eyes from his mouth.

He almost forgot what they were taking about. All of his intellect moved south. A volcano of ideas bubbled beneath his better sense.

Turning his chin away, he patted her twice on the shoulder. Using his body, he guided her so they were side-by-side. He linked their fingers and led her down the darkened beach. He would not take advantage of her. She was out of his league. The wife of his best friend. The widow of his best friend. Of his died-in-the-line-of-duty war hero best friend.

Liam was a high school teacher.

Squeezing her fingers, they headed for the first rental with lights on after dusk. They would figure out Lucky's motives. The others, too. He would be here for her. For her and Chloe. And that would be enough.

———

At nine in the morning, Aiden and Sam's friends were probably still in bed. If the boys had to spend summer days tutored in a course they sucked at, the least Liam could do was take class outside whenever possible.

The sun was high. Small and blazing. There wasn't a hint of a cloud. Yet, the steady breeze from the Gulf made him give it a perfect island morning rating. Willow doing her Pilates or yoga or something that made him dizzy and confused only helped the rating.

Aiden and Sam sat huddled together on an oversized beach rug, studying the materials he'd brought for this week's experiment. Positioned far enough away that the boys had their independence, yet close enough for supervision, he sat in his beach chair with Seth's laptop resting on his thighs. The experiment would be a potato cannon one day, but for today, it was a lesson in creating a decent log. It was August 1, and although concepts and vocab were strong, both of the boys' logs needed improvement. He had his work cut out for him, and little time left to do it.

The PVC pipes, adapter, coupler, plug, and reducer were already assembled. Since it had been two days since their last tutoring session, the glue had plenty of time to dry. To the naked eye, the cannon would look complete. To anyone in the know, it was clearly missing the ignition, acceleration, and combustion components.

Willow made it damned hard to focus, and since he was already multitasking with the laptop, her distraction was downright cruel. She stood on one leg like a sleeping ibis or great blue heron. As slow as molasses, she lifted her other leg with her arm until the leg was nearly straight up in the air. Was it touching her ear? He found himself craning his head to see if a horizontal view might make more sense.

The boys studied the electrical tape, spark emitter, trigger, and positive/negative leads. The hairspray accelerant and potatoes would have to wait for another day and farther away from humans.

Willow was right. The computer was clean of all pics, which made no sense. No external hard drive had been found in any of Seth's possessions. What photographer does that?

Liam had already tried over a dozen popular photo sites and couldn't find an account using Seth's email address.

Behind Willow's airborne leg was the sign for the only island drug store. The So Right Convenient Store. The light and height had always been a problem for the turtles during nesting season. How many had wandered toward it at night rather than the Gulf?

Shrugging, he typed So Right photos into the search bar, then began to log in using Seth's email. As soon as he typed the first letter, the site auto-filled the rest of it. He sat straighter in his beach chair and licked his lips.

Crossing imaginary fingers, he clicked the cursor into the password field, hoping on all hopes that the password would auto-fill as well.

A boom loud enough to shake the ground made him fumble the laptop, barely saving it from a sudden death in the sand. It was followed by loud bellows and cheers and then a dull thump as a potato landed in the sand between the boys and Willow and her, now screaming, yoga class.

The apparently fully assembled potato gun stood frozen and pointed to the sky. A contraband bottle of hairspray and the open bag of potatoes rested on the sand next to the offenders. It was one of Liam's proudest moments.

"Boys!" Liam yelled while chanting, 'Keep a straight face. Keep a straight face,' in his head.

Aiden and Sam stood like statues, their mouths shaped in large Os.

"We swear we didn't know it would be that loud." Aiden stood with both arms still around the cannon, hiding the C and the D in his ACDC t-shirt.

Sam lifted his arms in surrender. "Or go that high. Yeah, we swear."

Looking at the cannon still in hand, Aiden dropped it and lifted his hands as well.

Liam glanced from one side of them to the other. A few beach walkers down a ways. Aside from the freaked out beach yoga class, no one else was around. "You did it. No phones needed." Down by his side, he gave them a covert fist bump.

"All right." He stood and, with his hands on his hips, cleared his throat. "I want you to think about the abstract. Purpose, hypothesis, any major findings."

Sam snorted. "Like potatoes can shoot a thousand yards into the air."

Liam smiled from ear to ear. "Yeah, like that."

<hr />

With the sun straight overhead, it beat blistering waves on Willow's back. The jeans she always wore when handling larger turtles just made it worse. She used her cooling towel to wipe the sweat from her neck, then tucked the ends into her tank.

In the back of Raine's pickup, three loggerheads stirred their flippers under the wet beach towels used to keep them cool. The turtles might be large but were still juveniles. No way could she and her big sister lift a full-grown loggerhead.

"Ready?" Raine asked.

Willow checked her grip on the left side of the shell of number four. The stunning shapes of reddish-brown sections on its shell were covered in barnacles, and Willow could see part of a multi-pronged fish hook still imbedded in the thick, wrinkled skin of his neck.

The St. Pete's turtle hospital generally took care of hooks, but they were over capacity. Damned careless fisherman. So, the marine laboratory south of Ibis agreed to take care of and clean up the turtles.

An intern named Katie pecked on a tablet as Willow widened her stance. Katie couldn't have been old enough to be legal and was about half the size of Willow's willowy frame.

"Are you sure I can't help?" Katie asked in a tiny voice.

Willow's eyes opened wide. "No. No, but thank you for asking."

Raine had the other side and counted, "On three. One, two, three."

Using her legs, Willow hefted her side of the hundred pounds. Its flippers thrashed like mad. Another ten pounds and she and Raine might not be able to do this on their own, and the turtle had at least another few hundred to go before puberty when the gender would be apparent.

Chloe manned the hose, spraying the beach towels that covered the other three in the truck bed, as well as, inadvertently, Willow and Raine. Neither would complain about the refreshing spray, but Katie might. "Be careful, Chloe."

NINE

Grunting, Willow helped Raine give the turtle one more shove into the truck bed, then Raine craned her head around its backside. "He's clear. Let's close it up," Raine said and secured the tailgate.

Willow watched Chloe as Katie handed Raine some paperwork. "The marine lab is expecting them."

Raine already knew this but didn't say so.

"Back up, sweetie," Willow said to Chloe. "We need to get the topper on before we head out."

Chloe gave the new entry one more spray before she backed off as Willow and Raine lifted the topper over and secured it to the sides of the truck bed.

"Why are they called loggerheads?" Chloe asked Katie.

Katie looked around like the sky might have an answer. "I don't—"

"Sailors thought they were logs. Get in," Raine said. "I don't like them back there for too long in this heat."

To be fair, Willow didn't know about the sailors either. "Thank you, Katie. Good luck with your semester."

Chloe jumped in the middle of the cab as Willow turned off the water. As she climbed in, she heard Chloe let out a deep sigh. "They look really gross. Are they going to be okay?"

She wasn't talking to Willow. "Sure are," Raine answered.

"What will the marine lab people do?" Chloe asked as Raine pulled onto the highway.

Raine placed her free hand on Chloe's leg. "They are going to weigh them and feed them and clean their shells and get those nasty hooks out of their skin."

"Their dinosaur skin." Chloe curled her fingers, making two claws.

As she jiggled Chloe's leg, Raine smiled. "That's right."

"The biologists at the lab agreed to care for them until they can be released back into the Gulf."

Chloe craned her head over her shoulder and peered through the small window back to the truck bed before snuggling into Willow's arm.

Palm trees zoomed by. The 789 was one of the prettiest drives around. A muster of peacocks strutted along the side of the road to the east. Heat waves emanated from the Gulf water to the west. Stucco homes with yards framed in gama grasses or philodendron.

"Liam and Dane think the poem is a map."

You could have heard a pin drop, mostly because Chloe fell asleep. The silence was broken by an occasional rustle of a flipper in the back.

Raine kept her eyes out the windshield. "That makes sense."

"Yeah. I kind of thought so too."

"So, you and Zoe are the divers of the family."

"That's not true."

"Mostly true. The wet uncharted must be somewhere in the Gulf. Are you two going to look?"

Willow pulled her chin back. "What? No. When did Seth's obsessions ever turn out to be real?"

Raine shrugged.

"I couldn't care less about any treasure. That's Dane's thing. This is his idea."

"Of course, it is."

"People have been to Luciana's."

"People do that."

"Stop being a jerk. I'm serious."

"It's my job description."

"Different people."

"Spit it out, Willow."

"Blake Eaton."

"Wants to check out the competition."

"That's what I said." Willow folded her hands on her thighs. "Richard Beckett."

"Realtor with tons of property. You're renovating. Makes sense."

"Timothy Hart."

"The school superintendent? That's almost the entire dive team that went down with Seth's last dive."

"Exactly."

"What about Oberweiss and Mayor Green?"

Willow shook her head, not that Raine could see her as she drove, but then remembered. "The mayor, no, not that he couldn't have come when I wasn't there. Mr. Oberweiss rode his bicycle by. We spoke, but he didn't come in, only promised to show up for the grand reopening."

Raine let her head fall back long enough for Willow to fear for her life.

"What?"

"We probably need to tell the cop."

"Detective, and no."

"Wow. When did the role reversal happen?"

"I suppose, right now. So, what if the poem is a map? What if the divers of the Ibis think so, too, and want to go searching all over for it? We have circled back to the fact that Seth's obsessions never panned out, and who cares if there is a treasure? Law says the state takes ownership of it, and searching for that kind of stuff is not my thing."

"You've looked into this."

Willow sighed.

Raine asked, "Are you convincing me of this stuff or yourself?"

"One of Dane's treasure hunter friends came by too."

Raine pressed on the brakes and pulled off onto the narrow shoulder. "Lucky Nemo?"

"Are we there?" Chloe asked, wiping the side of her mouth.

"No, honey. Aunt Raine is having a moment." Willow kissed the top of her head. "Yes, Lucky Nemo. You know him?"

"Finding Nemo and his lucky fin?" Chloe asked.

"No," Raine said. "A bad Nemo. A man named Lucky Nemo, who isn't kind to sea turtles. Willow, he's suspected of vandalizing nests and—"

"Speak in code." Willow covered Chloe's ears.

Raine said, "We need to tell the c-o-p."

"I can spell cop," Chloe said indignantly.

"Why?" Willow asked as Raine pulled back onto the highway. "Who cares if they want to come and look at the poem? Take pictures of it. Go look for treasure. I don't want to jeopardize the investigation of Seth's murder."

"Okay," Raine said much too calmly. "It's going to be okay."

Looking down at her hands, Willow noticed they were clamped together.

"The marine laboratory is around the corner," Raine added. "Chloe is awake. Four loggerheads are about to have a safe place to heal. We are doing good here."

The huge white span of buildings came into view. Raine pulled onto the long gravel road that led to what Willow liked to think of as the service entrance. From the distance, she spotted Bobbi, her favorite conservation biologist. Braided pigtails hung close to her neck and over her chest. In her hand was a tablet much like one the intern had used.

"Mommy, can we see inside today? I want to see Milly."

Milly. The manatee that had been there for weeks now. Or, was that months? "We'll ask."

Bobbi waved and Raine rolled down her window. "Hello, Bobbi. Where would you like us?"

Bobbi peeked in the back. "Right where you are is fine. Four?" She checked her tablet, then scratched her head. "Let me grab some help." She disappeared around the first area with half-walls and four large water tanks.

Willow tried to blink back the tears without fully understanding why they were there. Look up and smile. Two proven methods to keep tears away. But, it didn't work. The first tear slipped over her cheek. "That pokes a hole in—"

Raine finished for her. "Motive."

Chloe asked, "What's motive?"

"A decoration on a t-shirt," Raine answered.

The motive for Seth's murder. She covered her mouth with both hands and realized they were shaking. It had always been the affair. The domestically abusive chief of police in a jealous rage over the affair Seth was having with his wife.

"What's the matter, Mommy?"

Willow shook her head. "Nothing at all, honey." She kissed Chloe on the top of her head.

"Roberts was caught in the act." In the act of trying to kill his wife and Zoe, too, for helping her.

"I'm sure you're right. There's Bobbi. Let's just be the ones to share with the cop instead of anyone else."

Raine let out a heavy sigh.

"Stupid cops," Chloe said.

Willow didn't have the energy to parent Chloe or scold Raine for teaching her that.

Raine lifted a single shoulder. "As primary permit holder, I probably need to make an appearance with the new chief of do nothing anyway. I'll go."

Willow cringed. "I'll go with you, but it is not a motive. Or a motif."

Bobbi and her helper opened the back of the topper. "Mind if we take her off?" she asked, referring to the topper.

Raine opened her door and got out. "Let me help you with that."

"Mind if we check on Milly?" Willow called to the back.

"Go right ahead," Bobbi said as the topper came off.

She and Chloe crawled out of the truck cab and stretched.

Small fingers took her hand and tugged her toward what she liked to think of as the marine life waiting room.

The concrete wall that separated it from the parking lot was about waist high and open to the elements above and to the awning. Walking through the entrance opening, Chloe dodged the hanging scale and ran right to tank number four. Milly's tank.

"How much longer until she gets to be free?"

"I'm not sure," Willow said and caught up to her.

Milly came over to investigate her small visitor. She'd weighed in at almost eight hundred pounds the last time they were here. The propeller wounds she was healing from were only some of the dozens of lines that covered her gray body. A whisker-covered nose came out of the water, wiggled, then sprayed them.

The first turtle was hauled through the door and set on a green blanket. Chloe ran over but kept her distance, making Willow the proudest mama ever.

She came up next to her, wrapped an arm around her short shoulder, and watched as the intern measured and recorded stats on the first turtle.

"Mommy, what does a chief of nothing do?"

Willow closed her eyes and smiled.

Raine agreed to pick up a bouquet of flowers. Without argument. Willow dropped Chloe off with her folks and waited in the shade next to the only door along the front of the Ibis Island City Hall. Leaning against the wall, she recognized how well the grounds crew kept the building as tidy as they did the rest of the public island buildings. The orange bricks were clean and the simple landscaping beds weeded.

Raine bumped into the parking lot and pulled her truck next to Willow's smart car. She gave her the stink eye over her steering wheel.

"I know, I know," she said as Raine got out of her truck. "I had a change of clothes at Mom and Dad's."

"It's probably good you told me to get smelly flowers, then."

"Fragrant."

"Yeah, that, because I smell like sea turtle."

"It was Zoe who said they had to be fragrant. I didn't ask why. You got a vase."

"You didn't say not to. Let's get this done," Raine said and held the door open with her free hand.

Willow recognized the flowers. Lavender and jasmine. To welcome Matt as the interim Chief of Police of Ibis Island? Squinting, she walked through the door and up to the reception desk. It was clean of anything and everything other than a clipboard with a pen attached by a string.

"Glory Studebaker." Willow walked around the desk with open arms. Glory was Zoe's year in high school, but since their parents had the three of them in three years, she and Raine knew her nearly as well.

After setting the nail file down she'd been using, Glory pushed away from the desk. "For me?" she squealed and tiptoed around on five-inch wedges and the tightest miniskirt Willow might have ever seen. "Zoe said she was going to send flowers. You Clearwaters are the sweetest girls."

Like just about everyone, Glory didn't remember Willow was really a Martinez. "We're here to see Detective...err...Chief Osborne." Willow appreciated that Glory turned to Raine and hugged her as well. The way Raine lifted her chin and quickly patted the top of the back of anyone who broke her personal bubble never got old.

Glory lifted her brows at the same time she smelled the bouquet. "Of course. Sign there on the clipboard, please." She motioned toward the empty columns on the paper attached to a clipboard. "New rules," she said, gesturing a thumb over her shoulder toward what would now be Matt's office. "I'll let him know you're here."

TEN

"We appreciate it," Willow said to Glory and elbowed Raine. "Yes," Raine said. "Thank you."

Glory pushed a button on her landline, then picked up her nail file. Raine took Willow by the hand, pulling her down the hall. "This place gives me hives."

They passed the empty mayor's office and the conference room that had a paper taped next to the door listing the dates the room would be unavailable. Monthly town board meeting. IPD officer and all staff meeting. She wondered who else would be included in the category of staff other than Glory.

Raine gave her another tug.

"I'm coming. I expect you to be on your best behavior."

Raine stopped short and craned her head to meet Willow's gaze. "You sounded like Mom there. It's creepy."

"I most certainly did not. It's just that Matt is my friend and a really nice guy."

"Sure he is, and he's here to make all sorts of changes for the better of Ibis Island. I bet he'll be there when laws are broken, enforce sea turtle codes, and show his face once in a while. Everything is rainbows and unicorns."

A few yards in front of them, a male voice cleared his throat. Matt stood in the doorway to the chief of police office. An empty nail stuck out of the center of the door where incarcerated Chief Robert's nameplate used to hang. He wasn't in uniform like Chief Roberts always seemed to be. Matt wore what she thought of as his detective gear. Dress pants. Buttoned-down shirt. No tie. Gun holster. The badge at his waist still had the letters SPPD engraved in it.

He tapped his finger on it. "New one comes today." He stuck his hands in his pockets and rocked back on his heels. "How did I get so lucky as to have a Clearwater and a Martinez on my first day?"

Like she did with Glory, she opened her arms. "Welcome to Ibis Island, Chief Osborne." She counted in her head, giving him a full three-second hug.

When she pulled away, she looked to Raine and even though she wanted desperately to smirk, willed her expression to that of innocence.

Rolling her eyes, Raine gave him the same hug, albeit shorter, that she'd given Glory.

Matt cleared his throat and said, "Come in, come in. I'll make room."

There was plenty of room, just no guest chairs. The same boxes that had been stacked in his St. Pete's office were now stacked in this one. She noted the differences from when Chief Roberts resided here. The stuffed fish were missing. Matt had hung diplomas—plural—and certificates of achievement as well as a few newspaper articles that she would read some time, only not when they needed to talk about her brother.

"What can I do for you ladies?"

Raine folded her arms and cocked a hip.

Matt nodded. "Let me get something for you to sit on."

"Be nice," Willow growled when he stepped out.

"Let's get this over with."

He came back dragging two padded chairs. "There. Those look good right there." He held his hand out for her and Raine to sit. "Can I get you some water? Coffee?"

"That's kind of you but no."

He sat in his chair and folded his hands on his desk. "I've seen Willow," he said as he looked to Raine. "But, I haven't had a chance to tell you how sorry I am about the delay in getting your brother's remains back to you."

"Do you mean former delay, current, or subsequent?" Raine asked.

Matt leaned forward on his elbows. "All of the above, I suppose."

"That's not exactly why we're here," Willow confessed. "It is likely inconsequential, but this is a small town."

"We think Seth left a treasure map." Raine swung an ankle on her knee. "This isn't big city St. Pete's, Chicago, or Reno. Small town means someone else who wants to blow it up to something bigger than it is. Small town people can do that."

Matt moved one of his hands to his chin and the other on a thigh. "Okay," he said, dragging out the word, then grinned.

"It's a poem," Willow explained.

Matt dropped his brows. "How about you tell me about this poem map."

"It would make more sense if I started at the beginning." She clasped her fingers together and squeezed. "My parents kept three pieces of furniture that belonged to our brother, two dressers and a desk. Seth and my father refinished or made them."

Matt nodded. His expression was patient and comfortable, yet she couldn't quite read him.

"Taped to the outside was a poem. It belonged to Seth." Deciding to qualify, she added, "It's not signed, but it's in his handwriting." She unlocked her fingers and waved her hand between Raine and herself. "We all know his handwriting well."

"Taped to the outside?" he interrupted.

It sounded worse saying it out loud in a police department. "Seth was eccentric like that."

"I see," he said as a statement. "And, you think it's a map?"

"It is a Haiku."

"A Haiku?"

"Three lines. The first and last have five syllables, the middle seven. It rarely rhymes." Why did she add that last part?

"I see," he said again.

She appreciated his patience. She was a good judge of character and this was a good man.

"Her Legacy," Willow said.

Raine set her hand on top of Willow's. It was gentle and careful.

"Seth as well as our entire family," Willow said. "We were raised to embrace nature, animals, and the land. Our parents were…are flower children. Becoming parents as teenagers, they struggled financially. My mother went to school in the day and my father in the evening. They learned to live off the land."

Raine rubbed her thumb over the back of Willow's hand.

"He took pictures as an art and a hobby. Land and underwater animals. He snorkeled. Could hold his breath under water for fifteen minutes. Honestly," she qualified. "Using sea shells, he created sculptures—some of them he framed—of the wildlife around the island."

"He had a reputation, well earned, of chasing rainbows. He graduated with a degree in nutrition. He tried to sell his photos, but that didn't take. Then, his sculptures but that was a failure as well."

Raine kept her gaze on Matt but wrapped her fingers around Willow's hand. She would be forever grateful.

"He lived inland as a delivery boy to pay his bills, and his next obsession was Luciana Bezan's dowry. I was there when Zoe told you the legend, and I expect you have a good memory."

"Thanks, I think."

"Seth lived it. Earned his scuba certification so he could stay down longer, search longer and deeper. People talked about him behind his back."

"Behind *our* backs," Raine added. "As the PPH, I can tell you, it's true."

"Primary permit holder."

Raine turned her eyes to Matt and pulled her chin back. "You've been doing your homework. So, Willow finds this poem. Her

Legacy. The wet uncharted. The cornerstone that is Home. The under under."

Willow shut her eyes and sighed as waves of warmth spread over her. She'd memorized it.

"Dane is a professional treasure hunter. Smithsonian professional. He thinks it's a map. We believe him. We just don't want it... don't think it," she corrected, "should make a difference in the trial."

Matt leaned back in his chair. "Ah." He turned and looked out the tiny window to the side of his desk. "Where would one find this poem?"

"Are you going to take it?" Raine asked.

"It is not evidence at this time."

It was a non-answer but felt more like the careful and gentle person she believed was Matt Osborne rather than elusive or dishonest.

Matt leaned forward, folding his hands again. "We have several witnesses who heard Chief Roberts threaten to hurt his wife and anyone she looked at. Miriam has agreed to testify. Torching Dane's place with her inside as well as your sister, since he saw Zoe as an accomplice, gets him attempted murder one. As far as your brother is concerned, we have a body, the murder weapon, and motive. We can place Roberts at the scene. I've seen suspects put away for less. What we don't have is a confession or physical proof linking the murder weapon to Roberts. He's still working on denial. He's getting out. We're all going to lose our jobs. Blah, blah, blah."

Willow set her fingertips on Matt's folded hands. "I think Zoe could get through to him."

"Your sister has been through a traumatizing ordeal." He squinted and pulled his hands away. "You don't seem like the type to put her in harm's way."

She knew what he meant. No physical danger, but emotional danger could be so much more.

Raine didn't move from her spot leaning back in her chair. "You don't know the big picture." She slung an ankle on her knee. "I've got the chief's back on this one, sister."

Willow craned her head. "Since when have you ever?"

Raine ignored her. "Zoe carries more on her shoulders in the form of guilt for the death of our brother than she does fear from the fire. He was a newly certified diver. Zoe agreed to be his diving partner and didn't show."

"Zoe didn't kill her brother," Matt said.

"I get that," Raine agreed. "Willow is the Zen master. Take her."

He rubbed a single hand along the back of his neck. "Bring in this poem. I'll take a look." He held up both hands. "I'll borrow it from you and consider your offer to bring one of your sisters along to an interrogation."

"Lip service," Raine said.

He stared at Raine. Awkward silence made Willow shift in her seat. Raine stared back. More awkward silence.

"I tell you what. I think Roberts is guilty. I think the jury's going to think so. We can say everything is rainbows and unicorns," Matt said using the term he must have overhead Raine say, "Or we can cast our net wide and get all we can on him."

He held back. Maybe a lot, but she and Raine had done what they came to do. "The poem is framed and hanging at Luciana's," Willow said. "How about a picture? I can—"

"I'll stop by," he interrupted and smiled.

Liam put the pontoon in reverse and gunned the engine enough to pull the end alongside the dock. Over the noise of the water that smacked between the pier and boat as it bumped against the buoys, he announced, "The bathrooms are inside the doors and to the right, there." He smiled at the ten eco tour passengers.

Lily was his assistant. That day, he was especially grateful for her work ethic and conscientiousness. As a college student at U of F, she was one of those kids that made a person think there was hope for the future of the world. He was distracted, and she took up the slack. No grumbling. No complaining. Grabbing the dock, she secured the back side of the boat before tidying up for the evening tour.

Liam stepped out to secure the front as he addressed the tourists. "Remember to check for your belongings, and thank you for using Sun Trips Touring."

As the last passenger crossed the mini-dock, Lily asked, "You okay, boss?"

Liam nodded, but it was a lie. "Tonight, we open the addition at Luciana's. Just got a lot on my mind."

Was the addition good enough? What would Henry think?

"Grand opening open?"

"No," he said, dragging out the O. "That's next weekend. We're taking down the plastic and plywood tonight for family, friends."

Lily looked at him like he was a little off, but he didn't expect her to understand. Lily didn't do the renovation or have fuzzy feelings for the owner.

"Why don't you get going, then? I can finish up here."

Liam opened his mouth to argue but stopped himself. "Thank you."

When should he get there, he asked himself as he wandered toward his Ford Ranger. What should he wear? Why was he thinking about what to wear?

A fist pushed his shoulder. "Earth to Liam," Zoe said.

He pulled his gaze from the gravel and looked up.

"Hey, Zo."

She was on her way in as he was on his way out. Stopping, she tightened the cowboy hat that served as her visor.

Liam decided on polite conversation. "How many do you have tonight?"

"Ten." She rolled her eyes and pointed a thumb over her shoulder. "I can smell the liquor."

ELEVEN

At the picnic table waiting area sat six college-aged boys and two middle-aged couples. Ouch. Two of the boys wore what Liam learned in his years of teaching high school to be do-rags. These were covered in skulls and crossbones. Tricky mix. Such a contrast to Lily.

"Your specialty." It was true. "How are wedding plans?" He expected her face to light up like the sun. That was what happened these days whenever he asked about her and Dane. Except, she didn't.

Digging both hands in the pockets of her denim shorts, she lifted her shoulders. "Not as much fun as I had hoped. This country is so full of expected traditions. Bachelorette parties, which are now weekend getaways, participant gifts included. Fancy invitations, bridal showers with elegant food and tulle-covered bride chairs. The table centerpieces and wedding guest gifts and cake and dinner and band and playlist and the dress. Good grief, the dress."

She'd lost him at tulle.

"This is going to cost as much as it would to provide clean water to dozens of third world villages for life."

He put an arm around her shoulder. "Spoken like a true Clearwater."

She sighed. "This is a happy time, supposed to be a happy time."

Giving her a one-armed squeeze, he said, "You're going to figure it—"

He gripped her shoulder and froze. On the other side of the picnic table was the new piece of land recently purchased by Richard Beckett, island real estate agent. It was going to be a remote parking lot for something. Liam's mouth hung open.

"What is it?" Zoe asked as she turned toward where he stared. Her mouth hung open as her insides erupted.

A giant crawled right over the gravel. A goliath. The biggest sea turtle he'd ever laid eyes on. And, since only females came out of the water, she came out for one reason. Still hanging onto Zoe's arm, he surveyed the gravel, the bulldozer, and the mess. "Layers of whoa." He pulled out his cell and yelled at it. "Call Raine Clearwater."

"What do we do?" Liam said as his cell rang, and he led the way toward the girl. "I've never seen one this big!"

"That's 'cause you've never seen a Leatherback. It's my first time too." She shook her head and marched with him. "Gotta be close to a ton."

"What do we do?" he repeated, knowing he was still yelling, but his heart beat so fast, he didn't care.

"Ibis Island Turtle Watch, please leave a message."

"Bah. Raine. Get your ass to Sun Trips! We've got a Leatherback!"

Each of the waiting ten in the sunset tour group rushed toward them. Zoe stuck her arms out. "We keep everyone clear of her and wait for Raine."

Okay, okay, okay. He could do that. He took the front of the girl and Zoe took caboose. "But the parking lot," he said, looking around at the destruction.

"I know," Zoe said then turned to the tourists. "Come on over, friends. My name is Zoe Clearwater." She waved her hands yet kept them outward and stood between them and the turtle.

Liam followed suit and held out his arms as well. Goose bumps as big as volcanos erupted over them. From the corner of his eye, he spotted Lily heading over. They were definitely going to need her.

The turtle made its way along the gravel like a behemoth swimming in slow motion; both flippers forward, dragging her body along the ground. Again and again, crunching over the gravel as if a dozen humans weren't following her.

Zoe was incredible. "I am not only your sunset tour captain this evening, but a certified member of our own Ibis Island Turtle Watch."

Both Skull and Crossbones boys maneuvered around the other side of Zoe, craning their heads at the turtle. "Back up, boys." She pointed at them. "You're welcome to watch, but you need to stay on this side of me."

The two didn't even pause and ducked right under her outstretched arm. "Mother fucker, man. Look at the size of it!" The taller one reared his head back and let out a rebel yell.

Liam charged them, his feet kicking up rocks. "Back off, boys," he said with his arms out in front of him.

"Lighten up, dude," the taller one said, dodging Liam's outstretched arms.

Liam grabbed the back of the boy's neck and squeezed.

"The fuck. Ow," the kid cried. "You can't touch me."

"Sea turtles are both threatened and endangered species. One more step and I call the cops. I promise they won't be as gentle." He hoped the kid didn't call his bluff and gave him a shove into his friend behind him. "As the lady said, you're welcome to watch but from a distance." He said the last three words nice and slow.

"Oh no," Zoe said.

With alcohol on their breath, Liam wasn't willing to turn around to see what was happening and, instead, glanced over his shoulder. The leatherback stopped and looked a lot like a cement mixer that anchored to the ground and outstretched its arms. "What's she doing?"

"Digging."

Stupid question. "Is that bad?"

"Very, very bad," Zoe said through her teeth and fake smile.

Sweat dripped down the back of his neck and not from the afternoon Florida heat. The turtle had stopped on the far side of the construction area in the smallest of dunes and used her massive front flippers first, then back ones to dig. Sand and rock flew behind it.

Her enormous shell looked like leather, and Liam thought that, other than Willow Martinez, he'd never seen anything more beautiful in his life.

He glanced around. Two of the guests from his eco tour had spotted the commotion and headed toward them. "Come on over," Liam said, then repeated what Zoe had said. "You're welcome to watch, but you need to stay on this side of us."

Zoe lifted her brows at him. He shrugged and grinned.

"This is a Leatherback sea turtle," Zoe began. "You are in for a special, special treat this evening as Leatherbacks are the largest of all living turtles and is the fourth-heaviest modern reptile. Other than its size, Leatherbacks differ from other turtles by their lack of a bony shell, thus the name."

The rest of the eco tour emerged from the Sun Trips Touring bathroom and changing area. Since they were probably going to come anyway, Liam waved them over.

The hole deepened. The girl maneuvered her butt like a pro. "Damnedest thing I ever have seen," he muttered.

"This is quite rare as Leatherbacks almost exclusively make their nests on the eastern side of Florida."

The group seemed to calm down and kept their distance, taking a plethora of pictures and videos.

Gravel crumpled beneath tires. Liam turned to see Raine's truck as it entered the parking lot. She skidded her tires to a stop, flew out of the driver's side, and stormed toward them.

She didn't speak and ignored Zoe's impromptu presentation. Instead, she walked around the turtle. She wore a shoulder bag with a sea turtle sewn on the flap. With both hands, she rubbed her face and the top of her head, then marched back to her truck.

Her hands were full when she returned and tossed the items on the ground about five yards from the Leatherback. A handful of wooden stakes, some orange electrical tape, a huge magic marker, and a rubber mallet.

"Hello, Raine," Liam said gently.

"Oh, hello, Liam," she said and pulled out a tablet from her bag. "Thank you for helping with this. I know you need to get to Willow's thing."

His eyes grew big. Luciana's. Checking his watch, he decided what he was wearing was just right. "What can I do to help?"

She nodded toward the six boys. "Keep frick and frack from getting too close."

He nodded and stepped closer to them.

"Are you Raine Clearwater?" one of the middle-aged women asked.

Raine rubbed a hand over her face. "Yes, I am. Hello. What a treat you have this evening."

"You have the best job in the world," she said to Raine.

Rained closed her eyes. It took her some time, but she finally said, "Thank you."

Obviously, word got out. It wasn't as if the soft opening was meant to be private or closed. The growing crowd and roar of voices was a good thing, Willow convinced herself through self-talk and deep breathing.

Not wanting to get in Paula's way, she mostly worked as bar back, which made her understand that managing and waitressing were more her cup of tea.

Paula was one of her favorite people. A red-headed bean pole with breasts the size of honeydew melons, which wouldn't normally mean a thing if not for the way she twisted, turned, and bounced back and forth from one end of the bar to the other, keeping the two newbies busy and tidying up in between.

Friends and family clustered around two kissing wooden spool tables. They sat adjacent to the beautiful, yet empty, dance floor. The brand new, extremely expensive beautiful, yet empty, dance floor.

She thought the area for dancing turned out perfectly. Picturesque. Early that morning, Liam had removed the temporary plywood walls that had hidden the construction. The plastic, the mess. Washed out planks lined the floor and roofing. The thick ropes that hung from it swayed in the steady Gulf breeze, almost keeping tempo to a song coming from the single-man band about cheeseburgers and paradise.

The transition between tucked away cabin-style booths and tables to the breezy, open dance floor couldn't be better.

"Stop worrying," Paula said.

"What?" Willow thought she hid her worry so well.

"It's written all over you." Paula popped the lids from two bottles of domestics, set them in front of Glory, the receptionist at city hall, and her date, and then turned to say, "The people will come. You carry way too much on those shoulders."

Willow skipped the obvious opening to a boob joke. "But, what if no one dances?" There. She said it.

Paula wiped down the counter with one hand and took Glory's date's credit card with the other. "It's not even dark yet. Simmer down, girl."

She could always make Willow smile. "You can't tell the yoga and Pilates instructor who also happens to be your boss to simmer down."

Paula tapped Willow's butt as she moved down the bar, then called over her shoulder, "Boss lady, we have a blown keg."

On her way to the backroom, Willow passed the group of almost everyone she loved in the world. Her mom and dad. Raine, Liam, and Dane. Greg and Lily from Sun Trips and several from her parents' restaurant, the Beachfront.

All eyes were on Liam, who stood, gesturing wildly with his long arms. "That mother was this big," he said, enunciating the last two words and spreading his arms wide enough that he could've been describing a whale.

She couldn't help but to stop and listen.

"She lumbered over the parking lot," he said, moving his arms and legs like a dinosaur.

A smile spread over her face as she crossed her arms and leaned in.

"Sand flew everywhere and on everyone. The drunk assholes—sorry, Harmony—were getting closer, and Raine hadn't arrived yet."

And, she was completely lost. His brown hair, cut tight around the sides. The way he ran his fingers through the longer part in front when that tiny curl fell on his forehead. The eyes that matched the hair and lit up any room he was in.

Liam had the most comfortable, attentive, and honestly truthful way about every part of him. And, he had no idea to any of it. One of his pretend flippers hit her as he spoke.

Jerking his arm back, he turned to see her. "Oh, hey, Willow." He wrapped an arm around her shoulder and pulled her in, continuing his story without missing a beat. "And the taller drunk guy stepped around Zoe, and I reached out my hand." He held out his dinner plate-sized finger span in the shape of a giant a claw. "I came down on the back of the dude's neck and clamped down. I said, 'Take one more step and I'm calling the cops.'"

TWELVE

Liam used his disciplinary teacher voice that was about three octaves lower and made her laugh. "A lot like a day in a high school hallway."

"Who's calling the cops?" Matt interrupted and approached the group with a draft in hand.

"Matt!" Willow said, her eyes betraying her and darting right to Seth's poem. "You came!"

Ducking under Liam's arm, she reached out and hugged the chief. She went to kiss him on the cheek, but while he hugged her back, he craned his head around to the direction of her traitorous gaze.

"Not that the cops would have shown," Raine said.

Willow's mother spoke up. "Now, Raine. Don't you start."

Liam put a hand on her shoulder. "Come now, Raine. You just had a Leatherback lay eggs on your island."

"This is Willow's night." Raine waved her hand dismissively.

"What's so special about a Leatherback?" Heads turned to Andre, the newest Beachfront waiter.

"They are quite rare, dear," her mother said. "And enormous."

Willow was more interested in her big sister. She looked more than worried. She looked sick. "Raine, what is it?" she asked.

Raine sighed. "That area never gets all that many nests, but it does get nests. That damned Richard Beckett doesn't care. He just buys it," she said, waving her arms around. "Plows it up, all to park some cars. I don't even know who he's selling it to or why."

Liam interjected, "Zoe said something about remote valet parking for Blake Eaton."

Raine ran her hands over her face, then the top of her hair. "Great," she said sarcastically. "Richard Beckett with Blake Eaton."

"Is this a story I need to know about?" Matt asked.

Raine only clasped her hands behind her neck like that when she was truly beaten down.

Before her big sister got herself in trouble with a snarky answer, Willow said, "Richard Beckett, prominent real estate agent and rental property owner on the island. He has a history of breaking sea turtle code and being a regular ass. Sorry, Mom. Blake Eaton. Bigger ass, actually. Not sorry, Mom. He owns Show Me's. Other than the Tiki Bar, it is the only other spot on the island with dancing."

"And non-turtle friendly lights and seating that goes way out onto the beach, and loud noises and lights past dusk from said seating." Raine took a swig from her bottle. "As far as caring about the turtles, Eaton makes Beckett look like a saint."

"Turtle code," Matt said. "It looks like I have homework."

Raine stepped to him. "Right," she said, drawing out the word.

Willow put a hand out. "Oh, boy. Whoa, whoa."

"Do we have a problem?" Matt asked.

"The problem is—" Raine stepped closer. "I was able to fence off the nest, but when hatching time comes, the chances of Richard Beckett or Blake Eaton following code and closing off that parking lot so the hatchlings have a path to the water is between zero and none."

Matt looked down his nose at her, his gentle voice a direct contrast to his body language. "I'm gonna tell you right now," he said, pointing a finger at her. "If when the time comes for the nest to hatch or come out or whatever it does, and I am still here, I will make sure that will happen by the books."

"Is that a campaign speech?" Raine growled.

Their father stood. "That's enough, Raine."

Everyone's shoulders fell, including Matt's.

"I'm sorry," Raine said, shaking her head. "You're right. I'm sorry." She turned to face Willow. "This is unbelievable. I'm so proud of you." Her eyes turned a shade of red.

Willow wanted so badly to wrap her arms around her.

"I have a mountain of data entry from the day," Raine said. "I will catch up with you soon." And at that, she turned and left without saying goodbye.

"Willow!" Paula called.

Oh hell. The keg. "Coming!" Willow said and jogged to the back room.

"Be right back," Liam said and followed Raine out the door.

Dodging a few tourists on rented bicycles, he caught up with her at her truck. She was already sitting in the driver's seat with her forehead on the steering wheel. He rapped on the window with the backs of his knuckles.

Without lifting her head from the wheel, she turned her eyes toward him.

Since it didn't appear she was going to roll down the window, he opened the door.

"I'm a bitch," she said.

Reaching in, he wrapped his arms around her and said, "Yeah."

Her shoulders shook. He hoped it was from laughter and not tears. Her chest filled and released. "You're the best replacement brother a girl could have."

"It's a job I take seriously. Are you sure you won't stay?"

She shook her head. "Nah. I honestly do have a mountain of paperwork, and I'm filling in for a beach walk tomorrow."

"I've got tomorrow off. I know what turtle tracks look like."

"Thanks, but sorry. You have to be certified."

He gave her a tight squeeze, then let go. "I'm going to hold that detective to his word. I won't forget."

She jerked her chin up once. "Right. Sure thing. See you around."

Starting her truck, he shut the door. "I mean it," he called through the window as she drove away.

He made his way back through the crowd and spotted Dane with Willow on the dance floor. It was a strange mixture of salsa dancer meets flower girl. Yet, it worked. Everything about her was contagious and full of life.

Harmony held her hand out for him as he approached their tables. He took it, and she pulled him into the empty seat next to her. "The renovation is positively delightful. Don't you think so, Detective?"

Matt squirmed on his stool and ran a single hand over the back of his neck. "The woodworking is exquisite, Mrs. Clearwater."

"But, that's not why you're here," she said with the knowledge that she and Willow always seemed to carry.

He nodded as he said, "But, that is not why I am here."

Liam guessed where this was going and held up a single finger. "Hold on a minute."

A few more customers had joined the dance floor. Liam made his way around gyrating bodies to where Willow reached to the sky and Dane sashayed. He tapped Dane on the shoulder. "May I cut in?"

With a dramatic bow, Dane gestured a hand to Willow while backing away.

Her hand was soft and her waist softer. Stepping in so their bodies pressed into each other, she whispered something in his ear. The feel of her curves apparently caused deafness.

"Isn't that great?" Willow asked.

"Huh?"

With the fog clearing slightly, he decided he ought to listen better. "Say that again."

She lifted on her toes, bringing her lips to his ear again. "People are dancing on your gorgeous floor."

Pulling back, he smiled into her eyes. "Our gorgeous floor." Over her shoulder, he spotted the detective. "Oh, yes. Matt is talking about the poem. Or going to, I think."

Willow's expression fell. She took Liam's hand. Together, they sidestepped their way back to the circle as the beat of margaritas claimed someone was to blame.

A tight circle that looked like a football huddle, clustered around a single table that had been pulled away from the other. A cowboy hat had been added to the mix during his deafening dance with Willow.

"Hello, Zoe. How was the tour?"

"Eventful. Where is the shrimp?"

Willow simultaneously tucked her hair behind her ear and pushed Liam back. "She's with her other set of grandparents."

"Jacob's birthday." Zoe took Willow's hand.

"You remembered." Willow smiled at Zoe. "I dropped her off after Raine and I went to see Matt."

"You and Raine went to see the detective?" Harmony interrupted with the same smile she used to call him out on why Matt was here.

Both Willow's chin and her gaze dipped toward the floor.

Henry stepped into the circle. "How about you tell us of this visit, Willow?" Everyone seemed to know, even the new Beachfront waiter, to shut up when Henry Clearwater spoke.

"So. Well." Willow fluffed the back of her hair.

Liam couldn't remember if he'd ever seen her do that before.

"Liam thinks Seth's poem is a map. Dane thinks islanders think it is a map to Luciana's dowry. Raine and I went to tell Matt, here, because it was the right thing to do, and you always taught us to do the right thing."

"Impressive," Liam had to say. "Throw everyone under the bus and finish with a suck up."

"Thank you," she said and grinned.

Henry was not as amused. "Islanders who?"

"Well. Right."

This was more interesting than grabbing the back of the neck of Skull and Crossbones.

Closing her eyes, Willow answered. "Richard Beckett, Blake Eaton, Miriam Roberts, Timothy Hart, and sort of Glen Oberweiss."

Henry said, "Sort of."

"I ran into him riding his bicycle in front of the pub."

"Does he normally do that?"

Willow shrugged. "I've never seen him do it before."

"And Lucky Nemo," Dane added.

Matt asked, "There is someone on the island named Lucky Nemo?"

"Named before the movie," the group answered in unison.

No one mentioned the potential change in motive for Seth's murder, and there was no way Liam was about to.

"Anyone know where the original is?" Matt asked as he took a sip of his draft.

This time everyone turned and looked at the bar.

"Because that," he said, pointing over his shoulder at the poem, "is a copy."

THIRTEEN

As Paula wiped down tables, Willow flipped off the neon open sign and let the front door close behind her. Liam would lock up the dance floor access for her while she waited for the Banana Bus.

"Banana bus?" one of the last two customers slurred as she clung to Willow for balance. "You're sending me home on a bus of bananas?"

No commercial restaurants or hotels called Ibis Island home, and years ago, the city set an ordinance that banned construction on anything taller than three stories. The mom-and-pop establishment feel helped make Ibis a safe place. It wasn't unheard of to spot a pair of women walking home at 2 a.m.

Except, these women were tourists, and Willow had no faith in their inebriated ability to find the way to their condo. "Banana Bus is the name of the island taxi service."

She heard it before she saw it. The twelve-passenger golf cart with giant bananas that covered the roof. The speakers boomed something about banana pancakes.

"Are you sure that's a taxi?"

Willow turned to answer, but one of them had gone missing.

She found her on her back in the small patch of grass between the sidewalk and the road. Ducking from the grip of the upright one, Willow hurried over to the one on her back before the bus ran her over. Her arms and legs stuck in the air like a turtle flipped on her back. "Up we go. Time to go to your condo, honey."

"Oh, thank you," the turtle woman said but didn't budge. "I broke my shoe."

Lifting her brows, Willow spotted the broken flip-flop dangling from her foot.

The bus came to a stop, leaving plenty of room between it and the woman in the grass. Thick, fake vines wrapped around each pole, dripping with artificial bunches of bananas. "Hello, Mando. It's good to see you."

Mando was round, caramel, and wore a t-shirt that read, Banana Bus, with the phone number on the front. She had him on speed dial. "Hello, Willow. Ladies." He tipped his Banana Bus ball cap. "All aboard."

Nine of the twelve seats were already full of swaying, sweating riders who chose the safe way home. "They're staying at the Coconut Corral."

"Oh!" The girl in the grass stood and limped onto the bus with the broken flip-flop dragging behind her. "This is lovely."

"Mando works on tips," Willow reminded them as they fumbled into the empty seats.

"See you next time," he hollered over the music as he pulled away.

Walking back inside, she noted she would have to serve as DD for her group. Zoe, Dane, and Liam were the only three left other than Paula, who never drank when she worked anyway.

"Goodnight, sweetheart," Paula said and wrapped her arms around Willow. "It was perfect. The grand reopening will be even better."

Willow pulled her head back enough to peer into her eyes. "Even sharing bar duties?"

Paula stretched as she made her way to the front door. She

called over her shoulder, "Almost perfect, but who's counting? I'll see you tomorrow at four."

Zoe, Dane, and Liam were nearly head-to-head around the same table they'd occupied throughout the evening. She had much to be thankful for. Peanut shells littered the floor beneath them. The tables had dried, so she began turning chairs upside down so she could sweep.

Zoe spoke with her hands. "I know where it is."

Since Zoe only spoke with her hands when it meant something, Willow stopped to listen. Everyone seemed to talk at once.

"How sure are you?" Liam said.

"One hundred and ten percent."

"What is 110 percent?" Willow asked.

Still waving her hands, Zoe raised her voice. "The wet uncharted. It is where I found Seth. It was uncharted on any map. He discovered it. He was there."

Dane shook his head, except it seemed to be more in disgust than disbelief. "I should have known."

Liam put a hand over Zoe's. "We will go with you."

Zoe nodded.

"It wasn't your brother's first time there." Dane's chest filled and released. "And, there is evidence something had been stored there."

"Stop," Willow said and wiggled into the group and turned to Dane. "What?"

"There were divots." Dane shook his head again. "I should have remembered."

Willow's chest tightened, and she clasped her fingers together on the table. "Maybe we should wait until tomorrow to talk about this."

"It might not be safe for me to drive after a few beers, but I know what I saw. Divots in the walls of the crevasse. Four of them."

Zoe nodded. "It made it look like a gray pillow stuck to the wall."

Zoe and Dane were the only two who had seen it. Zoe took pictures, but those had been confiscated by the St. Pete's Police Department. By Matt. She was sure the team that investigated the site and removed the skull had taken more pictures, but those would be locked up in evidence as well.

"The divots had been worn down with time." Dane pushed away from the wooden spool table and paced. "It was a pocket that got little to no current. It would be impossible to tell how old they are, but the divots could definitely, even likely, be the markings of where something had been kept for safe keeping. Drug dealers and treasure thieves use a net and spikes to secure their booty to the ocean floor."

"Or a crevasse in the Gulf," Liam added.

Willow reached out and put one hand on Dane's and the other on Liam's. "Except, Seth didn't find anything. He never found anything."

Dane ignored her and threw a punch through the air. "I was so occupied with finding Zoe the day she showed me the crevasse, I forgot all about the divots. And then it was the first time we—"

"Whoa, whoa, whoa," Liam interrupted and squinted like he bit a lemon.

"Nice visual," Willow said. "Thanks for that."

Dane went on still ignoring them. "I could kick myself. I'm off my game."

A heavy weight pressed against Willow's chest. Possibilities wrapped their hands around her throat and squeezed.

"We'll get Matt to give us copies of the pictures," Liam said.

"They're evidence," Zoe said. "He won't show them to us."

"Can't," Willow amended. "We've tried."

"Doesn't matter. We're going back down there to see for ourselves," Dane said. "First thing in the morning."

Liam wrapped his fingers around Willow's forearm. They were gentle and safe and made her heart slow several beats per minute. "Willow's got a thing. We'll go."

He remembered Jacob's birthday. He remembered and covered for her without making her talk about it.

Liam regretted drunk texting Raine the night before, pushing her into letting him substitute for her morning turtle beach walk. Now, everyone had to wait for him before the dive to the probable wet uncharted.

The sun had yet to make it all the way over the horizon. He waited for Harmony in the quiet of the morning at the public beach parking lot. It gave him time to consider Willow's visit to Jacob's grave and the fact that he hadn't been doing his part in this egg thing.

Harmony pulled into the lot driving their old Camry, her large straw hat taking up nearly the entire front seat.

"Good morning, Harmony," he called through her open window and pushed away from his Ford Ranger.

She pulled next to him.

"Thank you for coming out so early."

"Of course, dear."

He opened the door for her.

"Such a good boy." She got out and popped the trunk.

The comment took him aback. He wasn't entirely sure why other than the fact that she used the same words to describe Dane with his tattoos and leather jewelry.

He let her sling the backpack on her shoulder but stuck his hand out when she reached for the five-gallon bucket.

"I've got this." He recognized the telltale tools of a turtle conservationist in the bucket. Flags, the rubber mallet, brightly colored electrical tape. He spotted a cluster of wooden stakes and assumed they might be needed, so he grabbed them as well.

After maneuvering everything into one arm, he shut Harmony's trunk with the other and headed for the beach. Tropical Storm Ernest was well off yet but churned the waters regardless. Might take a turn west. Or it might not. A little hung over, he appreciated the breeze and even the cloudy sky.

Harmony pulled a paper grocery sack from her backpack and handed it to him.

She must have understood his look of confusion, because she placed a hand on his shoulder and smiled at him. "It's for garbage," she said without a hint of sarcasm as she pulled out a much larger and quite wrinkled plastic trash bag.

"Well," he said as they reached the end of the parking lot and toed off their shoes. "Now, I feel stupid. Why is yours bigger?"

"Mine is for discarded clothing and toys. I like to gather them and bring them to the local shelter."

As they walked over the sand, Liam understood. The beach was relatively clear, but even the occasional bottle of sunscreen, beach towel, or sand toy proved to be frustrating. Why didn't people pick up their stuff? With only a few hours of sleep, it was still a halfway decent way to wake before the dive.

"How far does this section go?" he asked.

She pointed toward the multicolored stucco cluster of rentals to the north. "Just to the Pineapple Paradise rentals."

"That all?"

She added a bright blue beach cover up thing to her bag. "I'm going with Willow today."

"Good. That's good." A selfish tinge of envy brushed over him. "Chloe will meet you?" He missed the shrimp since she left to spend time with her other grandparents. He made a silent promise to stop by and turn the egg or whatever.

"She feels the same way about you."

His feet stopped. "She's a good kid."

Harmony smiled and dipped her head. "That's not who I meant."

Oh. Awkward. "That's complicated." He made his reluctant legs move again.

She headed for a beach umbrella that had been left overnight. "I feel the need to be transparent and tell you that I am rather tired of that line. From both of you."

He knew his expression must have been something between disbelief and good old-fashioned pissed off since that was what he was feeling. "With all due respect, ma'am, my relation...my friend-ship," he corrected, "with your daughter is between her and me." Did he say that out loud? He should apologize, but he didn't know where to start and found himself looking around at the beach as if the answer might be somewhere in the sand.

She pulled a tag with string from the outside pocket of her backpack. "People are allowed to choose how and how long they grieve."

He might be a physics teacher with an MA in science instruction, but the only response he could come up with was, "Yeah." And, it sounded like it came from a sixth grader.

A side of the umbrella stuck in the sand. "It's more than that with Willow. I can't put my finger on it," Harmony said.

And for someone like Harmony, that must truly bother her. She went to affix the tag to the umbrella when she froze and said, "Oh dear."

He looked over to what she saw. "Oh. Oh. Oh, hell."

Without even correcting him for cussing, Harmony said, "You can't unsee that."

A butt naked man lay prone in the sand. "Where are his clothes?" Liam asked and checked around the area. "How can he have no clothes?"

FOURTEEN

Harmony pulled out her phone and dialed. "My emergency is that there is a naked man on the sand north of the public beach." She gave the guy a nudge with her foot. "I see his chest moving up and down."

Liam wasn't about to touch him.

"No. Yes. Can I at least turn him over? Size matters, you know."

Liam forced back a laugh and ended up snorting like a girl.

"They're sending someone over." Harmony reached down and put a no overnight furniture tag on his big toe, then another on the umbrella. She turned back north as if nothing happened. "You're diving Seth's crevasse today." It wasn't a question.

He left the naked man with the small penis and followed. "How do you always know everything?"

"I wish that were true, dear."

It was, he thought, but didn't argue. "We meet at nine."

"Henry is going to join you."

He didn't even ask how they'd already learned about the dive and that Henry was joining them. These were Clearwaters. He knew better. It would be nice to have a diving partner, and he wasn't about to argue with Harmony Clearwater.

Willow sat with her mother on the bench that was twelve rows from Jacob's flat marker. She needed this time before she stepped to the one that read his name.

Stuffing her betrayal was impossible here. As it should be.

She liked this bench. The grass was trimmed today, and the rains made everything green and welcome. It gave her a moment to look out over the thousands of markers and headstones and ponder the sacrifices and what they meant. Clouds covered nearly all the blue.

Her mother's fingers tightened around Willow's. Looking down, she noted how her own shook around the small bouquet of artificial zinnias she'd brought. A tear spilled over their hands, then another and another.

"What is it?" her mother asked.

What a strange question in this place. Yet, if her mother only knew. Willow looked up and forced a smile. The two proven methods to stop tears did nothing to halt the torrent of water that dripped from her eyes. "My husband died," she said. It was sarcastic and rude, she knew. "Come." Standing through the weights on her shoulders, she tugged her mother toward the inevitable.

Her mother didn't follow or let go, causing Willow to nearly fall on her lap. She looked down at the power grip on her hand, then to her mother.

No tears. No smile. "There is more, dear."

"I can't." The flowers fell at her feet, and she wiped the tears with her free hand. "I have family and a daughter and, and, and a business, and family and a daughter," she stuttered. Why wouldn't her mother let go? She fell to her knees in the grass in front of the bench, sitting on her heels and rocking as she cried. She cried harder than she did when the men in green rang her doorbell five years ago.

Her mother sat next to her, wrapping her arms around her and rocking with her as if she were a child, and like a child, Willow defiantly said, "Don't you say a thing about Liam. This has nothing to do with him."

"I know, honey." Her mother pulled her in and ran her hand from the top of Willow's hair down her back again and again. "I wish I knew what it did have to do with. This is too much for one person to carry alone."

"I am strong. I am smart. I have family and a daughter."

"And, we love you unconditionally."

"I'm sorry. I'm so sorry."

"It's okay, dear. We forgive you."

"I wasn't good. I wasn't a good wife." Her eyes clamped tight, and she pushed her forehead into her mother's shoulder. "I-I had thoughts, dreams. About another man. Other men. I flirted." Was she saying this out loud? It made it too real. "Jacob was fighting in the desert, and I was safe on an island flirting and having fuzzy feelings for other men."

Her mother didn't waver, just kept rocking. Willow had to get up. Had to get to Jacob's grave marker. Stick the flowers in the grass. Be ready for Chloe and his parents. What did any of this matter?

Pushing away, she wiped her face and ground her teeth together. "Why aren't you saying anything? Asking me how could I? I did it. Why aren't you saying anything?"

Her mother tilted her head and lifted the corners of her mouth, making the lines age her ten more years than they should. "I don't think you want to hear what I have to say."

"Of course, I don't. How could I? Now you know. You know why I can't. I can't. I just can't."

"I've had fuzzy feelings and I've flirted."

Willow fell on the backs of her heels and let her hands drop listlessly to her thighs. "What?"

"Everyone dreams, dear." She said it so matter-of-factly, Willow didn't know what to say, what to think. Her aged hands reached up and wiped a new tear as it escaped Willow's eye. "Everyone's eyes wander. Did you act upon those dreams?"

"What?" she repeated. "What? No. Never. But, I wanted to. And, not Liam. I'm tired of everyone pushing us together."

"Oh, honey." Her mother put both hands on the sides of Willow's face now. "I had thoughts and dreams."

"Why are you telling me this?" She knew why she was telling her this, but she didn't want to know, so she argued, "Dad is your soul mate."

Her mother let go and waved a hand at her as she leaned her back against the bench. "One does not happen upon their soul mate. We make our mate into a soul mate. He wasn't my first choice."

"What? Why? What? You were sixteen."

"Yes." Her mother smiled a blissful smile.

"You see?" Willow said. "You're smiling. It's that smile. The one you always have when you talk about Dad. It's a smile a soul mate smiles. A forever soul mate who doesn't flirt with other men."

"My first choice—"

"I don't want to hear this."

"Wasn't available." She was still smiling that damned smile. "His parents didn't let him sneak out at night with their bottle of whiskey to have sex on the beach like your father's did."

Willow covered her ears, but she could still hear her.

"We got pregnant with Seth." Like she was sixteen again, she crossed her legs in the grass and placed a hand on each knee. Willow could swear the ten years disappeared into thin air. "My parents wanted us to adopt. His wanted us to abort."

"We wanted him. It was our choice." Her soft blue eyes turned to Willow now. "We made each other into soul mates. That was also our choice, not our destiny." She took Willow's hands between her own. "Your father is the best man I've ever known. He makes me a better me every day, but he wasn't my first choice. I had dreams and thoughts, and I flirted with that first choice, but like you, I changed. I worked to be a better me. That's what soul mates do."

"But, what if I—?" The tears flowed freely in streams down Willow's cheeks.

"What in the world good is it to go there?"

She was right. Somewhere in Willow's heart she knew this. Possibilities called in the back of her mind, but she couldn't quite allow herself to listen.

A single thumb lifted Willow's chin. She opened her eyes even though her heart told her not to.

"Do you think Jacob didn't have thoughts or dreams? He was a man without his wife for months at a time. Henry? We are humans, my sweet, sweet girl."

"You think he cheated?"

"Not at all. He loved you. He was a good man."

"I never. I would never. I swear, Mama. I loved him. I did. Not like you and Daddy, but I loved him." Willow wrapped her arms around her mother's neck.

"You would have gotten there, and if you hadn't, you would have been faithful. You were a good wife. You are a good mother. I am so proud of you."

Willow looked into her mother's eyes. It took her several minutes to gain the courage before she whispered, "Liam."

Her mother leaned in and said into her ear, "Yes."

The sound of tires brought Willow back to the bench. She picked up the flowers, wiped the tears from her swollen eyes, and smiled at her mother. "Thank you."

"Mommy!" Chloe's happy face ran from the Martinez car.

Mr. and Mrs. Martinez stepped out and smiled.

"We had a tea party," she yelled as she ran. "And I had a crown and a dress and cookies."

A few feet from Willow, she jumped into the air. Willow had to drop the flowers to catch her.

"And we went to the zoo and saw elephants and monkeys," she continued as if she hadn't risked both of them tumbling to the ground. "I liked the alligators the best."

Willow pulled back to see her lovely face. "You live in Florida, and you like alligators the best?"

"Uh-huh." She craned over to see the discarded flowers, almost knocking the two of them over again. "You brought flowers for Daddy? You've been crying, Mommy. Let's go give Daddy his flowers. It will make you feel better."

"Let's."

The Gulf waters churned, smacking between the pier and the boat. They warned of the coming storm. It had been too long since Liam had made a dive. He wouldn't let that happen again.

Henry parked the Camry. Liam spotted Zoe in the passenger seat.

Dane took a swig from his water bottle, paused, and turned to him. "Listen, man."

Liam hauled his tank and diving bag over the side of the boat. "Hmm?"

"I mean about the last few days."

Glancing over, he spotted Dane scratching the back of his head. "Oh, right," Liam mumbled.

"I shouldn't have—"

"I get that—"

"And then, when—"

"No worries, man," Liam said.

"Don't say, man, dude. It's not you."

He wasn't wrong. Liam smiled. "Apology accepted."

"She's at the cemetery today?"

"Yep." Liam stowed his gear in front of the passenger seat. "Jacob's birthday."

"So, we're good?" Dane asked.

"Yeah."

Dane nodded. "You're still a jackass, though."

"You're still stupid."

Dane nodded and jumped onto the pier, jogging over to Zoe and Henry.

It wasn't as if they were going to find hidden treasure or human remains, but a search for possible clues? The place where Willow's brother was murdered? Adrenaline raced through Liam's veins. He looked out over the Gulf without seeing it as he turned the ignition to the Sun Trips boat. "All aboard," he said as they climbed on.

"Thanks to Ernest, the Beaufort scale is at five with a steady wind coming from the south at 21 knots. This is Liam Morrison, and I'll be your guide for the morning."

Zoe smacked his shoulder with the back of her hand. "You're weird."

Liam shrugged. She wasn't wrong. She kissed him on the cheek, Dane unhooked the boat, and Liam gunned the motor. With only professional divers on board, he had no reservations about opening up the engine.

FIFTEEN

Dane tilted his head back and let out a yell as the tail wind helped them cut through the waves. The way back wouldn't be nearly as much fun, but he wouldn't worry about that now.

As he drove, the three pulled on diving skins. Willow would be just about saying goodbye to Chloe at that time. Jacob's parents were taking her to Busch Gardens before they headed north to their home. Willow took her mother to the cemetery this time. That was new. It was good, he decided. Yes.

A pod of dolphins swam with them portside. He spotted a marlin fin farther inland. There was no place better than this.

"So, we know," Dane yelled over the engine and the wind. "There will be no treasure in this crevasse, but I want us to be vigilant with our surroundings anyway. Treasure hunters are not the safest types, and those who are can flip as soon as they think they're close to a score. Word's gotten around about this. We don't know what, exactly, those words include."

Liam shook his head. "Always the treasure hunter at heart, ma —, du—, Dane."

Dane laughed as he wrapped both arms around Zoe. "Babe, we haven't been diving without a tour group in too long."

"I think I should partner with my dad," she said.

"What?" Dane said. "I mean, of course."

Liam would have preferred Henry, but he couldn't say that now. Had Henry been in Seth's crevasse before today? It didn't feel right to ask about that either.

"Three hundred yards northeast." Zoe pointed. "There."

Ahead, crowds of tourists poured onto St. Pete's beach, claiming their spots until the slightest of drizzles chased them away. By tomorrow night, the only tourist on the beach would be Ernest. Evacuations hadn't been called yet, but that was only a matter of time.

The Clearwater family all resided in ground-level homes. Dane, too. Liam's apartment was one of four in a building with stilts and became their place of refuge, if Ernest decided to turn into a hurricane.

"This is good right here," Zoe yelled.

Liam let up on the throttle, then brought the boat to a stop. Dane tossed the anchor overboard.

Liam couldn't help himself. "This here is some earnest wind."

"Oh my gosh." Zoe hit him again.

Dane froze. "Dude. Shut. Up."

Henry held out a fist for Liam to bump.

Their hair flipped around in the wind as they finished with their gear. "One long and two shorts if it comes to that," he said. "We follow Zoe."

She stood in full gear with her mouthpiece dangling by her chin. "With this choppy water, the opening won't be visible. Trust me. I know where I'm going." She stuck the mouthpiece in place and walked off the end of the swim step like a soldier and vanished.

Henry waited for her to dive a safe distance away from the entry point, then saluted and did the same.

Dane looked out all sides of the boat. "Not now, but after I jump, I want you to look at your 3 o'clock. Who rents a boat in this weather?" Like a kid, Dane sat on the swim step and fell sideways.

Glancing over the boat like he was waiting for his turn to jump, he lifted his eyes to the rental. Bright yellow. That meant Yo-Yo

Rentals. He jumped feet first, piked, and threw his legs straight up and let his weight give him a good push downward.

This was home. Up there, it could rain, and people could visit cemeteries or go to their jobs. This was island life for Liam.

He caught up to Dane, who kept about ten yards between him and the Zoe/Henry team. They passed the cavern the girls liked to call the palm tree cavern. He craned his head at it. If you asked him, it looked like a rock star with eighties hair.

Underwater wildlife took cover behind the rocks, in the plant life, and the caverns they passed. They knew what was coming. He wondered if they watched in confusion at this group of humans who swam in the open as a storm brewed. The humans swam close enough to the smaller caverns along the peninsula wall that Liam reached out and brushed his fingers along each like one of his high school students running a hand along the lockers between classes.

Zoe took a sudden vertical dive toward a dark blue shadow. His heartbeat picked up, and he stopped to tread water and watch. She held up a finger, then pointed. There was nothing there. Mapping was her thing as much as physics was his, but the scientist in him saw nothing. She said to trust her, so he did and swam close enough that their elbows touched.

The three men waited as Zoe inched her way to the deep blue line of nothing. From within the churning particles, a row of jagged teeth jutted out.

Instinctively, Liam put his arms in front of Dane and Henry as if he might be protecting one of his high school students from flying through a windshield. Dane grabbed Liam's wrist and shoved it away.

Dane swam toward Zoe as two yellow eyes appeared. Moray Eel. Zoe stood her ground. At that moment, she definitely won coolest person of the day award. Even Dane paused at the sight.

It slithered out and darted directly to Zoe. She held out a hand, and the thing put his head under it, swimming along like a golden retriever copping a feel on his way around her. Much like Zoe had done, the thing took a quick vertical turn and disappeared somewhere below.

He realized he was breathing too hard for scuba diving and closed his eyes long enough to regain a slow pace. She went first, vanishing into the nothing until only her calves dangled out of the invisible opening. Her flippers turned in two full circles, the beam from her flashlight showing around them.

She spent a solid few minutes checking it out. He, Dane, and Henry didn't use the waiting time to explore the wildlife, rocks, or plant life. They each kicked their fins enough to keep their places as they eagerly faced the direction of the hidden crevasse. Liam would be a liar if he didn't admit that he kept a watchful eye in the direction of the disappearing eel.

She emerged. Henry turned to face Liam. Liam pointed a finger toward the crevasse. It was only right for Henry to be next.

Dane and Zoe circled each other, then he pulled her toward a nearby cluster of rocks. Liam watched for Henry as a cloud of black ink exploded near his friends, followed by a small octopus that darted from the rock cluster. It swam away from the two of them and right in front of Liam. He followed it with his eyes as it raced away from the human intruders back the way they'd come.

A diver. Male. Not fifty yards from them. He faced them with his arms out as he treaded water.

With a diving knife gripped in his hand, Dane swam next to Liam.

Where was the diver's partner? Liam did a 360. Did the man have a diving buddy? They made a circle, the three of them, back-to-back. A hand landed on Liam's shoulder. He grabbed it and jerked himself around. It was Henry.

He nodded, then turned back in the direction of the diver. Nothing. He was gone as fast as he'd appeared. Or was he?

Dane's expression was dead. He pointed to Liam, then to the crevasse.

Shaking his head, Liam copied the gesture for Dane to go next.

Pushing Liam, Dane shook his head again. Liam didn't argue this time. He leaned forward and swam to the crevasse. The opening was barely big enough for him and his tank. Flipping on his flashlight, he saw why Zoe called it a baseball cap. It made a lot more sense than the palm tree cavern.

No signs of life of the plant or the animal variety. He shined his flashlight near his hand as he ran it along the bumpy gray walls. Over the deep crack that must have held the knife. Over the four smaller divots that may or may not have been used to secure a netting full of drugs, gear, or Luciana Bezan's treasure. A chill ran through him. He may not be claustrophobic, but he cut his turn short and pushed himself out anyway.

Dane's turn. He took the knife and gripped it in his hand. He seemed to be considering, looking at the knife, all around him, then to the crevasse. Curiosity must have won out, because he nodded and disappeared into the wet uncharted.

Pulling her smart car into the Beachfront parking spot meant for electric cars, Willow turned to her mother. "I'll be by before the dinner rush is over. I promised—" She decided against telling her mother she had agreed to attend a Chief Roberts interrogation. "—Matt I would stop by."

Her mother set a hand on top of Willow's as it rested on the steering wheel. "Don't spread yourself too thin, dear. Today was a lot."

"I feel oddly energized." She grinned at her mother. It was sincere. "Thank you for…for everything. I love you so much."

Her mother opened the door. "I miss Chloe already."

"Me, too," Willow said. "Three more days."

She waited for her mother to disappear through the drizzle into the employee entrance of the restaurant before she pulled away.

Expecting to be a little shaky, she held her phone in both hands. Waiting for it to come was fruitless, because they didn't shake. Texting wasn't juvenile, she told herself. This was important, and he was diving. Probably. She covered her mouth with one hand and used her thumb to press the message feature on her phone.

i need to talk to you

There. She sent it. Now, he would get back to her when he could and—

He answered so fast, she almost dropped her vibrating phone.

Is everything okay?

She didn't have time to think of what to say when he texted again.

Is it Luciana's?

Liam and his text punctuation. She sat alone in her car and smiled like a teenager.

Chloe?

Did she never contact him about anything else? Hurrying before he called 9-1-1, she texted him back.

everything is great. just want to talk.

Want to. There. That was less cryptic. Or not.

I have a tutoring makeup class. Can I come by later?

She was due to check in at Luciana's and close at the Beachfront that evening. Her mother was right. She had herself so busy. A heavy weight fell on her shoulders. Also, juvenile.

no worries. will catch up with you soon

Laying her forehead on the steering wheel, she closed her eyes. What was the hurry? There was no hurry.

She turned on the radio. She chose WIIN and listened to the storm update.

"Repeat. This is not a mandatory evacuation. As a precaution, it is recommended to sand bag any ground-level structures. This is not a mandatory evacuation. Sandbagging volunteers are still needed at the bay access bridge. Stay tuned for updates."

As her car was not exactly one for flooded streets, it looked like it would have to nap for the weekend. She could call one of her sisters or Liam for rides. Liam. Definitely Liam. Something stirred inside of her that had been asleep for a long time.

SIXTEEN

The ring of her phone made Willow jump. Why was she doing that lately? Caller ID said it was Matt. She tapped the answer button on her Bluetooth.

"This is Willow. How are you doing this morning, my friend?"

"Very well, sunshine. You coming?"

"ETA is five minutes."

"Use the northeast entrance. Leave your gun at home."

Gun? Did he know she was born a Clearwater? "Are you joking?"

"About the entrance, no. About the gun, yes."

"Okay to both, then. See you in a few."

With nowhere to go, the water already pooled along the sides of the roads and the low spots in neighborhood yards. So many turtle nests. She hoped they would make it.

Tourists mostly headed inland for the few days. A steady row of cars lined the official evac route along the west side of the island, so she took the east.

He waited at the back door. His face was covered with a rain poncho, but she could tell it was him. A true islander would never wear a rain poncho in this light drizzle.

She parked in one of the two electric car spots, plugged in her car, and walked toward him. The cool spray from the water refreshed her face and her soul. She stopped in front of him as the rain fell. "You're dirty."

Lifting his chin, he raised a single brow as he peered at her from under the plastic hood.

"Your pants." She took both of his hands. "And, your hands."

"Hello, Willow." He didn't try to pull his hands away. "I washed them."

His nails were dark brown. His palms reddened. "You've been sandbagging."

This time, he did pull away and opened the door for her. "It seems to be that time, yes."

She walked through. "I feel I should explain. Chief Roberts was chief since I was a little girl. I can't remember a single time he managed the sandbagging, let alone doing some himself."

"I see." They approached the doorway that led to the handful of cells in the county jail. "I'm not sure mentioning it to anyone would be helpful this afternoon, but I'll keep that in mind."

She'd never been back there. If she judged the building correctly, this was the other side of the wall from city hall reception. The single sliding glass window was tiny, and no one seemed to be manning it. As they approached, she spotted two ladies sitting at small, individual desks facing away from the window.

As if they had eyes in the backs of their heads, the two of them turned to the window. Willow recognized them but not enough to remember names. One was close to her mother's age, the other much younger.

The younger one pushed away from her station and walked the few steps to the window. "Good morning, Chief."

"Not sure when I'll get used to that title, Lucy." Matt lifted off the wet poncho. "How are you doing this fine day?"

Ah. Lucy Green. Mayor Green's daughter. "Pretty good. Dad's back next week." She tapped a clipboard. "I'll call to have Mr. Roberts ready for you. Sign here."

Mr. Roberts. Willow thought that sounded much better than Chief Roberts.

Matt signed his name, then pushed the clipboard back to her. Name, time, reason for visit, and a little box that said when a visitor had left the premises. Lucy set a plastic basket on the counter, then slid it through the small window.

Matt really did have a gun and set it, along with the rest of the contents of his pockets, in the basket. Willow reached up to add her purse and phone, but Matt placed a hand over hers as Lucy set another basket on the counter. Ah. Willow put her purse and cell phone in it.

"Have a nice visit, Chief." Lucy nodded her head toward a white door with a hooked handle. It clicked, and Matt reached to open it.

After a metal detector, a waiting room, and instructions to head to Interrogation Two, Matt held the back of her elbow and led her to where Interrogation Two must be. "You ready for this?"

She truly was. "Just trying to get him to crack enough to slip up. Got it." And, it was like she'd told her mother in the restaurant parking lot. A strange energy filled her.

A guard stood outside the door. He was young and stiff but obviously knew Matt already and tipped his chin up at him.

Matt opened the door. He'd told her to be prepared, told her to let him do the talking, but she could feel her expression give her away. She'd known Chief Roberts almost her entire life. It had only been a few weeks, but she swore his face was thinner, his hair longer, and she didn't think he'd shaved since he tried to kill his wife and Zoe with the fire at Dane's home.

"What is this?" Roberts demanded.

The room was bare. Gray painted concrete brick walls and a single metal table in the center with four folding chairs around it. His hands were handcuffed to the table with a metal ring.

"Good afternoon, Neil. How are your accommodations? Everyone treating you well?"

No answer.

"Good to hear. Willow, here, found something you might be interested in."

Or, already knew about.

Matt pulled out a chair for her, and she took it. She folded her hands on her thighs and squeezed her fingers.

Matt leaned toward Roberts and took out a folded piece of paper from his back pocket. It was as dirty as his fingernails. "You'll have to forgive me, Neil. I've been sandbagging."

Roberts huffed a single disgusted breath and craned his head away from the paper.

Willow assumed the huff was multilayered and she couldn't help but appreciate Matt at that moment.

"You're wasting your time," Roberts growled. "Big news is coming. I'll be out of here within the week. You don't get who I am."

"So you keep saying," Matt said and unfolded the paper.

She knew what would be on the paper.

"This is a screenshot I took. It's a copy of a picture Willow has hanging over the back of the bar at her pub."

"Luciana's," Roberts said through his teeth. A little bit of spittle flew out as he spoke, but he still didn't look at the paper.

Matt set it on the table and flattened each fold, one at a time. "Not sure if these people who are getting you out within the week mentioned this map, or maybe chose not to."

Roberts' eyes dropped down his nose and onto the paper. His gaze said he read it several times, then he looked to Matt before reading it again. Sweat seemed to pop from along his temples and in his mustache. "This is hanging? In the bar?" He still hadn't acknowledged her presence.

"That's right," she said and smiled. "It's been a delightful addition. So many of our island family have come by to see it."

"I want to see my lawyer." He shook his finger at Matt. "I have something to say, and it's big, but I'm not talking until I see my lawyer."

"Of course, Neil. I'll get that together right away."

Matt stood. She looked from him to Neil. That was it? She tried to push away from the table as if she expected it. Matt refolded the paper and stuffed it back in his pocket. "I'll call on my way to the bay bridge. It sure is raining out there."

Not yet, she thought.

Since it protected them from most of the drizzle and Ernest's prewind, Liam chose the high school courtyard. After this makeup, Sam and Aiden had two more sessions. Liam nodded to himself at how far they'd come.

"I don't know, Mr. Morrison." Sam stood in the grass next to a folded table, two-liter bottles of Diet Coke, and a pocketful of Mentos. "Not that I'm complaining or anything, but these experiments feel more like chemistry than physics."

Their understanding of the difference as well as their ability to create a decent log was more than he could have imagined in their few months' time.

The need for physical and verbal direction had been trimmed. Liam's goals for the boys had been to achieve a level at which they could confidently pass physics in the fall. They'd exceeded those expectations and beyond. These were only a few of the reasons he stayed in this profession.

A lab barstool would have been too much to balance, so Liam borrowed a folding chair from the teacher break room. The courtyard grass wasn't too soggy yet, so he leaned back on two of the legs. "I'm glad to hear you ask that, Sam. Today we're going to experiment with nucleation, which is a physical reaction rather than a chemical one."

The look on Sam's face was like the first day of summer tutoring. It could have been mistaken for a trance, especially with the mist that covered his face.

Liam cocked his chin at Aiden. "If you roll your eyes any farther in the back of your head, they could get stuck there." He smiled as he turned on Seth's laptop. "Our objective here is the lab report, which, by the way, have been much better."

As the boys worked the legs of the eight-foot folding table, Liam adjusted his large umbrella and opened the net. Clasping his fingers, he flipped his palms away from him and locked his elbows in front of him. Since So Right was his only possible lead, he went there first, typed in Seth's email as the ID, and stared at the empty password box. He rubbed his chin between his thumb and forefinger and took a stab at a few. Treasure. Treasure4. 4Treasure. Miriam. MiriamTreasure. TreasureMiriam.

The distinct sound of an opening two-liter bottle of soda distracted him enough to realize his efforts were ridiculous. He noted the bottle of Mentos rested safely next to the liters of Diet Coke and unused umbrellas as the boys scribbled in their log books.

He took out his phone and texted Willow.

Do you have any ideas on passwords Seth might have used?

Slipping his phone under his thigh, he stared at the site again, hoping an idea might come to him if he stared long enough. LucianaBezan? Luciana'sDowry? Nope. Nope. His phone dinged.

sorry no any chance u can come by at my dinner break

He pulled his chin back and turned his head to look at his phone through the corner of his eyes. He answered her question with a question.

Is everything okay?

u keep asking me that lol

He took in a deep breath and was ready to respond, but she beat him to it.

3turtlesisters

What?

What?

Oh. He typed in the suggested password as his phone vibrated.

He didn't get a chance to read her response due to the geyser of Diet Coke that shot twenty feet in the air and covered Sam from head to toe. The boy stood hunched over, arms out, with soda dripping from his chin. Aiden held one hand against his Def Leppard shirt as he bellowed with laughter and pointed at Sam with the other.

SEVENTEEN

Liam tried not to laugh, but it came out as a snort, and he really did drop Seth's laptop this time. Sam looked angry enough to start swinging until his face cracked, and he started cackling as well.

Liam stood and made his way to the mess. "One would think you would have learned your lesson from the potato gun."

"We," Aiden said and sucked in air before he continued. "Did," he finished and walked in a circle busting his gut.

Shaking his head, Liam spotted both journals, dripping wet with sticky soda. "I hope this was worth it."

"Dude," Sam said to Aiden as if Liam weren't there. "Take my picture." He opened his mouth, paused, looked to Liam this time, then continued. "No wait. We've got more supplies, let's video it. Your turn."

Interestingly enough, Aiden agreed. The rain wasn't nearly hard enough to rinse them off. So, Liam gathered the laptop, tucking it under his arm as he headed for the courtyard door. "I'll see if I can round up some rags. That roll of paper towels isn't enough."

He made it as far as his classroom before curiosity got the best of him. Trying not to get his hopes up, he lifted the top of the laptop. In the center of the screen was a title that read My Photos, and under it, a handful of files with photos of Miriam Roberts as the covers.

Afraid to jinx this or break something, he pulled his shaking hands away, then used the tips of his fingers to scoot the machine from the edge of the tall lab counter in his classroom.

After rapid blinking through the multitude of possibilities, he covered his mouth with one hand and battled a short tennis match in his head between his fierce curiosity and the ethics of taking this right to Willow. Or not. She asked him not to come until seven.

The quick question of why she wanted to see him over her dinner break for the first time in...ever, brushed through his mind before he found his fingers clicking on folders.

Pictures of Miriam on dark beaches, in Seth's apartment arranging shells, dressed in jeans, sneakers, and a tank on a boat, selfies of the two of them on his couch. The next folder contained underwater sea life. None of the folders were titled, only dated.

A drip of sweat stung his left eye. He wiped it away with the back of his forearm.

The sound of squeaky shoes echoing through the empty halls made him slam the laptop shut so hard, he feared he may have broken it.

"Mr. Morrison?" The shoes squished into the classroom. Sam held out his phone. "You have got to see this. Watch."

It was all Liam could do not to order the boys out of class.

Liam didn't care what time it was, where she was, or if she was on any kind of dinner break, on an errand, in a meeting, or in the damned bathroom. He had to tell her, show her. Setting the laptop on his passenger seat like it was a...a...a duck egg, he checked his watch and decided she'd be at the Beachfront right about then.

The rain changed from a drizzle to a steady falling shower. The wind pulled his truck along as he changed his wipers from delayed to low.

He'd been too scared to look at the pictures again and too

freaked out to exactly know why. Getting the boys out was easy. With the color that had left his face and the sweat dripping down his temples, they assumed he was sick. Which he was. He could lose his lunch at any moment.

Hands still vibrating on the steering wheel, he glanced over to make sure the laptop hadn't somehow disappeared. What if? He parked in the spaces across the street from the Beachfront before allowing himself to complete the thought. Whatever this was, it belonged to Willow.

A lone set of customers carried their plates from the open porch to inside and away from the increasing wind. He'd been so engrossed with the images of the photo files, he barely noticed the ones hustling to their cars. Even the locals seemed to be either rushing for cover or staring at the Beachfront in raingear as they waited for a ride.

Willow was there. Her quick movements so fluid, it was hard to tell that she was rushing. Smiling as she spoke to the rushing duo, she reached for the cord that released the plastic barrier to keep at least some of the rain away as it became nearly horizontal in the wind. Their eyes met and she paused.

She wore the black dress pants and polo that all Beachfront employees wore. He preferred her colorful oversized shirt and yoga pants things, yet she looked stunning in anything she wore. Her blonde hair was in a low ponytail and draped over and down her shoulder. There was something to her expression. It was sincere and warm and anxious all at the same time.

He hadn't even opened his door when he heard the crack. It was deafening and ripped through the voices, rain, and blowing wind. He was out of his truck and halfway across the road as the entire roof that covered the restaurant patio plummeted a full two feet before jerking to a shaky stop.

Panic threatened to freeze his feet where he was, but he stuffed the panic as he sprinted for her. She lifted her arms as if she could somehow stop the inevitable. "Move!" he yelled as he made it to the patio edge, but he wasn't fast enough.

Just as he reached the railing that surrounded the area, the roof collapsed on the best person he'd ever known. His Willow. His life.

"No!" he screamed as he yanked on the pieces of railing that stood between him and her. Splinters dug in his hands as he fought the wooden spindles. She lay lifeless beneath broken white planks and the corrugated metal roof. Tears burned the backs of his eyes as he reached her. "Willow. Willow, please," he begged. "Say something. Please."

He slipped a hand beneath her limp neck and assessed her body, limbs, and breathing. His hand covered his mouth at the blood that dripped from high on her forehead. Her right arm and shoulder seemed to be wedged between the roof and floor.

People poured out of the Beachfront door. "You!" He pointed to two men. Blinking, he recognized both of them. Realtor Richard Beckett and the Show Me's owner, Blake Eaton. "Call 9-1-1!" he yelled to Beckett, then moved his pointer finger to Eaton. "Call Turtle Watch and tell Raine."

Straddling her like a catcher at the plate, he wedged himself between her and the fallen roof. With all his might, he pressed his back against the wooden roof, pushing with everything he had. His entire being shook as he grunted then yelled. The roof creaked and fought him but lifted enough for Eaton to pull her free by her feet.

"Willow." Liam dropped to his knees next to her.

She opened her stunning blue eyes, blinking until they found his. Her shoulder turned in a way no arm should. Torn clothes and rain falling on her face, she looked at him with much the same expression she had when their eyes met moments before. Reaching over with her good arm, she took his hand and closed her lids again.

Willow woke to a scent so strong, it burned. The multitude of sounds all blurred into one. Sirens, people, voices she didn't recognize. Rain, the distinct smell of bandages, and the metallic smell that could only come from blood. The scents and sounds combined with a searing pain that shot through her head and right shoulder hard enough that the dark threatened to return.

Through the pain, she inhaled slowly through her nose and exhaled through pursed lips.

"No, no, no, honey." The voice sounded female. Willow didn't recognize it. "Stay awake now."

Willow held up a single finger on her good hand before the smelling salts came back to assault her.

"Put that away. She's awake." It was Liam. "She does that," he barked.

Even though it was his angry voice, it made the backs of her eyes burn with a relief of safety.

He caused the fear in her soul to relax enough to assess the outward. Rain thrummed around her but not on her. The distinct sound of the plastic that protected the Beachfront patio flapped madly in the wind. There were no sirens, but red emergency lights made their way through her closed eye lids. Anxious whispers, none of which she recognized, buzzed in the perimeter.

Reality rushed through her fast enough to make her head spin even with her eyes closed.

The Beachfront.

The customers.

The storm.

"The beam." She said this last thought out loud as she opened her eyes and searched for him. "Liam." She found his wrist and clamped her fingers around it.

A hefty woman in navy blue paramedic's gear kneeled next to her. A stethoscope hung from her neck as she took Willow's vitals. "It's good to see you awake, honey."

"Thank you," Willow said automatically. The expression on Liam's face distracted her from what she wanted, what she needed to say.

Clumps of brown hair stuck to his forehead, his eyes glossy and bloodshot.

Lacing their fingers together, he brought her free hand to his lips and kissed the back of it. "You're crying." She'd never seen him cry before.

A smile that was in direct contrast to the tears that fell down his cheeks spread over his face. "You're awake."

"Liam," she said but looked cautiously to the paramedic. "I have to tell you something. Listen to me." She squeezed his fingers.

"I'm here. I'm here." He placed his free hand on the side of her face.

She turned her cheek into his palm and realized her head was covered in bandages. She couldn't let even this discovery keep her from what she needed to tell him. "The beam. Look for it, Liam. A weight-bearing beam was cut." She squeezed their fingers tighter.

His eyes peered first to the paramedics, then to the patio roof.

"With a saw, Liam. A diagonal cut. Just enough to slide apart in the wind and rain."

The female paramedic interrupted. "We need to get her head and neck secured now."

Liam nodded.

"Honey, because of your head injury, we need to secure your neck," she said, then nodded to someone on the other side of Liam that Willow couldn't see.

"Wait. My head?"

Without answering her, the paramedic looked to her partner and said, "Possible concussion."

Liam shook his head. "Doubtful. She's like that. She has a high tolerance for pain and is able to use chi or breathing or meditation or something like that to stuff the bad."

"You have a laceration on your forehead, honey, a possible concussion, and a broken arm. The doctor will have more conclusive information for you at the ER."

"I'm going with her," he said in his handsome teacher voice.

The paramedic's eyes moved to her. "Is he family?"

"Yes," Willow lied without hesitation, then turned to focus on him. "But, what about the beam?"

"It's not going anywhere, and I'm not leaving you."

Since his tone said he wasn't ready to negotiate, she paid more attention to the something behind her that distracted him. He lifted his head and yelled, "You people move aside. Give the family room to get through."

Even without the sight of what was going on over her head, she assumed everyone scrambled to follow directions. She didn't ask which family he spoke of. Her focus was on the fact that Liam Morrison kneeled next to her. "You're here." She wouldn't have realized that she said this out loud if he hadn't responded by looking down into her eyes.

With one arm still held straight out like a human stop sign, he said, "Always," and made everything okay.

EIGHTEEN

As Liam backed out of the way, he spotted Henry and Harmony walking in. Family trumped friend, so Liam backed away and gave them room. He took the time to text Chief Osborne. He didn't know if Matt saved his number, so he introduced himself.

This is Liam Morrison. There's been an accident.

That wasn't right, so he deleted the second sentence.

A beam was cut at the Beachfront. The entire patio roof collapsed on Willow. It appears as if it was meant for her. She's headed to the ER now. Please come investigate.

Harmony kept her distance as the paramedics transferred Willow to a spinal board. She covered her mouth with one hand and reached to Willow with the other. "My little girl," she cried, then turned to Liam. "Is she going to be okay?"

Forcing a smile was one of the hardest things he'd ever done. He pressed send and shoved his phone in his pocket. "Of course," he said, then repeated the reason for the spinal board. Next, might be *the* hardest thing he'd ever said. "You'll be in the ambulance with her. I'll bring your car and meet you there."

Without taking her eyes from Willow, Harmony shook her head. "No. She needs you."

"Give me your keys, son," Henry added.

Liam looked from Harmony to Henry but neither paid any more attention to him. He was speechless, which was a good thing since the relief that flooded his body wouldn't allow him to say anything otherwise.

Willow gave a thumbs-up as they loaded her. He assumed it was to reassure her parents, but it made the entire crowd cheer. There was no cheer anywhere in his being.

The outer edge of the patio roof crushed the wooden floor-boards. He found the beam she spoke of, both pieces. Someone did this to his Willow. Premeditated and purposely. That someone was going to pay. For now, his focus needed to be on her. His Willow? She wasn't. Had he really declared her as his life?

He dug in his pocket and took out his keys. Tossing them to Henry, he followed the gurney and jumped into the back of the ambulance.

As the sirens blared, the male paramedic pointed at a spot for Liam to sit next to Willow. He lowered to the seat next to her as the female inserted an IV into Willow's good hand.

"Uh," Liam stammered. "I'm Liam."

The guy nodded. "I got that." He pulled a latex glove from his right hand. "I'm Paul. This is Carol."

Carol wasn't willing to sacrifice the glove and extended a crooked arm. They elbow bumped before she continued with the IV.

"Liam," Willow croaked.

"I'm here."

"You stayed." She grinned a toothless smile and made everything better.

Her blinks became longer. Remembering Carol's reaction to the unconscious Willow earlier, he looked in her direction and lifted a single brow.

"It's okay. I gave her something for the pain."

Relaxing in his seat, Liam gently rubbed the hand of her potentially broken arm and watched the paramedics work. The IV bag swayed as the van drove around evacuation traffic on the wrong side of the road. Carol adjusted and added bandages to Willow's head. He definitely thought it needed stitches. Maybe that was the ER doc's job.

The bandages around her head looked like an oversized sweatband. Paul dug through one of the dozen metal cabinets that lined the inside walls. Carol checked Willow's blood pressure. Again.

It all caught up with him, and he found himself wanting Willow to do her magic and make everything calmer. Zoe called Willow a Zen master. Except, now he needed to be the Zen master. He could be the boss when he had to. Stand back and let it be until needed, even a mixture of both. But, this was as heavy as the wind and rain that beat on the windows and roof.

He wondered if the ER would be busier than usual with the coming of the storm and tried to focus on that. It took his mind, if not at least slightly, from the beam and the laptop and when and how he would share the former with the chief and the latter with Willow. And, this need for Willow to be his.

"You stayed," she repeated in a mumble.

His shoulders lifted and fell. He'd be damned if her words didn't Zen master him. "Always," he said and drew circles around the back of her hand.

"That feels amazing," she said, barely audible over the rain and the siren.

His phone vibrated in his pocket. The paramedic named Paul dialed his own cell as Liam checked the screen for who'd texted him.

Liam swiped as Paul spoke.

"Female, age—" Paul elbowed Liam.

"Twenty-eight," Liam said as he read the message from Zoe.

what the frigging hell happened

"BP one hundred-ten over sixty."

The roof collapsed at the Beachfront. She was under it. She's awake.

With closed eyes, Willow slurred, "If I don't make it, you need to know I'm in love with you."

The phone fell out of his hands. He looked down to her. Paul leaned over, picked up Liam's phone, held it out to him, and continued his briefing of Willow's condition to whoever was on the other end of his cell. Carol tapped the end of a syringe, then added something to Willow's IV. Willow turned her hand over and opened her fingers.

Her expression was not that of someone that just declared love. It was the drugs.

Paul cleared his throat. Liam looked up and realized the guy still held Liam's phone in the air. "Right. Thank you," he said and took it from him.

Placing his hand over Willow's open hand, he linked their fingers.

Without opening her eyes, Willow said with the smallest of smiles, "I can't stop thinking about you. About what our babies would be like."

This must have been a bigger drugged declaration than what the paramedics were accustomed to, because it made both Paul and Carol stop what they were doing. Only for a moment, but Liam noticed.

"She's…" Liam began. "You know."

Paul ended his cell conversation and said, "Happens all the time, man."

Not that Liam didn't have enough to juggle at that moment. He was a school teacher. He could juggle a lot all at once, but this? This was their taboo. It was a rule written in imaginary stone and silently agreed upon by all parties involved. Friends only. Both of them followed this rule. It wasn't a case of one was the more resilient. They had an agreement. A pact.

As he decided whether to move to Alaska or possibly fist bump the air, the hospital came into view. He spotted his Ranger in the parking lot and wondered how Henry had managed that one.

The island was too small to justify a hospital, so the ambulance had traveled all the way inland on the wrong side of the road. Dane tiptoed into the room and joined Liam along a side wall. He noted that Willow's parents and sisters didn't notice Dane as they huddled around the unconscious Willow.

"Is it okay if I'm in here?" Dane whispered to him. "It's a lot of people."

It was a double room with the bed closest to the door empty, but it was still crowded. Too crowded. The news played on the television in the corner, updating the stats on the storm and adding to the noise. Liam agreed and wanted to tell everyone to go, or at least to be quiet and let her rest. The line across his back that he'd used to pry the roof from his Willow burned like hot coals.

He rolled his shoulders as he whispered, "The more the merrier, seems like. The nurse already tried to thin the herd, but apparently the ER doctor is an old-time friend of Henry's and gave a nod to the crowd."

Henry had also explained to the doctor that Willow would never agree to narcotics, so the drip was discontinued and the IV used for saline only.

"How is she?" Dane asked.

"Six stitches high on her forehead, and a concussion that was determined to be minor due to her coherency before the narcotics."

Dane craned his head to him. "You don't sound convinced."

Shaking his head, Liam said, "No, I'm not convinced. She's good at managing under pain and stress." He was, at least, relieved the head bandages were reduced to a patch that went from below her temple to the center of her forehead.

"You sure that's not just protective boyfriend coming out?"

"Ya know, I am about as up for your bullshit as a…a…shut the hell up."

Dane held his hands up in surrender. "Sorry, man. Really. S'up with her arm?"

"Bruised rotator cuff. So much wrong." He wasn't going to share the extent of the wrong with Dane. Not there. He had to be patient. Had to wait. It was a lot easier to do in a classroom filled with thirty-two teenagers than an emergency room with the woman he had declared as his life.

The nurse came in and announced, "If you don't mind, I need some room to take her vitals."

The woman had to be frustrated that the doctor overrode her directive, but if she did, hid it like a pro.

As the Clearwaters all backed away, Chief Osborne came in out of breath. He stopped short when he saw the crowd.

The nurse said, "Oh, why not?" There was the frustration. She placed a clip around Willow's finger and a blood pressure cuff around her arm.

NINETEEN

"I heard," Matt said, but he didn't mention that he'd heard it from Liam.

"As of yet," the reporter on the television announced, "the biggest structural damage by far is the Beachfront restaurant on Pine and Palm."

Everyone quieted so they could hear the rest.

A reporter in full rain gear stood in front of the Beachfront. Yellow crime scene tape circled the patio. Two emergency vehicles remained, a fire engine and a squad car with its lights still circling. "As you can see, the patio roof collapsed in the wind. A safety inspection will determine if the structure was up to code. Manager Willow Martinez suffered minor injuries and is listed in stable condition at the Florida Gulf Inland Hospital."

"Safety inspection," Liam barked. "Minor injuries?" Stepping forward, he took a deep breath. "It wasn't the storm that knocked down the roof."

Everyone except the nurse turned to face him completely. His eyes traveled to each of them before he said, "It wasn't an accident."

"And you're telling us this now?" Raine barked.

As if it had been that long?

Henry held out a hand. "Let him talk."

Dane joined the circle and slipped an arm around Zoe's shoulder.

"There is much to say." Liam clasped his hands on the top of his head and paced. "She's lying there unconscious. I don't know what to say or when is the right time to say it. She would want to be part of it. I don't know what's the right thing to do, only that it wasn't an accident, and we have to find out who did this to her."

"She would want you to share what you know," Matt said from the door.

Raine asked, "Is that the friend Matt asking or Chief Matt?"

Matt was soaking wet and dripped over the floor. His clothes were spotted in mud and his pants ripped at the knee. Regardless, he didn't give a snappy comeback. "I'm very tired. There's a lot going on out there, and I came up here in the middle of it as both."

Liam stepped deeper into the mix. He ground his teeth, then explained, "Someone cut a support beam."

He heard a few gasps but didn't look to see who they came from. He wanted to see if Matt would add anything.

"It's true. You saw the yellow tape on the news. I've been down there and declared it a crime scene. Don't know why the reporter said storm damage. I'll be speaking with him." Matt lifted his foot to take a step closer but looked down at the puddle he'd made, then set his foot back down.

From behind, the nurse showed up with a handful of towels. She set some on the floor and handed Matt the rest.

Matt nodded and gave a small bow. He held the towels and, without attempting to use them, said, "There's more. I'm sorry this is such a bad time, but I don't want you to hear it elsewhere. Neil Roberts was found dead in his cell. I'm not able to tell you how he died, but I can tell you that I'm treating it as a homicide."

A length of deafening silence followed as each person in the circle processed this information. Time seemed to stand still.

No one made a sound until Zoe let out a torrent of sobs and buried her head in Dane's chest. Everyone knew it wasn't over the loss of the former Chief Roberts.

Henry wrapped both arms around Harmony.

Raine grabbed clumps of hair from both sides of her head and began pacing.

Each person knew what this meant, Matt included. No one verbalized it until Willow.

"That means he didn't kill Seth," she said.

Instantly, the circle reconvened.

Her eyes were far too alert. "And, it all means his murderer is still out there."

"Willow." His Willow.

The silence returned, each person filling their lungs. Matt stepped into the circle.

"Willow, what all did you hear?" Harmony asked. "You need to rest."

"I have a concussion. I get that. I need to stay overnight for observation. I get that, too." Her eyes were open, but her blinks still long. "What I need is for each of you—" She looked to Liam now. "—to leave me and find out about the vandalism. Find who killed our brother."

Flexing his jaw muscles, Liam forced his shoulders back. "There's something else."

Raine was uncharacteristically quiet. In fact, no one offered a smart remark or chided him for keeping more from them. This family. This family he loved was beaten and broken. Their dreams had been shattered, healed, and shattered again.

"I found Seth's missing photos."

"What missing photos?" Zoe barked.

Willow answered, "Liam and I realized Seth would have had pictures of him and Miriam. None were on his laptop or any external hard drive. I asked Liam to see what he could find." She looked to Liam again. "Did the password work?"

"It did." Feeling the stares that drilled into him from all around, he kept eye contact with Willow. "I'd been searching higher end photograph sites, entering Seth's email to see if he had an account. I had my students on the beach one morning when you taught your yoga class."

"Pilates," Willow corrected.

"Pilates," he conceded.

She added, "The potato gun day." Of all things, she smiled. Behind the bandages, her face softened and glowed.

He nodded. "Yes. Sorry about that," he said and noted that the rest of the people in the room were a distant part of that moment. "I spotted the So Right sign behind you and thought, 'Why not? They do photos.'" The silence in the room and attention on him should have made him sweat. "I entered the first letter of Seth's email, and the rest populated immediately. I'd been trying every password I could think of." He shook his head. "It was dumb. I know. Willow came up with it right away."

"Not right away."

"Well, I got in. There are pictures of Miriam." He lifted his gaze and let it travel around the room. No one seemed to judge him for looking at the photos. That might come later.

Everyone spoke at once. Liam's body was tired, and his mind was full. "I can go get the laptop. It's on the passenger seat of my car. But, is this the right time to—?"

"Son," Henry interrupted him. "I drove your car. There was nothing on the passenger seat."

Liam's eyes grew big. "No. No, no, no, no. I locked—" Did he?

"There was a lot going on," Henry said as an undeserved excuse for Liam.

Liam turned his head away and clamped his eyes shut. "The man." He looked around the room as if he might find answers in the air.

"What man, Liam?" Matt asked.

"There was a man. He was tall, and I think slender. He wore head to toe rain gear. I assumed he was waiting for a ride, but why would he do that there and not under shelter? He was watching the Beachfront. He was watching Willow. He would have seen me. Could have easily gotten into my car."

"I'll check the street cameras," Matt said. Everyone looked to the new chief for direction. Apparently, it was Matt's turn to pause as he obviously considered his words. He finally stopped his gaze on

Liam. "How about you meet me in my office first thing in the morning?"

"I'm not leaving Willow."

"Liam," she said as tears dripped over her face. "Please. I'm hurt. I'm not broken. I'll be home tomorrow. Please, help my family find who murdered our brother."

It was already basically tomorrow, but he wouldn't argue the point.

———

Liam drove through the rain, his fingers clenched around the steering wheel. None of the tension was due to the storm.

He turned his wipers to low. Ernest had been an ass but was no match for the islanders of Ibis. This wasn't their first rodeo. Sleeping in their dry beds, they waited patiently for the water to subside, so they could venture out and begin helping one another with clean up.

To keep an eye on the water around the sandbags, Raine had stayed with Henry and Harmony. Since Liam had spent the night at the hospital, and Zoe's home wasn't on stilts, she and Dane had crashed at Liam's place.

Turning into the drive of his four-apartment building, he punched the garage door opener for his unit. He stopped, wrapped his fingers around his phone, and shook his head. He had no idea when the right time would be to share what he found in Seth's photos as Willow had slept through the night.

Both Dane and Zoe's Jeeps fit end-to-end in his garage. Their tires sat in water. With paper coffee cup in hand, he splashed through the warm puddles to shelter. He checked around the corners of his garage as he made his way to the door that led upstairs to his place. Everything was elevated and secure. This wasn't his first rodeo, either.

He took off his hiking sandals at the bottom of the stairs, next to what he recognized as Dane's and Zoe's. Taking the stairs two at a time, the smell of coffee told him Zoe was already awake or possibly, like him, hadn't slept.

She sat in one of the two seats at his kitchen table, her face unusually pale and her eyes so swollen that if he didn't know better, he would have thought she'd been in a fight.

What would she do with what he'd found? He wanted to tell her. Certainly, it would cheer her up. Or, would it? This was not the time.

Since she turned her head away from him, he decided to give her some room. "Morning, Zoe," he said as he walked to his bedroom.

He'd told Willow he would shower. He just didn't say when and decided a quick change of clothes would do for now. Peeling off his jeans and Sun Trips t-shirt, the shirt snagged on a small splinter he'd missed. The white end stuck out of his palm. He stood in his boxer briefs looking at it, then closed his fingers in a fist and clamped his eyes shut.

His Willow. His life. Lifting his chin, he looked in the mirror. The image was of himself but all he could see was her. She'd made him promise, and he left her.

After the quick change and a toothbrush through his mouth, he came out to find Zoe hadn't moved. He walked to her and slipped a hand under her mug. It was cold. She wore what looked like, to the common passerby, compression socks on her forearms. Anyone who knew her knew she was tired of explaining the bandages and decided on a disguise. Taking the mug from her, he stuck it in the microwave.

Between the blame she placed on herself for Seth's demise and the near-death arson that had almost killed her and Miriam Roberts, Liam felt a sudden wave of pity mixed with guilt that his focus had been single-sided. If she only knew.

Handing the warmed mug back to her, he began to speak. "We're going to find him." Or her, he corrected in his head.

No answer, and other than accepting the mug, no movement.

"Is Dane still sleeping?" It was rhetorical and a pitiful attempt to get something out of her.

"I'm going with you this morning."

Oh boy. Not what he was looking for. This was awkward. "I, uh, Matt sort of—"

"I haven't told him, told you, everything. I'll drive myself if I have to, but I'm going with you."

He nodded. "Okay," he said, drawing out the word. Taking a deep breath, he knew when to concede to a Clearwater. He reached for a to-go cup from his cupboard and gently took the mug from her hand, pouring the contents into the paper cup. "Well, come on, then."

Considering a dry pair of sandals, he decided that would be stupid and slipped on the wet ones. As Zoe did the same, he spotted a newspaper tucked under her arm. He didn't ask.

"Raine is getting your mother to the hospital this morning, then taking care of Willow's beach section," he offered as small talk. "And, the rest of the island, of course."

Flashing sawhorses stood in the especially deep puddles and blocked off the roads impassable even to jacked vehicles such as his. He was a local. He knew the roads to avoid.

TWENTY

Giving up on small talk, Liam was a professional at patience and drove in silence the short trip to city hall. The lot was empty but the lights were on, and he could see Glory talking to an officer who stood next to her desk.

Zoe clenched the newspaper like it might get away. He stepped out into the rain. He would have left the umbrella if not for her. Instead, he opened it and went around to get her door.

Matt showed up in reception and reached the front door before he and Zoe did. He didn't show surprise at the sight of her and propped open the door for the two of them. "Liam. Zoe. Come on in," he said. "Your family doing all right so far in the storm?"

The sound that came through the door was such a contrast to the empty parking lot, Liam paused. Clicks and voices, ringing phones and barked orders.

Liam shook out his umbrella and left it in the foyer.

"It's been a busy night," Matt said as he led the way.

Liam had never been in the office to the Chief of Police before. There were people everywhere. It was like a real city hall. Liam had no idea the Ibis Island Police Department had this many people on staff.

A rookie Liam didn't recognize grabbed his hat and raincoat as he hustled to catch up with a veteran Liam did recognize but couldn't remember the name.

He and Zoe followed Matt down the single hallway alongside a common room that housed a number of metal desks arranged nose-to-nose. "Everyone is tucked away safe and sound. How is your first welcome-to-Ibis storm?"

"It's been a busy night," Matt repeated as he stepped into his office. "I'm learning, that's for damned sure." He held out a hand toward the guest chairs in front of his desk. "Have a seat. Please. Coffee?" Glancing at the cups in their hands, he amended. "Refills?"

Zoe shook her head and sat in the farthest chair.

Liam held his cup out as he sank into the one next to her. "I'd love a warmer, Matt." His knees hit the desk, so he scooted the chair back as Matt used a coffee maker on a file cabinet to top off the cup.

"I found your rain gear man on the street cam." Matt handed the cup back to him and he placed a file in front of them.

"May I?" Liam asked as he reached for the file.

"Go on," Matt said.

Sliding the file closer to Zoe, he flipped open the cover. It was him all right. "I pegged him on the height."

Matt nodded. "And, that's saying something with how tall you are. There's a close up in there too."

Lifting the first pic, he noted the second wasn't much help.

Zoe took it from him. "It's not Miriam Roberts."

"Right," Liam agreed. "She's too small, but we really don't have her on our radar though, right?"

The third was a pic of the man getting into his car. "Damn it," Liam said. He closed his eyes and shook his head.

Zoe slipped the newspaper over the file. "I don't mean because the man is too small. I know it's not her for another reason I haven't shared." Her eyes lifted to Matt as a tear fell on the paper. "Forgive me."

Smooth as a detective, Matt didn't flinch as he lifted the newspaper. "This looks like the publication with the break-in at Seth's old apartment," he said, all but ignoring the apology.

"It is," she said. "Since she broke into my parents' home and mine searching for the love letters between her and my brother, everyone assumed she was the one who broke into Seth's place for the same reason." Zoe looked down at her hands as they clutched the newspaper. "I questioned her about it."

Matt paused at that but only for a quick moment. "How's that?"

"It was at the celebration of life dedication for Seth. When we were on the boat. I asked her what she was trying to find there. If it was the letters she'd been trying to find in my parents' home and in mine?"

It seemed as if the tears had dried up, her cheeks red from the salt.

"She was honestly shocked. Hadn't heard of the break-in at Seth's apartment before. I'm sure of it." Her lungs expanded slowly, then released in a rush. "Sure of it and never told anyone."

Because that would mean an unknown person broke into Seth's apartment and would cast doubt on Neil Roberts as Seth's murderer. "The cornerstone that is Home," Liam said.

Zoe blinked. "What did you say?"

He added, "The damage done to Seth's old apartment. The hole in the wall. It was a corner between the kitchenette and the hallway, right in the center of the place. The cornerstone. Whoever knocked out that wall was looking for treasure."

Matt slid his hand across the desk. "Slow down there."

"Do I get charged with obstruction of justice or something?" she asked. "Withholding evidence?"

Matt lifted his brows.

Liam hoped this was the time. It had to be the time. "That isn't the half of it. While Willow was sleeping, I got back into the So Right site. Look." He tilted his phone, so the three of them could see it at the same time. "In case the man in the rain gear figures out a way to get into Seth's account." Or, if Liam left it unlocked and it opened when the laptop was lifted. "And, removes the photos, we have copies."

He flipped from one photo to another. Solid gold toilet seats, enormous marble candle sticks, jewel encrusted water goblets. All covered in barnacles and clearly secured in an underwater cave with wire roping.

Zoe stood, almost knocking over her chair. She placed both hands on the sides of her head. "Are these pictures from a museum? From a magazine?"

He knew she didn't really believe that. "My mind went there too," he said. "At first. Except, these are under water."

Lifting his arm from the desk, Matt held out his palm. "Guys, guys, guys."

Ignoring Matt, Zoe squealed, "Are you trying to say that Seth found…treasure?" Her voice squeaked the last word out. She moved her hands to cover her eyes so that she was looking at the slideshow Liam gave her through her fingers.

He said, "It looks like Luciana Bezan's treasure."

Matt leaned over his desk and held out both arms between them. "Whoa. Guys. Seth's wall, the cornerstone that is Home? These pics of some legendary treasure? I can tell you want this, but—"

"He did it? He did it!" Zoe jumped up and down, stomping both feet in a circle as if she held a winning Powerball ticket. "He did it!" Jumping in the air, she wrapped her arms around Liam's neck and nearly knocked him over.

Then, her hands moved over her mouth. "And, he was killed for it," she said through her hands. "Because I wasn't there with him."

"Or," Liam argued, "you could have been killed with him."

"You're jumping to conclusions, Zoe." Matt was nearly yelling now. "It didn't fare too well for us last time. Liam, give me that ID and password. I'll get the account locked down."

She stopped and slid to the ground, then turned to Matt. "What about Liam's phone?" Her voice turned obedient. "The pictures that he copied and saved?"

Matt sighed and stuck his hands in his pockets. Shaking his head, he let his eye lids drop to half open. "What pictures?"

Her mother sat next to Willow on the hospital bed as the nurse read over discharge instructions. Raine's patience impressed Willow. No sitting on the edge of the guest chair, tapping her foot. Raine leaned back with a leg slung over one of the armrests.

She couldn't begin to imagine all Raine had to get to out there. And now, she had to add Willow's section of the beach to her list. She wanted to ask Raine how many nest wash outs Willow had in her section, if her beach walkers had all stayed through the storm to help, and about any other damage that had happened. She decided not to bring it up.

With a long blink and smile, Willow nodded at her as the nurse spoke. Raine winked back, then crossed her eyes and stuck out her tongue.

Fortunately, the nurse's focus was on the discharge papers. "You can alternate ibuprofen and Tylenol every three hours. If you wash your hair before your check-up, make sure to cover the stitches with the waterproof bandages in the bag."

The one-long, two short knocks at the door was the Sun Trips emergency dive signal. She knew it was Liam, and anything else the nurse said became a blur. His smile took her breath away and was almost as big as the bouquet of yellow roses he carried.

Maneuvering around the wheelchair meant for her, he dipped his head and stepped next to Raine, who even though patient, sat with Willow's discharge bag and the plant she and their mother brought that morning.

Although his smile and gaze were aimed at her, his head tilted to Raine as they whispered back and forth.

The nurse checked over her shoulder at Willow's sudden distraction, paused, then asked, "Any questions, Willow?"

"No. I feel almost good as new and am truly grateful for your excellent service."

Behind the nurse, Raine set the bag on her lap, stuck a finger down her throat, and pretended to vomit. Willow was an expert at how to keep a straight face when her big sister baited her.

"Oh," the nurse stuttered. "You're welcome. It's our pleasure. Who is taking you home?"

"He is." Raine gestured with her thumb thumbed an elbow to Liam.

He was?

"I am?" Liam's expression said that idea was not part of their whispered conversation.

What about the Beachfront? What about Luciana's? They'd told her to trust them to take care of it. She closed her eyes and inhaled through her nose, then out her mouth. She was helpless to all of it.

As the nurse stepped to him, her mother set a hand on her knee. "Raine needs to get out and take care of the island, dear."

"Right." Willow shook her head, knowing all that was needed out there. And, with the sling and bump on her head, how useless she was to help.

"Remember to call Chloe," her mother reminded her. "Be as honest as you can. You don't want her to fear for your safety every time she leaves you."

Raine stood. "Okay. Well. We'll get this stuff to your place, check around for water issues, then let you get some rest."

Liam lifted a pointed finger. "Before you leave—" He looked to the nurse, then to the floor. After far too long of a pause, he shook his head. "Let me assure you I'll take good care of her."

His words should have soothed her, but there was something more behind them. Squinting, she stood and cradled her right arm as she moved to the wheel chair.

"May I?" she asked him and held out her good arm.

His look of puzzlement melted her soul.

"The flowers," she said.

"Oh," he said and handed them to her.

As the nurse began to push her toward the elevator, Willow dug her nose in the roses and inhaled.

The bumpy thresholds and elevator floor seam gave her cause to second-guess her decision against narcotics, but she kept her poker face intact.

TWENTY-ONE

illow waved to Raine and her mother as they pulled away
from the hospital circle drive and Liam pulled in. On her
lap, she held the half dozen yellow roses.

She had so much to tell him, to share with him, to ask him.

She considered whatever it was he began to tell the three of
them in the hospital room before he'd decided against it.

She didn't mind the puddles or the rain or Ernest's tail wind.
The scent of the island woke her senses and appreciation for family
and friends.

"Is there anything else I can get for you?" the nurse asked as
Liam pulled up.

Willow sighed and grinned a toothless smile. She shook her head
and said, "I have everything I need."

"Someone call for a taxi?" Liam jogged around the car to get
the door for her.

There was nothing the matter with her legs or her left arm for
that matter, but she complied. Anything to get out of there. When
her legs were clear, he shut the door, and she waved to the nurse.

Collapsing against the headrest, she sighed as he pulled away
from the circle drive. "It feels like I've been in there for days."

"Or not even a full one." He reached over and took her good hand. "I'm glad you're well enough to leave." Then, he did a double take. "You are well enough to leave, right? You didn't pull a Zoe or anything, did you?"

"Nope. Narcotics are out of my system." Fortunately and unfortunately. "They gave me this nice little tape to cover my six stitches, and I can't even feel my bump." The last one may have been a stretch, but he'd beat himself up enough already.

"Good." He squeezed her fingers before letting go.

The taking of her hand was amazing and the letting go disturbing.

"I have something I need to tell you," he said. "So much has happened."

"Did they find who cut the beam?"

"No, not that, but Matt is looking."

She nodded. "Good." She realized it was in the same platonic tone he'd used. "Matt is good." Now, she could kick herself. "I have something to tell you too."

A lonely dry spot appeared in the parking lot ahead. "I need ice cream. Can we pull over to Joe's?"

Jerking his head toward her, he gave her a look that said he didn't believe the narcotics were out of her system but pulled over anyway. "You eat ice cream?"

"Every five years," she said. "Religiously."

"I'm not sure if they're open." He craned his head toward the front door.

"You have something on your nose." She used her good arm to balance on the seat between them, leaned in, and laid her mouth on his.

His lips didn't move. It wasn't what she'd imagined as a first kiss, but that was not what this was about for her. And, since her eyes never closed, she noted that his didn't close either.

She smiled around their joined lips. She couldn't help it. He looked like someone just dumped Luciana Bezan's dowry over a cliff. She pulled back an inch or two and studied his eyes at close range. "I'm sorry, but I've had a lot happen this weekend, and I need you to know that I'm in love with you."

No response.

"I'm not sure exactly how you feel in this regard." Why did she sound like this was a job interview? "And, I'm not trying to say I want sex. I've only ever done that with Jacob." She waited for the stab of guilt at the mention of his name and smiled bigger when it didn't come.

Still no response from the object of her dedication.

"I only sleep with forever." She was talking much too fast, but she couldn't help it and just went with it. "And in this day and age, I don't want to give you the impression—"

He leaned in and pressed his lips to hers. The long fingers from both of his hands cupped her cheeks, then traveled around to the back of her neck and laced through her hair. Pulling her into him, his lips opened and explored. Lips and tongue. It was like a mixture of fireworks and of coming home.

Her eyes rolled in the back of her head, and she closed her lids. She forgot the pain, forgot her arm, her head, her anything else. As she let herself go in the safety of his lips and all that was Liam, a hand wrapped carefully around her head and gently pulled her closer into him.

His mouth was warm and gentle, needy and sexy.

Setting his forehead on hers, he pulled his lips away. She opened her eyes, but he kept his closed as he spoke.

"I don't know what to say." His head rotated back and forth against her forehead.

"Tell me I'm not crazy."

His eyes opened to hers. Gold specks she'd never noticed before danced in the dark brown. She felt no fear, no nerves. He was her safety net, and no matter what he felt, she loved him.

Parting their foreheads, the tiniest of smiles lightened his face. A thumb brushed back and forth across her cheek, then landed over her bottom lip. "When I reached you. When you were lying there under the roof." He paused to take a deep breath and turned his gaze to hers. "I kept running two thoughts through my head." He brushed a strand of hair away from her stitches and behind her ear. "That you are my Willow and my life."

———

It was hard to mention the idea of leaving the parking spot in front of the ice cream shop they never entered. Willow could have sat there for days, facing him with her leg cocked on the seat and the good side of her face resting on the headrest. The sound of his voice covered her in peace and the expressions on his face in joy.

"I need to make an extra stop before we go home," she said.

He inhaled deeply, then sighed. "I have—" he started to say, then reached across his face and scratched his cheek. "It can wait."

She wasn't sure if his sigh was from the idea of making an extra stop or from what he needed to tell her, but intuition said not to ask.

"I want to stop by Miriam's. Even after all he did, Chief Roberts was her husband. I feel like I should check on her."

"You could call?" he said as a question.

Knowing you could say almost anything with a smile on your face, she grinned at him and shook her head. "This is one of those times, I believe, it is important to show up."

As he drove toward Miriam Roberts' apartment building, she glanced down at their joined hands. So much right in the midst of the wrong.

He approached the four-way stop that would have been completely under water a few hours earlier. A pickup came from the left fast enough that he let go of her hand and draped his arm in front of her.

The pickup went through without even pausing.

"He might simply be distracted," she said.

"You see?" Liam exclaimed. "How do you do that?"

"Do what?"

"Keep your calm like that. Give everyone the benefit of the doubt." Taking her hand again, he gently accelerated.

"What if he had an emergency? What if he lost his job?"

"Statistically speaking, he's a jerk who's not paying attention."

"Maybe," she said and laughed at statistically speaking. She was in love with a high school physics teacher. "Probably." She turned to gauge his expression. "A wise person once told me you can tell a lot about a person by the way they drive."

"Does that person happen to have gray hair, grow herbs on her front porch, and have goats that graze on the roof during the day?"

"Blonde gray, but yes. She might indeed."

Much of the water had displaced. Yet, he still turned down the roads islanders knew would be safer. He glanced over to her. "What does a jerk who blows off a stop sign and nearly runs you over say about a person?"

"I understand that odds say he is a jerk, but since there is nothing I can do about it either way, I choose to give the person the benefit of the doubt. As for your driving—"

"Whoa, whoa, whoa there now."

"You didn't get angry. Frustrated maybe, and I love it when you say, 'whoa, whoa, whoa,' by the way. You didn't yell or shake your fist at him."

"I called him an ass in my head."

"But kept it to yourself. Says all the more about you, and all of it good."

"Okay, but now I feel driving pressure."

"Thank you for agreeing to this," she said, bringing the subject back full circle.

"You're welcome, but I don't feel right about it. Are you sure?"

"I am," she crooned but noted the throbbing in her head began to take over. "Just this stop, then I'll be ready for an afternoon of rest."

Miriam Roberts. The new widow of former Chief Roberts. She hadn't married a good man like Jacob or like Liam, only had an affair with one.

"You're doing this, because, regardless of what Chief Roberts had been like, you know what it's like to become a widow."

"How did he die?" she asked.

He paused and took a deep breath as if he was deciding whether to tell her. "Knifing."

Prison knifing. That made sense.

"What are you going to say to her?"

"I have no idea. It just seems like the right thing to do."

"Like giving a pass to an ass who cuts you off at a four-way stop?"

"Something like that, yes." The throbbing became stronger. She had an hour yet before her next dose of ibuprofen. "Then, I probably should get home and rest."

"Paula and I will take care of Luciana's. Chloe comes back in two days. The egg has been easy. We can do this. You and me."

She stared into the brown and saw that the gold specks were still there, even in this light. "You and me," she repeated, and noted the blanket of peace it brought.

"Did you say anything to Chloe about the attempt on your life?"

"Attempt on my life?" That seemed like a stretch. Was it? "I told her there was an accident."

He drew circles around the back of her hand as he turned into Miriam's lot and parked. Turning off the car, he shifted into park and looked down at their joined hands. "There's something I need to tell you. It's important as well." He shifted in his seat. "Not as important as this." He lifted their joined hands and squeezed her fingers. "But, it's important for me to share it with you, and I can't seem to find a good time to tell you."

She'd never heard that many words come from him all at once before.

"We think your brother may have found treasure."

She leaned forward in the seat. Her body and mind woke, and she may have yelled the subsequent flood of single word questions. "What? How? When? How?" Her mind told her that wasn't possible, which sounded condescending, even if in mind only.

With his free hand, he took his phone from his shirt pocket. "The what is that I found exactly two hundred sixty-three pictures of Miriam and of treasure that were on the So Right photo site. The how is the password you gave me. It worked. The when is a mixture of—"

"Seth was a semi-pro photographer," she interrupted. "He would never use such a low-quality developer as So Right."

"I tried the better ones when you were doing your yoga thing on the beach that day—"

"Pilates."

"Yes. That. And, I spotted the obnoxiously bright sign behind you and decided it couldn't hurt to try. Maybe he thought no one would ever look there. At first, I spotted only the ones of Miriam. I was so shocked I slammed the laptop shut. It would have been wrong for me to look through the rest without you."

He paused and grinned.

"Or, maybe Sam and Aiden came in the room, and I didn't want them to see. I knew you'd understand. I did drive right over to you." His eyes clamped shut. "And, I found you. I'll never erase the image of you lying on the patio." The muscles in his jaw flexed and released.

"I'm here. It's just a bump and scratch. Wow. Can you forward me the pics? Have you told anyone else?"

TWENTY-TWO

Liam nodded and turned to look up to the two-story Bayside Apartment complex. "Matt, yes. Zoe was with me."

"Zoe? What was her reaction?" A stab of pain shot through her arm as she reached for the door handle.

"Don't. I've got you." As he'd done in the emergency room circle drive, he hopped out and jogged around the vehicle. "Zoe acted like a kid who stepped into Disney World. Matt, not so much." Holding out his arm, he guided her out of the car. "Are you sure about this?"

"I am. This is the right thing to do."

As easy as the sun, he joined hands with her. "Okay, but I need to be honest with you that I never know what to say in loss situations, let alone one that involves an abusive estranged husband who tried to kill his wife as well as one of my best friends."

He acknowledged that this was important to her and went along with it. She had hooked the best, smartest man on the planet. She might be slow, five years slow, but she was brilliant.

She climbed the stairs and knocked on Apt. 2. There was shuffling behind the door, but no one answered. She glanced up to Liam. He shrugged.

Waiting another moment, she heard footsteps creak to the door, then stop. Miriam must have been at the peephole. She opened the door. The size of her smile was in direct contrast to the pale color of her skin and dark rings beneath her eyes. Her black dyed hair looked like something might have nested in it. The tank she wore exposed the entire nicotine patch stuck on her left upper arm, which would be impressive if not for the lit cigarette in her other hand.

"Liam. Willow, hello."

Willow paused before asking, "May we come in, friend?"

"Of course," Miriam said and stepped aside. The living room was a combination living room/kitchen/dining room. Other than the strong smell of burnt coffee and cigarette smoke, it was OCD clean.

"I heard about your arm," Miriam said through the cigarette that dangled from her lips.

It hadn't even been twenty-four hours.

"And, you about my husband. Small town," she added as she placed a hand on her hip, fingers pointing behind her. "It's why you're here?"

Crossing her arms over one another, she grabbed each elbow. Dark circles ringed her eyes. "I'm surprised you're out of the hospital." Lifting her cigarette hand enough to reach her mouth, she took a deep drag.

"I, we wanted to let you know we love you and are here for you. Are you okay? How are you holding up?" She placed her good hand on Miriam's arm. It was ice cold, and Willow could feel the goose bumps beneath her fingers.

Taking a deep breath, Miriam blew smoke into a fallen clump of hair stuck on her forehead. "Best day of my life, really." She blinked and looked Willow in the eye. "Oh, and for you, too, right? Case is closed?"

"Right," Liam answered for her.

He was smart not to let on about what they knew. Still, it seemed deceptive.

Liam added, "There is that, but we are still sorry for...everything."

"Yeah. There is that." She turned away and grabbed the back of her head. "Sorry about the mess. I've been busy."

There was no mess. She still hadn't offered for them to sit. Willow sagged more and more by the minute and wasn't sure if she would make it long enough for a sit visit anyway. "What have you been doing, if it's okay for me to ask? We really must have some coffee soon. Did you hear the Coffee House is offering a free cup in exchange for a bucket of beach garbage?"

"No, I hadn't heard that."

Awkward silence followed, especially since she hadn't answered Willow's question. "Well, we won't keep you. I'll call in a day or so about that coffee."

"You do that, yes. Get better, Willow."

As he pulled into Willow's drive, Liam made a list of things to do. Clean up fallen brush, trim the grass, shape the palm trees, and power wash the siding. He knew keeping busy was his knee-jerk to calm all that had happened in the last day or so, but he also knew he wouldn't be able to properly process until he'd gotten some sleep anyway.

"Did you hear me?" she asked.

"Of course, I did. I'm a guy." He had no idea what to do with this new thing that was them. Or, how it happened, for that matter. His delirious mind was full of the recent events and turns in everything that was anything. It might be that this was all a dream or drunken stupor, and he was going to wake up any second.

He grinned as he pulled his Ranger next to Raine's truck. "Okay." He shifted into neutral, set the emergency brake, and turned to her. "Tell me again. I'm listening." It was hard with her arm in a sling, a bandage on her forehead, and the most incredibly soft lips he'd ever kissed speaking to him.

"We need to have a family meeting. Go over everything. Make sure everyone is on the same page. Invite Matt."

Spoken like a Clearwater. He sighed and added, "Heal from the damage of a building falling on your head."

"Roof," she amended. "How is your back by the way?"

Reflexively, he arched. It was sore as hell. How did she know about that? "Good as ever."

"You are such a liar." Her arm lifted toward the door handle, then pulled back again. Smart girl. He jumped out of his Ranger and around the hood as he noticed Raine on the side of the house, checking on the water. "How is it?" he yelled as he opened his passenger door.

Her eyes met his, but she didn't answer.

He stared at Raine as she went back to what she was doing that didn't look a thing like checking on water.

He forced a grin as he held out an arm for Willow. "May I?"

She took his arm and eyed Raine as much as he had. "My place is a mess."

"So?"

"So, you're neat and organized."

"And, you're attentive, giving, and the best mother I know."

Her eyes watered. He assumed it might not be from pain.

Standing in the drizzle, she said, "My Love Languages are gifts and words. You brought me flowers and personal compliments."

"Oh, well. That's good, right?" Rubbing his chin with his thumb and forefinger, he said, "I don't know my love speaking thing."

"Touch and words, I think. So, we've got words down and need to pay attention to gifts and touch."

She reached up around his neck and lifted on her toes. Pulling his head, she laid those softest lips he'd ever kissed on his. How? When? Why? Yep. He was sleep drunk.

"What? Oh my gosh." Raine marched from the side of the house and walked right by them. "Why the hell not?"

Willow covered her mouth and laughed enough for her shoulders to shake. The wince on her face had him placing his hand on her back and guiding her toward the door. He'd thought for sure Raine would be gone by the time they got there and definitely that she wouldn't be coming in.

Toeing off his shoes, he set them straight next to Willow and Raine's discarded pairs.

"Mom is home?" Willow asked.

"Yeah. We've got forty-five wash outs so far," she said, referring to turtle nests, he assumed. "I dropped her off, so I could get out there." Raine moved the crumpled blanket from the side of the couch and sat. "Come sit. I have something to tell you."

There was a lot of that going on, and he had a feeling it wasn't about catching him and her sister kissing.

Willow sat next to her, and he took the armchair.

"I want you to know that I've called Matt. All of your windows are locked as well as your front and back doors."

He did not like where she was going with this and stood.

"Just," Raine said and held out both arms to him. "Be calm, Liam. She needs you to be calm."

"Would everyone please stop treating me like a glass doll?" Willow barked.

Raine raised her voice. "Or, someone who had a building fall on her last night?"

"Roof," Willow said. "A roof that paused halfway before falling to the ground, and what the hell is wrong with my yard?"

"Someone's been back there. Your plants are all stepped on." Raine looked to Liam, then back to Willow. "Around the corners."

The sound of tires over Willow's gravel had Liam take the three long strides to the front door. Looking out the glass crescent window at the top, he spotted a squad car. Matt.

He didn't come to the front door but meandered around the side of the house.

"You told him about my plants?" Willow asked.

Raine nodded. "How long has this—" She motioned between him and Willow. "—been going on? Am I the last to know again?"

Willow sat up straighter than her already straight body. "Nope. The first." Did her face light up as she said that, or was that his sleep-deprived delirium?

"But," Liam interjected from the front of the house. "There's something I need to tell you."

"The treasure," Raine finished for him. "Zoe called. Mom and Dad know." She leaned forward and rested both forearms on her thighs. "I realize this might not be the time, but give me your phone. I want to see the pics."

He nodded and swiped open his phone. As he handed it to her, she said, "Willow needs to get some rest, and I have to get out to… Oh. My. Gosh." Raine stood as she swiped. "Look at these. I mean…" She started pacing. "Zoe said, and I believed her, but maybe not, because…look at these!"

"I know," Willow said as a fat tear fell down each cheek. "He did it."

"If you don't mind," Liam said, "I'd like to check the windows and doors myself."

Raine nodded as she paced and swiped.

He stepped into Chloe's bedroom first. The room was blue with a Dora bed and play kitchen set under the window. It was dusted and organized with the comforter turned back exposing freshly laundered sheets. Splitting the blinds between his fingers, he saw that the locks were secured.

What had Chloe's reaction been when Willow told her about the so-called accident? Was it his right to ask? He rotated on the balls of his feet and went next door to Willow's bedroom to check her locks. She was going to stay with him at his place. He would make her. He wasn't a chauvinist. Mostly. And, he knew she could take care of herself…had taken care of herself and her daughter on her own for five years, but this was different.

Her room was just as dusted, but her bed wasn't made and small nests of clothing were scattered everywhere. The blinds were open. His feet stopped as he imagined someone like Lucky Nemo searching in and around his Willow's house for millions of dollars' worth of treasure.

The locks were secure, so he closed the blinds and went to see about the rest of the house.

150

TWENTY-THREE

Liam returned as Matt came in the front door.

Taking a deep breath, he marched in, ready to make his first demands as Willow's what? Boyfriend? He would be much better after a good night's sleep.

"Liam," she said before he had a chance. "Can you stay here with me?"

He lifted a finger, shook it, then opened his mouth. "Oh. Yeah. Okay," he answered. Spoken like a true graduate with his MA in physics.

"The whoever already searched my stupid cornerstones, and we're both really tired. When Chloe comes back, I'd really like to stay at your place as you have no cornerstones that could be home, or potential under unders since you are not family in that regard."

He opened his mouth, paused, then said, "Yeah, okay."

Raine sat with her arms folded and Matt the same, only standing. "You two done?" Raine asked.

"Raine is right," Matt said. "Someone's been out there. I can't tell either of you not to stay here, but can't recommend it either."

Raine stood. "I say, Liam's about to fall over where he stands, and Willow is getting whiter by the minute. Let's let them get some sleep. We'll be ready for their call and can powwow at that time." It seemed to be a rhetorical suggestion as she turned to Willow to finish. "I'll call Mom and Dad and update them on the way to the beach."

Matt swiped an arm toward the front door and said to Raine, "Bosses first."

"Screw you," she said but went ahead of him anyway. "I'll keep my phone on," she said as she slipped on her shoes and left.

"Lock up as we leave?" Matt asked as he stood in the front door.

Liam lifted to his feet and headed after him. "I checked the rest of the house, too, yeah."

Securing the deadbolt, Liam checked his watch. "Time for your ibuprofen."

Yawning, she said, "Will you help me to bed?"

Oh, boy. He nodded much too fast, then quickly rubbed a hand over his face to cover.

"I just need to step into the bathroom."

Digging his hands into his pockets, he followed her to the bedroom, rocked on the backs of his heels, then decided to make her bed. Was that too presumptuous? He didn't want her to think he looked down on her because she wasn't as organized as him. He was overthinking. This was going to make him insane.

She came out wearing a fresh pair of black pants things and an oversized Turtle Watch t-shirt in her good hand. "Help me?"

With the shirt? He knew his eyes opened wide but thought he caught himself and turned calm and collected fast enough. "Yep."

She turned away from him and slipped out of the good sleeve of her Beachfront blouse. No bra. Rubbing his hand over his face once again, he opened the neck of the blouse and guided it over the sling.

Her shoulder was strong and smooth. Any fear of arousal at the sight of them disappeared at the bright red bruises that covered them.

"Is it bad?"

No sense to lie. "Yes. It's bad."

He rested his hand on her upper arm, and she covered it with her own.

"I love you too." It just came out. He was too tired to be nervous about it. All he cared about at that moment was her, about her and about keeping her safe.

She kissed his fingers, and he helped her with the Turtle Watch shirt.

"You made my bed." She said it like he'd given her a dozen roses, which made him remember the flowers in his Ranger. He would get those later. "There is nothing better than getting into a made bed." Turning to him, she held out her good arm. "Sleep with me?"

He knew she didn't mean sleep with, but it made him swallow hard anyway.

She slipped in the side closest to the only nightstand. "You have dark rings under your dark rings."

He covered her up and said, "Let me get you some water and that ibuprofen, and I will stay with you."

Willow opened her eyes to morning sun shining through her windows. Her first instinct was panic that she'd slept through her Turtle Watch section check-in from today's walker. Or worse, a call to say there was an emergency.

The pain in her head and her shoulder shook her back to reality.

Turning to check the time, she spotted him. Liam Morrison. He was in her bed. He'd stayed. He slept with her without a hint of sleeping with her.

They weren't touching, mostly because he'd spent the entire night in his jeans sleeping on top of her comforter, but she could still feel his warmth and the strength of his body next to him. He was lying on his back, his arms folded on his chest. She wasn't sure why that struck her as funny, but it did.

He should be snoring lying on his back like that, but he wasn't. His chest rose and fell. He'd kept his shirt on. It was all beyond disappointing.

But, he'd stayed.

She wasn't just not alone; she was with her best friend. Her best friend who turned out to be an incredible kisser. The clock read 7:46 a.m. She was due for Tylenol in fifteen minutes. He'd been setting his phone alarm.

Deciding on letting him sleep through this one, she reached over to get his phone from her nightstand.

"I'm not sleeping," his deep, groggy voice mumbled.

"Oh." She took the phone anyway. "I guess I don't know your passcode."

"Who do you appreciate?" he whispered.

What? Oh. She laughed to herself as she swiped, then pressed 2-4-6-8. The photo app was open. She stared at a jewel-encrusted goblet laced with seaweed next to pieces of matching silverware embedded with green and brown jewels.

Rubbing his eyes, he propped himself on his elbow and faced her.

She swiped through photos. A solid gold toilet. A crown? Each was clearly under water and in a cave, she decided as she squinted.

He placed his hand over the screen. "I'm not going to suggest that you let it go until you're feeling better, although I wish you would. I don't know that I could if the situation was reversed, but Matt had some good advice."

She turned her eyes to his. The gold specks were gone. Only the smooth, strong brown remained.

His fingers left his screen and traveled to her good forearm. The ibuprofen and Tylenol mix definitely left some to be desired. She could be pain free if she'd accepted the stronger stuff. But also, not on her A game.

"We assumed Neil Roberts killed your brother. We were wrong. He says let's wait before we decide if it is Luciana's, or even treasure that he'd found."

She wanted to disagree. Letting her lungs fill completely caused pain in her shoulder, but she did it anyway. Nodding, she said, "You're right. He's right." She swiped the phone open again anyway. "Both that we shouldn't assume and that I can't focus on anything without looking through these first. How about you get me some Tylenol and water and we can go over the facts?"

Wide awake now, the condition of her teeth and unshowered self became a reality. She rotated her legs off the side of the bed, sat, and assessed if she was going to be dizzy. "A mysterious diver that rented a boat in a coming tropical storm."

"Likely a yellow Yo-Yo boat."

Shuffling to the bathroom, she added, "All of those people who came to see Seth's poem, and now a mysterious man who stole Seth's laptop."

"And, whoever stomped around the cornerstones of your house."

Liam opened the door for Willow and saw Glory positioned behind her city hall reception desk.

"What in heaven's sake are you doin' out, girl?" Glory shuffled around the desk on impossible shoes and gave Willow a wide A-frame hug. "You barely got out of the hospital."

"Heard there was a family meeting," Willow answered, giving Glory a tight squeeze with her good arm. "I am part of the family, and there is nothing the matter with my brain."

Glory pulled her chin back and gave her a convincing expression of shock. Rolling her eyes, she jerked a thumb toward her desk. "Sign the clipboard on your way back. They're in the conference room."

Liam signed for both of them, and Glory didn't argue about it. Either because Willow's right arm was in a sling or because she had a magazine she needed to get back to. He noted the pertinent names listed before theirs on the check-in form. The only names listed before theirs on the check in form. Henry, Harmony, Zoe, and Dane. They were only missing Raine.

The bell on the door dinged. He guessed it was her before he looked.

"I hoped Liam would talk you out of this," Raine said. She wasn't nearly as PC as Glory.

"She insisted," Liam interrupted. "I made her eat some protein, get ahead on pain meds, and drink plenty of water."

"Can we discuss me as if I'm not here in the conference room, please?"

Raine scribbled on the clipboard and followed them in. The long wall of blinds was closed but not the one on the door. Through the glass, Liam spotted Matt as he stood at a whiteboard, scribbling notes. The rest of them sat around the table.

Liam knocked and opened the door at the same time. Predictably, the room became silent. "Don't look at me," Liam said. "There's no stopping her." He stood out of the way for Willow and Raine to walk through.

Henry stood and stepped to Willow. Carefully, he wrapped his arms around her and held on for a signature Clearwater three-second hug. "You look tired."

"Thanks?" she said as a question.

"I'd ask what you're doing here," Matt said. "But, that would be obvious. So, sit down. I'll catch you up."

"Hello, Chief," Raine said and pulled out a chair.

"Hello, Raine."

Matt stepped out of the way of the marker board. "We've come together today," he began as Willow placed a hand on Liam's thigh.

Out of the corner of his eyes, he glanced to her. Were they public? Her expression said she didn't realize what she was doing, and he had no idea whether to scoot away from her or set his hand on hers. He decided on acting as if he didn't realize it either.

"To gather all the facts," Matt finished. "All the facts," he repeated.

Like a school teacher, a boring one, Matt pointed to the words on the whiteboard as he read them verbatim.

Obsession with Luciana Bezan's dowry

Time searching Gulf-side caves

Ah. A chronological list of Seth's pertinent actions before his death. And sure enough, facts only, it appeared.

Affair with Miriam
Plane tickets
Photos sent to So Right

"Wait right there," Liam said. "He used So Right only for the pictures he wanted to hide. He knew no one would look there for him to develop anything."

"We talked about that, yes," Zoe said.

"Which we would have known," Willow said not at all gently.

He liked the sound of we.

Willow finished. "If you would have let me know when you were meeting."

"We did let him know," Zoe said, ratting Liam out. So much for the we.

Matt continued.

Murdered in cave
Apartment wall damage
Poem displayed

Reluctant to interject yet again, but not enough not to, Liam said, "Did you want to add the long list of divers who came to Luciana's to get a look at the poem that absolutely is a map, firsthand?"

Matt looked around the table.

Henry nodded. "I think that's a good idea. Willow?"

Looking much like her father, she nodded but closed her eyes. "Lucky Nemo, Richard Beckett, Blake Eaton, Glen Oberweiss, Miriam Roberts, and Timothy Hart."

Zoe leaned forward. "And Mayor Green?"

Willow shook her head. "No, and his daughter, Lucy, mentioned he wouldn't be back until next week. Remember?" she said to Matt.

He nodded. "I remember." Then, finished adding the suggested names.

Liam had a feeling Matt wasn't telling all he knew, and probably had a whiteboard like this one hiding somewhere in his office. Liam found himself empathizing with Raine's aversion to the police.

TWENTY-FOUR

Willow picked up Liam's arm by the wrist and checked his watch. "The mayor doesn't get back for another five days."

Raine asked Willow, "When were you with Matt talking to the mayor's daughter?"

Willow blushed, then lifted her chin. "When we interrogated Chief Roberts."

"Former chief," Zoe amended.

Matt stepped between Willow and Raine. "Our objective was to get him to slip up either in interrogation or afterward to whoever it was he kept alluding to who was going to get him the hell out, sue us all, and make him scot-free." He rubbed a hand over the back of his neck. "Didn't know it might get him killed."

"You think he was murdered for this?" Liam asked.

"I can't say."

Except he did just say.

Chief Roberts found dead

Tall man in rain gear

Beachfront vandalized

"No," Liam said to the last part. "Change that. Vandalism is something done by kids wanting to stir up trouble. This was attempted murder. This was to scare us, to send a message."

"And we're not scaring," Willow finished for him.

Matt ignored their circling of the wagons and drew a vertical line separating the chronological list of what they knew from the rest of the board. He made a title that read, Haiku.

Her Legacy

The wet uncharted

The cornerstone that is Home

The under under

Liam noted that Matt had it memorized.

"Let's just say," Matt began, "that her is this Luciana Bezan. At least, in Seth's eyes."

"And in the heads of the other treasure hunters," Dane interjected.

Matt nodded his head back and forth in a way that said he would go along to get along. "And, the wet uncharted is the scene of Seth's mur— The scene of the crime."

"The knife," Zoe blurted. "The knife. It was…" She waved her hand in circles. "Was ornamental. Gaudy. Gold and jeweled like the treasure in the pictures Liam found."

Matt's lungs filled. He didn't look too happy that Zoe made that connection. "An area of Seth's apartment wall that could be considered a cornerstone of his home was destroyed." His eyes traveled from face to face. "The outside of Willow's home has evidence of a person or persons searching the corners."

Zoe blurted out, "For treasure."

Harmony covered her mouth. "Ours too," she said from behind her hands.

"Raine? Zoe and Dane?" Matt said. "What about your homes?"

They shrugged. "I'll check," Dane said.

Raine nodded. "I will too."

"I'm going to send a patrol out to all four of your homes to take pictures, and I'm going to investigate myself."

Raine opened her mouth to say something, but Matt steamrolled her. "This is my island, for however long, and I'm going to look over any potential crime scene with my own eyes." He stood tall and placed his fingers in his front pockets. "I don't want any of you to be concerned when a squad car shows up at your homes, and I am looking around taking pictures."

"Can he do that?" Raine said, looking around for backup.

Matt answered for them. "He can, and he will."

"You see," Matt said and capped his dry erase marker. "This is what I find puzzling." He paused as he moved his eyes to each of the Clearwater family, including the one that was really a Martinez. "Interesting and puzzling. Impressive, definitely. I've heard each of you cheer that Seth had found actual treasure. I get that. Talk about the others who might be looking for the treasure or more of it. You've even pushed back a number of times in defense of invasion to your family. But, none of you have mentioned a single word about finding the treasure for yourselves."

"Well, I've sure as hell gone there," Dane said. "For Seth, if nothing else. He wouldn't want it to fall in the hands of someone like Lucky Nemo. The location of the treasure from the pictures? Was that the cornerstone that is Home? Or, was it the under under? Or, is it even the booty he was killed over?" he said as he wrapped an arm around Zoe's shoulders. "If we find the treasure, we find the killer."

"Possibly," Matt said. "Or, we find someone in the know." He drew another line and wrote, going forward.

This was what Liam wanted to see.

Seth's apartment
Clearwater and Martinez homes
Richard Beckett
Blake Eaton
Timothy Hart
Lucky Nemo
Yo-Yo Rentals

He listed them automatically in alphabetical order by last name. Matt truly was steeped in this case.

"Why not Glen Oberweiss or Miriam Roberts?" Zoe asked. "I

notice you often stay quiet as the people around you share what they know."

Matt lifted a single brow at her. "Fair enough." He nodded. "As soon as I'm sure everyone is safe from this tropical storm, I'm going to have one of my men inventory the items from Seth's treasure photos, then begin a search to see if items matching this description have been purchased or sold within the last two plus years. As far as Oberweiss and Mrs. Roberts are concerned, we might question them down the road, but for now, they're short."

Dane jerked his head around the room. "What does that mean?"

"It means that Zoe and Liam are right," Matt said. "The traffic cams show a tall, slender man in rain gear watching the patio collapse. It shows him getting into the passenger side of Liam's car."

Car left unlocked, Liam amended in his head.

"Oberweiss and Roberts are short people. Is the tall man responsible for the attack on Willow? And yes, I am calling it an attack. I can't say against Willow specifically, as of yet, but definitely an attack."

He rotated to face the whiteboard and its three columns.

Liam took out his phone, turned it to mute, and took a picture of it.

"We have to remember that it's in the realm of possibility that each person of interest you've mentioned to include on this board is just that. A person of interest. The person responsible for the Beachfront might be someone completely different. Same with your brother's murder. I can tell you from experience, it's important to keep an open mind." He pulled the cap from his marker one more time and wrote WHO HAS THE ORIGINAL POEM in all caps. "This might be the most important detail to lead us to it all."

Willow faded fast, but she wasn't about to give Liam any indication of it. The back of her neck where her sling rested was knotted and her shoulder throbbed.

"You're fading fast," he said.

Rolling her eyes, she halted their trek down the long beach access and looked up to him. "I'm—" She wanted to argue, but then decided that would be pointless. "Going home right after this and crashing, yes." His eyes were void of the gold specks and the rings beneath them that continued to grow darker said he might be fading as much as she was.

She brought their joined hands to her lips and kissed his fingers. "You've stayed."

Letting out a small grin, he nodded. He released her hands and opened his, setting them on the side of her face.

"What is this thing we're doing?" he asked.

She understood he didn't mean the checking on her beach section two days after she had a roof fall on her head. With a small shrug, she said, "Following what is meant to be?" That sounded forever-ish. A small rush of heat ran up her neck.

The brown in his eyes seemed to lighten and bore warm holes into her soul.

After setting down the bucket he carried for her, he took her face between both of his hands, leaned down, and laid his mouth on hers. His lips were testing and careful, a few gentle pecks before she lifted to her toes and dove in.

A small croon escaped her throat, and he slipped his hands down to cradle the sides of her neck. His thumbs traced her jawline as she tilted her head and explored this new part of her best friend.

He pulled away much too soon. She tried not to pout, but was probably as effective as she was with fooling him about fading fast.

"We have all the time in the world for this," he said as he tucked a stray strand of hair behind her ear. "You should focus on healing."

After picking up the bucket, she tugged him along toward the beach. He hadn't challenged her on how long checking her section was going to take.

As she approached the opening that led to the northern most end of her section, she sat on the closest bench and toed off her sandals. Inhaling, she closed her eyes and took in the coastal breeze. "There's something about the clean, crisp air that follows a storm."

The sand was cool beneath her toes, and she wondered how many nests of hatchlings would wake that night and emerge from the cooler ground temperature.

"I'd like it if you'd rest at your parents' house," he said and sat next to her.

It wasn't like him to make demands. He was the kind of person who picked his battles, or in this case, demands. She moved her thigh to touch his, then gestured for him to hand her the Turtle Watch cinch sack he'd carried for her.

"You've been patient with me. Carted me around town to check on Luciana's and drive by the Beachfront."

He handed her the bag. "I didn't do those things to guilt you into staying with your parents."

She pulled out her nesting chart and checked which ones were close to the water. "There are people in this world who are takers. There are those who are traders, and there are those who are givers. You, Liam Morrison, are a giver, not a trader. I will rest at my parents' house for you."

She bit the side of her cheek from the inside and turned to look at him. "I think we should keep this thing about us between us."

"Oh," he said and nodded. "Right."

It was his pout face. The corners of her mouth lifted. "Chloe hasn't even seen me hurt yet, and with the death of Neil Roberts, I think our focus should be there."

Still nodding, he patted her three times on the knee. His physics teacher nerd insecurities would have his mind buzzing. "You did, you know," he mumbled. "Put your hand on my leg in the city hall conference room."

"No one noticed," she said, checking on the chart.

The nod became slower. "And, Raine did catch us, you know, kissing."

This was unethically fun. Running her finger down the nest location column, she added, "Raine is a vault. My mom will know."

"Right." He looked around the sand at their feet. "Harmony has a reputation of figuring this kind of thing out."

"She'll think we are having sex."

TWENTY-FIVE

L iam choked on the air.

It was the first time she remembered laughing since Raine caught them kissing. "She thinks dating means sex."

He rubbed his hands over the top of his head.

She stood and faced him. Using her good hand, she tugged him to stand. "I love learning new sides of you."

He stood tall and gripped her waist.

It woke things inside of her that had been sleeping for a long time. "I'm falling hard."

"Chloe, Seth, and this," he reminded her, brushing his fingertips over the bandage on her forehead. His eyes glossed over, and the whites turned a shade of pink.

He was so good at stuffing, she didn't realize until that moment how much all of this affected him. "Come. Let's get this done and hit up my mom for some raspberry tea."

He tucked the cinch sack back in the bucket and joined her.

The first nest was her section's nineteenth. It was a recent hatch that happened after her accident. "My team has been unbelievable." The hole left from the hatchlings was more of an indentation after Ernest. "They all stayed. Oliver took care of the stats and got them to Raine himself." She took her nesting chart and made the notation that the nest would be due for excavation the following morning.

"The next nest is two blocks south." She didn't mention her plan to check the ones on the way. Locals began emerging. It seemed anything and everything that could happen brought people to the beach. The calming effect was known to reduce stress and aid in sleeping patterns.

Down the beach, she spotted Raine in the Ibis Island Turtle Watch ATV. It looked like she was working on a nest relocation.

"You've been suspiciously quiet," she said as they reached nest number eighteen.

His jaws flexed and released.

The response was disconcerting, and she took his hand.

"Everywhere I look I think I see him," he said as he glanced up and down the beach. "The man in the rain gear. I should have known no one stands in the rain and wind."

"You're not honestly blaming yourself for this."

"Not that. Sort of." His shoulders fell. It wasn't a lot, but she noticed. "Someone out there hurt you. Purposely hurt you."

He stared blankly, then out to the horizon. A few locals with garbage bags walked the beach, picking up trash that the winds blew in. "Was he trying to scare you? Make a point. End you?"

His hand trembled over hers as he said the last few words. Shaking his head, he inhaled deeply and turned to look at her. His eyes were terribly sad.

He added, "I expect that's what you and your family feel in regards to Seth." He looked to one of her eyes, then the other. "Do you? Do you wonder with every person you talk to? Is that him? Is that the person who killed your brother?" His voice got louder and louder. "What about all those people that came to see Seth's poem at Luciana's. How do you do it? How do remain cordial?"

"I think of the person who killed my brother as a weed among the flowers. I choose to water the flowers, not the weed."

"I'm in love with you."

The backs of her eyes instantly burned. It was like she could do anything, solve anything, endure anything with this new pillar of strength that supported her.

"Let me explain this," she said, hoping to provide a distraction. It was her nesting chart. She kept it in a clear plastic cover. "The nests are listed in order of when they were laid. Here's the column with the dates. We had the first one on May 19. The next column is the watch for hatch date column, followed by the actual hatch date. State law requires an excavation and tally three days after the hatch. Here is where we record the number hatched and unhatched, and the final column is the location." She pointed toward the bottom of the page. "These are the ones I'm worried about. Mary Jane already texted me that two of the nest wash-outs were in my section. That's actually pretty good, considering."

The anticipation of her section began to trump all else. She stood and held out the hand on her good arm. "Come. I see Oliver."

His fingers were strong and safe. Yes, everything he said was true. The looking over her shoulder. The analyzing everyone she saw or met.

Close to the water, she spotted a handful of white balls bouncing in the surf. She resisted sprinting to them but picked up her pace and pulled Liam with her.

The stakes were still in the ground but leaning toward the water. The white balls were exactly what she thought. Eggs.

Liam seemed to read her anxiousness as he turned the bucket over, dumping the contents onto the sand. She began gathering eggs. The surf chipped away at the sand around the nest, exposing more and more of the eggs with each wave.

The wet sand was compact and heavy. Some of the eggs popped as she scooped, each time causing a shudder to run through her body.

"Let me," he said and stepped into the water with his back to the waves.

She stood to a hearty head rush but decided to keep that to herself. The tide was rising. He seemed to notice, kneeled in the water, and dug faster. Out came a dead hatchling and one that had only nearly formed. Liam made a gagging sound.

"Are you going to be okay?"

He nodded as the water overtook the rest of the nest.

Clutching his forearm, she said, "Enough. It's over." She forced a smile. "We saved a lot of them. We'll go find a safer place and relocate them."

He grabbed a bigger shell and chucked it down the coastline. There was so much more here than lost turtle eggs.

Liam watched as she slept. He sat next to her on the side of the futon in Henry and Harmony's den. She fell asleep almost as soon as her head hit the pillow. The expression on her face said she was content, but what did he know about when she slept?

How did they get here? She hadn't given him a clear answer about that. Was it a change in heart caused by a near-death experience? No. He shook his head to himself. It didn't feel like that was it.

Her lips parted as she seemed to melt into the pillow. He couldn't begin to wrap his head around how tired she must be from all of this. The room had once been Willow and Zoe's, but that was in another life. Her injured arm rested in the sling and across her chest. The doc said it was a sprain, so no surgery. The bandages on her forehead peeled at the edges. If he craned his head to peer beneath, he could see the stitches. Since it was already a little creepy watching her sleep, he decided not to.

The waiting was hopeless. The wondering helpless.

Taking the light blanket folded at her feet, he shook it out and covered her up to her chin. He rested his lips on the good side of her forehead and kissed her goodbye.

Henry sat in his ancient recliner in the front room reading *Fahrenheit 451*.

"She's sleeping," Liam said to him.

Without taking his eyes from the pages of his book, Henry responded. "Seemed to be doing that standing when she got here."

"Right," Liam said and couldn't decide whether to sit. "I probably should have insisted we come here earlier."

"A lot of good that would have done you," Henry said as he turned a page.

Liam understood that Harmony might know about the two of them but wondered about Henry. He and Willow never came close to one another unless in private, but Liam had definitely been around more. Rode in the ambulance, took her home from the hospital.

"You were quiet at the city hall family meeting," Liam said. Quiet even by Henry standards.

Without lowering the book, Henry turned his eyes to him. They were green like Zoe's. Willow had her mother's eyes. Blue.

"I have my hunches. Waiting on some things."

Liam nodded. "Cryptic."

Returning his eyes to his book, Henry said, "I suppose so, but I don't like to jump to conclusions or assume. Not my style."

Digging his hands in his pockets, Liam rocked on the backs of his heels. For whatever reason, it felt a lot like high school. Standing in the middle of the living room meeting the father on a first date. "What if said jumps or assumptions could lead to facts?"

Henry nodded but didn't look at him. "I'll take that into consideration."

The sound of sea shells crunching under tires told Liam a car turned onto the Clearwater drive. Stepping to the window, he saw it was a police cruiser. "Matt's here. Probably to check out the cornerstones that might be home."

"Already been to Raine's, I hear."

Gathering evidence or checking locales off his list. Doing the things cops do.

He wandered out to watch. Matt's newest hire, Officer Applegate, rode shotgun. Matt got out first.

"Howdy there, Liam."

"Matt," Liam answered and held out a hand. "Officer Applegate."

Matt turned to Applegate. "Get the pictures. I'll be right there."

Noticing Matt waited until the officer was out of earshot, Liam perked his senses.

"I'm the new guy around here."

"Yes," Liam said slowly.

"People don't always take too kindly to a new guy."

Ah. "I can see that happening, especially since your predecessor was a lazy ass. It doesn't help that the island's primary permit holder doesn't too much care for you, either."

Matt rubbed the back of his neck with his hand. "You see, there it is. I need you to explain that to me, since the primary permit holder doesn't too much care for me. I also need to give a visit to the owner of the boat rental place."

"Yo-Yo?"

"That'd be the one."

"You're smart to take a local. The owner is Big Joe. He and Sunset Touring go way back. He sends over his scuba divers and we send him over any personal water craft customers."

"See? I knew I could count on you." He pointed a thumb over his shoulder. "I'm going to go join Applegate. Can we leave in twenty?"

"Twenty minutes?" Liam asked. "From now?" He glanced over to the house. That wasn't exactly in the lesson plan book. "I guess. Why not? Do you mind if I join you in back?"

"Of course. Maybe we can go over why the primary permit holder seems to hold all the weight around here."

"PPH," Liam corrected.

"See?" Matt said as they walked past the giant mermaid. "Helpful already."

TWENTY-SIX

Matt made Applegate ride in the back. Whatever Matt's reason for it, Liam was grateful. He wasn't sure how he would have explained riding in the back of a cruiser to every islander they passed on the way to Yo-Yo.

A full-sized laptop stuck out of the dash, attached to something that looked like a swiveling television stand. Liam thought of it as the mother of all texting and driving but decided against saying so.

"So, PPH?" Matt asked.

"From what I know, every beach or maybe every island has a PPH. This is the person in charge of sea turtle conservation. If the PPH does a good job, the beach or island is awarded grant money and beach nourishment."

"Beach what?"

"Nourishment. Civilization messes with the beaches. Sand is lost. This is why it's illegal now to destroy sea oats. They help reduce erosion."

"I'm not following."

"Beach nourishment is the process of siphoning sand from offshore and dumping it onto eroded beaches. It takes a lot of enormous equipment and the military. The government will only agree to it if the PPH has a handle on the endangered species."

"Military?"

"Yep, and it takes millions," Liam said as they turned into the Yo-Yo parking lot. "That's Big Joe, there. In the hut."

It was a mom-and-pop place. Liam couldn't remember how long Big Joe had owned it. Before Liam's time, for sure. He kept it small, outdated but with reliable equipment.

At the sight of Matt's squad car, he came out from around the counter in the hut.

Big Joe was burly, middle-aged, and with deep brown skin and a thick beard. "He could scare away a prize fighter," Liam explained. "But deep down he's a pretty good guy. Sucker for his grandkids."

The windows were down, and Liam stuck his arm out and waved.

"Excuse me, sir," a young woman in a swim suit cover said as she stepped into Big Joe's path.

Reluctantly, Big Joe turned his attention to his customer as Matt pulled into one of the six Yo-Yo parking spots.

"How about I introduce you?" Liam suggested.

Matt opened his door. "I was hoping you would say that. Applegate, you wait in the car."

Big Joe schmoozed the customer. "The gentleman and his friend are due back any minute, miss," he said as he slipped his thumbs inside the straps of his overalls. "You're the first in line for those personal water crafts, and I will say they are—"

"Two of the best," Liam finished for him. "Big Joe, here, won't steer you wrong." Liam held out a hand and shook with Joe. Regular shake to a thumb grasp to fingertips and snapped apart.

She seemed convinced and stepped away to the single picnic table waiting area.

Big Joe may have participated in the island handshake, but his eyes remained on Matt. "Man, why are you bringing brass in my parking lot?" Big Joe whispered.

"This is the interim Chief of Police," Liam answered. "Chief

Osborne, this is Big Joe. He owns the place. We need to know who took out one of your boats the day before Ernest."

"I don't know the island shake, but it's good to meet you, Joe." Matt held out a hand. Joe eyed him before he held out his hand.

Joe scratched his beard. "I don't remember anyone taking out one of ours that day. You sure?"

He was lying; Liam was sure of it. He didn't know the first thing about confidentiality and hadn't asked if Matt needed a warrant. "Did you hear about Chief Roberts?"

"I don't live in a hole in the ground." Joe crossed his arms over his substantial belly.

"Then, you know the prime suspect in the murder of Seth Clearwater is no longer."

The muscles in Joe's face fell as he connected the dots. "The Clearwaters may be kooky, but they're good people. That stuff doesn't happen on Ibis. Not Seth or Roberts. Let me check my books."

"Thank you kindly," Matt said.

Joe walked back to his hut while Liam and Matt waited. Three sets of couples, all young, waited for Yo-Yo equipment at the picnic table.

"I hope that was okay," Liam said to him. "We didn't really make a plan."

"You did great." Matt nodded. "You're hired."

Liam shook his head. "Ha."

Joe came back sans his records book. "What does this rental have to do with the Clearwaters anyway?"

Matt stepped forward. It was just an inch, but he made his point. "Might be nothing, really. The person or persons who rented your boat last Sunday might have seen something we can use."

They were losing Joe, even Liam could tell. He shook his head and squinted his eyes.

Matt smiled. "I see that the folks of this island take care of their own. It's why I asked Liam to join me when we came out to see you. He and Dane are the ones who recognized your boat out on Sunday."

"I wasn't working that day," Joe said as his eyes zoned in on a spot on the page of his appointment book.

"Right." Liam nodded. "We need to talk to him."

"Them," said Big Joe. "The mayor and Oberweiss."

Two, Liam thought. Not one.

"Why would locals who are avid divers need to rent a boat?"

"I'm sure there's a good explanation, and that the mayor and owner of our fine island museum will be happy to answer some questions."

There went Matt again with his homework. He knew Glen Oberweiss owned and managed the island museum.

Willow sat with her legs crossed on the living room floor next to Zoe, who flipped through the pile of bridal magazines she'd checked out from the library.

Zoe turned her head toward Willow's legs and cringed. "I know that's called the easy pose in yoga, but it doesn't look easy. It looks painful."

Glancing down, Willow shrugged. "It is easy." She straightened her legs. "You see? You crisscross your legs." With her good arm, she hoisted her right calf on top of her left knee. "Then, remaining centered, lift one leg on top of the other. It's okay if your knee pops up. It takes time to train your hips to do this."

"I'll take your word for it," Zoe said and flipped through more pages. "I've been thinking."

"That's always a good thing," Willow said and wrapped a hand around her knee.

"I think I'm giving up on all of this."

"What? Are you sure?"

Zoe shook her head. "I don't mean the ceremony. I mean all of this...stuff. We really aren't inviting very many people."

"That's how it starts," Willow warned.

"No, really. Just family and a few close friends. I'm cutting our wedding budget to two thousand, donating the extra money Mom and Dad gave us to Turtle Watch." Zoe looked at her with big eyes.

"Two thousand." Willow tried to run through the list of things needed for a wedding in her head. How much of it would be missed? "Does this include rings?"

"No. Look." Zoe set the laptop on Willow's crossed legs.

On it was a screenshot of a floor-length skirt covered in tulle and a no-sleeve, lacey, short blouse. It was adorable.

"Seventy-five bucks apiece. I've already got white sandals." She flipped to a new screen. "I really only need bouquets for me, Chloe, and the two of you. Some flowers for the men and Mom and Dad."

She stood, then, and started pacing. "Table decorations are not needed. Tables are not needed. Sit down dinner? Nope. DJ? We can crash Luciana's and use the juke box."

"Whoa. Wow. Hold on, there."

"Why? No! It makes sense." She burned a path in the carpet with her stomping back and forth. "Why would we start out our marriage in debt for a single day of festivities? This is about a commitment. When did our country decide we need weekend bach-elorette parties and party favors and—"

Willow stood, grabbing her with her good arm.

Zoe stopped and turned. "What? Are you okay? What's the matter?"

"I'm so proud." She brushed Zoe's long blonde hair over her shoulder. "Promise me you won't skimp on the pictures."

Zoe nodded, deep in thought. "Yes. Pictures are forever. I've already made my own invitations. I only need to add a date. It'll be fun."

"And, don't get rid of the cake."

"All right, but we don't need a fancy one. Screw the Jones. I don't need to keep up with anyone. And, I'm not waiting. Dane and I have been trying to figure out how fast we can put all of this together. A minimalist wedding with only close family and friends means we could have it next weekend."

"Zoe, slow down. I mean it."

As if she hadn't spoken, Zoe said, "As long as Dane's parents can make it from Alaska on this short of notice. Oh, Willow. I know Mom and Dad set aside money for this, but think of what that money could do for Turtle Watch."

She was literally bouncing. Ignoring Willow, definitely, and bouncing. Or, maybe it was gliding.

Their mother walked in carrying three empty baskets. Willow knew what that meant. Picking herbs, or maybe the last of the tomatoes.

"What money for Turtle Watch?" her mother said as she handed a basket to each of them.

"Hey," Willow said. "I'm injured."

"You're in charge of mint and basil. Use your good arm. The fresh air will help."

Zoe took the expected basket and draped it over her arm. "I've been stressing about this wedding."

"That generally comes with the territory," her mother said. "Just ask Willow."

Flashes went through Willow's mind. Of Jacob and their young wedding. Of Liam. Heat crept up her neck and over her cheeks.

"Are you okay, dear?" Her mother placed a hand on her arm. "You don't need to help us if you're too tired."

"No, no. Liam is helping Paula close Luciana's tonight." After working a scuba dive, she thought and sighed. "No, I can help." She went to run her fingers through her hair, then remembered her stitches and that awful bump. Willow opened the door to a steamy afternoon and inhaled. She wouldn't trade one day or season, hot or no, for anywhere else in the world.

Zoe bounced around them, then stopped and turned. "What am I picking?"

"Hollyhocks and honeysuckle."

"Got you," Zoe said and took the three stairs at once. "I'm capping my wedding at two thousand."

"Oh?" her mother said as a question.

It made Willow smile from ear to ear.

"Ah. And, the rest can go to Turtle Watch." Her mother chose the best lemon balm leaves and placed them in her basket.

TWENTY-SEVEN

It was blistering hot, but Ernest's tail provided a decent enough breeze. Liam was a Floridian. Floridians were pros at blistering hot. The sun, the breeze. The waves, the Sun Trip's newest boat. The water was a sea of emeralds, the white caps like the sun reflecting off the gems. And, to think he'd been internally whining about having to captain the boat for that evening's diving group.

Zoe's constantly buzzing phone was a whole other issue. It went off in the little pink purse thing she carried. Again and again. And, since she was currently diving with a novice group thirty feet under, he might be listening to it a while yet.

Tuesday meant lighter boat traffic. The day after a tropical storm, lighter still. That was something anyway. Working on his best Willow Martinez impersonation, he tried not to dwell on the events of the last few days, including the love of his life sitting alone while she healed. The unsolved murder hanging over said love of his life and now, where the hell was Luciana Bezan's dowry that Seth had found?

Inhaling the Gulf air, he stood tall. A fever of stingrays hunted port side. A small pod of dolphins dove over one another starboard.

Zoe's phone buzzed again. He sighed and gave up and dwelled

on all of it.

Walking around the perimeter of the boat, he checked the lines and instrument readings, checked his watch, then glanced over the boat for any signs of life of the human form. That was when a buzz came from his pocket and not from the little pink purse thing.

There. See? He had friends too. "This is Liam," he said as he answered.

"Liam, it's Raine. Are you with my sister?"

"That all depends on which sister you speak of."

"Gah," she barked. "Zoe."

"I'm friends with Willow too."

"You are not *friends* with Willow," she said.

Why did he always seem to be on the wrong end of the gotcha moments?

"It's important," she added.

"Sorry, then. Yes, I am with Zoe, but she's in the water with a diving group right now. Can I help with anything?"

"Hell." Awkward silence. "We want to have a family meeting without the cop," she said.

"I don't know what to say."

"Just don't tell the cop."

"I'm not a tattle."

More awkward silence. "It's 'I'm not a nark,'" she corrected.

He shrugged. "That, too."

"Have Zoe call me when she's up."

"Of course."

"Thanks. The meeting is at Mom and Dad's tonight. You should come." And she hung up.

He should come? It was a family meeting, and Raine thought he should come.

Movement sounded starboard. "Mother fucker!" a younger male voice yelled from the waves between sounds of spitting water. The new diver. Liam understood his excitement.

"Great job," Zoe's voice said next. "Slow down your breathing some, a little work on the accuracy of your safety stops, and you'll be on your way to certification."

"This rocks, dude."

Liam glanced over the side, ready if the new guy needed help with his gear. Zoe's charge climbed as she gave him room. She popped up, keeping the others in her sight while supervising his handling of the equipment.

So it wouldn't get knocked over, Liam moved the newbie's air tank shoved under the seat and out of the way. "The shark," the novice said. "Did you see it? Dude! It came close enough I could have touched it."

Liam doubted that.

Another splash. It looked as if the entire team was ready to call it a day.

Since the divers would be post-dive thirsty, he took out bottles of water and handed one to each as they settled. One by one, the group shared their tales from below.

He leaned over and nudged Zoe. "I need to tell you something," he said.

She glanced over at him and nodded. "Everyone," she announced. "Remember to turn off your tanks and disconnect your regulators. Line up the tanks by the onboard compressor. I'll come by in five and do a check."

She stepped over to Liam and squinted at him.

Her damned phone buzzed again. She turned toward it, but must have decided he was more important. Zoe turned her cheek away from him but kept her eyes on his. "What is it?"

"Just Raine. You know how she gets. She wants, or maybe everyone wants, to meet without Matt."

She fell back in the closest seat, her arms falling between her legs like wet noodles. Nodding, she looked up at him. "How do you feel about that?"

"I had the same reservation you seem to be having. I don't see anything illegal about a family getting together to discuss an investigation."

She seemed to be looking right through him as she nodded.

He may have taken the way back to Sun Trips a bit too fast, but the speed and the wind made it worth it. As soon as he steered around the bend, Liam spotted her. His heart sped up like he was seventeen again. He craned his head forward as if that might give him a better look.

The noise from the engine, the splash of the wake behind him, the loud bantering from the five students as they talked about the dive. Even the wind he'd just craved. It was all white noise to him by then.

Zoe spoke from the passenger seat. "Is she waiting for you or me?"

He looked over at Zoe as she adjusted the strap on the cowboy hat she used as a visor. He shrugged and got out his phone. No missed messages from her. "I don't know. Do you?"

"I got nothin'," Zoe answered. "I know she puts on a good show, but she hasn't taken any of this well, you know."

Zoe was one to talk, Liam thought, but wouldn't call her out on it.

"We're about to dock," Zoe said to the customers as she turned in her seat. "Gather your gear. You were incredible down there, and see you in a week."

Pulling up next to the pier, Zoe jumped out and grabbed the line. Willow sat with her legs crossed on top of the farthest picnic table under the waiting area shelter. Her back was straight, and the waves of her long blonde hair blew behind her like a goddess.

Zoe cleared her throat.

The boat. Right. He tied the stern to the pier and began straightening equipment, preparing the boat for tomorrow's diving reservation. Zoe headed toward her sister.

I think we should keep this thing about us between us. Willow's words rang in the back of his mind. Sitting back in the driver's seat, he checked the day's student diving logs. Willow slipped down from the table as Zoe approached her. Air levels, depth of the dives, how long they were down there. Zoe turned toward the break room, but Willow didn't follow.

Her expression. He couldn't quite read it, but she wasn't moving from her spot in front of the table. So, he finished as quickly as he could and made his way to her.

"Did you rest?" he asked in lieu of a greeting.

"I did. Very well, thank you." They stood for a long moment. Her smile was slight yet potent. "Did you hear about the secret meeting?"

"It sounds deceptive when you put it that way, but yes."

"I need to make sure my house is secure and picked up before Chloe comes home tomorrow."

"Her room is spotless."

She mouthed the words, 'I love you.'

He should have smiled or returned the gesture. His facial expressions betrayed him as he felt his brows drop low. "Let me get my backpack from the break room." He tried not to be obvious as he rushed to get it.

Zoe came out as he went in. "See you later tonight," she said. "It shouldn't be long."

Long? Clearwater family meetings could last hours.

Liam squished through the soggy grass along the front of Willow's home. He noted some spots in the foundation that needed tuck pointing. It was an older home. So, that made sense.

The landscaping was substantial, mature, and hid most of the cracks and peeling paint. He stopped when he got to the first corner. No hiding a damned thing there.

With his hands dug into his pockets, he stared at it and ground his teeth together. The greenery was trampled, some of the branches of the bushes snapped.

Clamping his eyes shut, he curled his fingers into tight fists. An intruder, likely a killer stood in the spot he was standing. A murderer.

He lowered into a squat to get a better look. Running his fingers over the concrete slabs, he checked for any loose pieces. The siding didn't give. He could fit his fingers underneath it but barely. Using his fingertips as tools, he poked around the dirt to see if anything wasn't right. Anything other than the fact that someone had been trespassing on Willow's property a few yards from her bedroom window.

It felt stupid and was probably useless, but he walked to the other corners. Had Matt done the same? Surely, he'd been back here by now.

Everything was maddening. He found nothing compromised and itched to go check the other Clearwater homes and Seth's apartment on his own.

When he found himself at the front door, he made himself pause. His hand on the front doorknob, he lifted his chin, blew out a breath, and stepped in.

He found her in the middle of the living room, sitting with her legs out unnaturally, doing her yoga thing. Or was that Pilates? Her back was to him, but surely, she heard the opening door. She didn't say anything. With her back straight, she lowered her chest toward the floor, cradling her injured arm like a baby until it brushed the carpet.

It had to be wrong that he thought, other than the sling, it was damned sexy.

Leaning against the doorjamb watching her was probably borderline creepy, but his head was all wrong anyway. The overhang to the Beachfront outdoor patio would be fixed in days, yet Willow would be in pain with a useless arm for who knew how long?

As he watched, he realized her long blonde locks looked darker and flatter than usual. "Why don't you let me wash your hair for you?"

She didn't jump at the suggestion, but her body stilled. Her chest slowly expanded, then contracted as she rose to an upright sitting position. When her eyes turned to meet his, the blue was sultry and inviting and definitely sexy. "You would do that for me?"

He swallowed hard. Of course, he would. "I would."

Pulling her legs in closer, she crisscrossed her ankles, then lifted as she unfolded like an accordion to a standing position. "I set up some stuff in the kitchen. I was going to try and do it one-armed after I got some kinks out."

TWENTY-EIGHT

"You shouldn't have any kinks." The heat of frustration radiated up Liam's back.

Turning the side of her head toward him, she tapped her forehead and said, "I already put the waterproof bandages over my stitches." She stood tall and made circles with her good shoulder. "You have kinks of your own. How is your back?"

He headed toward the kitchen to see about this stuff she had set out. "It's nothing," he said. Or, at least nothing in comparison.

"Lifting a fallen roof with your back isn't nothing."

As he turned, she unzipped her sports jacket. She started to wiggle out of it on her own.

Even though an enormous frog seemed to leap into his throat, he kept his head enough to take a single long stride to her to help. Beneath she wore a blue tank with spaghetti straps. It had the thinnest line of white lace along the top.

She stepped to the sink and craned her head so that her long blonde locks partially covered her face.

He was useless. Frozen, mesmerized, and useless.

"Are you sure about this?" she asked.

Reaching around her, he turned on the water. She smelled like the flowers her mother planted in the planter boxes on her porch. Taking a towel from next to the sink, he folded it in front of her, then laid it over the rim. Gently, he placed his hand on the back of her head and guided her to the ceramic bowl. Using the hand spray, he checked the temperature and moved her hair around to one side.

He cupped his hand along her hairline to keep the water from running over her bandaged stitches. Her eyelids dropped closed, and the sound that came from her throat almost made him drop the sprayer.

Reaching around her head, his body pressed against hers. This was going to be a problem.

He forced himself to think of basic physics symbols. The wavelength system international is meter. Angular Displacement, radian. Mass, kilograms.

"I think it's wet enough," she said.

He meant to say okay, but instead he said, "Temperature, Kelvin." He was reasonably sure he yelled it.

Her shoulders shook. Her laugh was contagious, and he began laughing as well.

Setting down the sprayer, he took the shampoo and poured a teaspoon amount in his hand. Looking at her hair, he turned the bottle over and poured some more.

"Why didn't you ask someone to help you with this? You have two sisters." And you have me. You will always have me. Using his fingertips, he spread the silky bubbles over her scalp. Massaging, cleaning. He could get lost in her crooning.

The muscles in her back relaxed, and she melted beneath his fingers. The basic symbols didn't help, so he rotated the front of him away from her and was thankful for long arms.

Rinse and repeat. Conditioner. He tried to be thorough yet fast, except he'd never done this before. She'd laid out a towel. After he was sure about the rinsing part, he shut off the water and wrapped the towel around her head.

He helped her upright and reached for the other towel, but she used her good hand to grab the back of his neck and pulled him down to her.

This was not the purposeful, careful Willow she had been with him thus far. This was aggressive and needy. She maneuvered around him until it was his back that was against the sink. She pressed against the length of him as their tongues moved and hands explored.

He gave up on hiding what his body felt and pressed back into her.

Her strong arm snaked between them, and her hand fisted the front of his shirt.

His mind, his heart. They would never come back from this.

Breaking their connection, she gasped for air and said, "Say it again."

He pulled his chin back and glared in her eyes.

She bit her bottom lip and said, "Tell me the two things."

He grabbed her face with both hands. "My Willow." He kissed her once. "My life," and kissed her again.

Willow sat in the passenger seat alternating between staring at their joined fingers and at him. Contemplating. Planning. Scheming, even.

She wasn't stupid. Okay, she may have been stupid for much of the past five years, but she'd wised up since her epiphany with her mother in the cemetery. It might be called something more like digging in her claws or hooks or whatever people said these days, but she was over it.

She was alive and felt pretty and wanted, desired even, for the first time in longer than she could remember.

"You're quiet," he said and rubbed his thumb over the back of her hand.

She took a deep breath. "Just thinking." Calculating.

"It's not safe for you and Chloe to be alone."

"Oh?"

"I'm not saying you can't take care of yourself. You have for years. I know this. It's simply that there is room at your folks'—"

"Raine is staying with them. My dad put his foot down."

"I know I'm not your father, but I don't want you staying alone either."

"What are you suggesting?" It was clear what he was suggesting. It was cruel, she knew, but far too much fun to watch him struggle.

"I can sleep on your couch." He held up a hand as if he expected her to argue. "Until we catch whoever was creeping around your home."

"I can stay in Chloe's room with her. You take my bed."

"I know you think—what did you say?"

"I agree with you. I have to think of Chloe. And, the thought of having you at our breakfast table fills my heart. I love you."

He opened his mouth, then shut it again, squeezed her fingers, and turned into the bump at the end of her parents' drive.

He parked his truck next to the low spot in their yard that always flooded, then jogged around to get her door. She stepped out and reached for his hand.

Pulling his away, he said, "Keeping this between us for now, remember?"

The words seemed harsh. Had she been the one to say them a short time before? A fake grin was all she could offer.

There was no smoke coming from the back, so she decided the front door was a smarter choice than the backyard where they generally held their family meetings.

The mint leaves called to her. She plucked a handful for a well-deserved mojito.

He opened the door and held it ajar for her to walk through. "Is that enough for everyone?" he asked.

"Point taken," she said and ducked under his arm to pick more.

She could hear them through the open door. They must be in the dining room nook area, sitting around the table. Taking note that each window and door was closed, she began to understand.

"They think they might have spies." Liam said what she was thinking.

"That's got Dane written all over it."

"He knows what he's talking about," Liam said and held the door open for her.

He always had Dane's back. "Did you save us seats?" She spotted two, even if they weren't together.

He took the farthest one, and she headed to the kitchen. She could hear just fine from there. She would make a half dozen. If that was too many, she'd sacrifice herself on a second. It wasn't like she'd be driving home that night.

She heard Raine's voice first. "We've felt, nudged, and picked at every cornerstone to anything we can think of might have been considered a home to Seth."

"What if we're wrong," Zoe said. "That the pictures were of anything he found."

After taking down six tumblers from her mother's glass front cabinet, Willow washed the mint leaves, then sprinkled about ten in each cup.

"No," Henry interrupted. "There's no other explanation as to why the pictures of the treasure were stored, hidden if you will, in the same place as the photos of his mistress."

She'd taken a gamble some limes would be in the fruit basket and won. There were several. She chose a few that weren't yet yellowing and had the right amount of give to the rind.

"I still can't get over it," Dane said. "Your brother found buried treasure right here around Ibis Island. He's a legend."

A slice in each glass, and the mint and limes were ready for crushing.

"Where did he find it?" Raine said. "What if the cave isn't the wet uncharted? What if the cave is really the under under, and the wet uncharted is still out there?"

Zoe said, "The cave where I found him was uncharted. I'd have never found it if it weren't a calm day when I swam near it."

The group turned silent. The strong smell of minty lime woke her senses. Or, was that limey mint? She smiled at her silent joke and added a few more lime wedges. A lot of ice, some rum, and the rest carbonated water.

She plopped the glasses on a tray, then realized she wouldn't be able to carry it. Frustrating. She carried a single glass to the dining room nook.

"You washed your hair?" Raine asked loudly.

"Liam did it." She set her glass down, then ran her fingers through it to help with the drying in the Florida humidity.

Liam leaned forward at that time. "Since I can't believe Dane hasn't asked this yet, I'll be so bold as to say, where is the treasure now? I don't mean any that is hidden in a cornerstone that is home or an under under. I mean the treasure from the photos." He stood. She thought it was to make a point, but he walked toward the kitchen and added, "Maybe it's still secured in the cave from Seth's pictures. Nothing has been in the news about ancient Cuban dowry items surfacing. No one on the island became suddenly wealthy two years ago."

She sat down as he disappeared.

"Not that we know of," Dane said. "Most treasure hunters do it for the trophy, not for the sale."

Liam entered the area with a tray. "We could smell the mint out here," he said. "Has Matt, er, Chief Osborne been out to investigate around each of your homes?"

A chorus of yeps, uh-huhs, and general nods came from each person around the table.

Raine said, "We need to find out which one on Matt's short list is the biggest suspect."

"Remember he said to also be looking around for other possibilities," Zoe reminded her. "The person responsible for this might not have been in the original diving team the night Seth was killed."

"I think former Chief Roberts is key." All eyes turned to Willow and the mojito now. "He was certain he was getting out of jail soon. When he saw the poem, it was as if he'd seen it before."

Harmony said, "Matt pointed out that it is a copy."

Willow continued, "Yes, and it was when Roberts saw Matt's copy of it when he changed his tune and asked for his lawyer. He turned white as a sheet."

"Then, he shows up dead," Liam said.

Willow sighed. "I don't feel any closer to finding out who's guilty for stealing Luciana Bezan's dowry. Or who killed Seth."

Liam added, "Or cut the beams in the roof to hurt you."

"Oh, but we are," Harmony said. "He is coming out. He had Neil Roberts killed. Tried to hurt our Willow. He knows we will know this and are looking for him."

Henry finished for her the way couples who have been together forever seem to do. "We also know that we have treasure hunters among us."

"Hey!" Dane argued. "I resemble that."

Her father offered a rare grin toward him before he continued. "The person or persons who followed us to what we now call the wet uncharted as well as those looking around the corners of our homes may or may not be connected to Seth's killer, but we are being watched by a murderer for certain and potentially a slew of treasure hunters."

TWENTY-NINE

Liam brought sweats this time. He wasn't sleeping in his jeans again, but even though Willow was in Chloe's room, sleeping in Willow's bed in his boxer briefs seemed…he wasn't entirely sure what, but not right.

Running his toothbrush around his mouth, he realized exhaustion hadn't really hit him until then. Relocating a sea turtle nest, questioning Big Joe at Yo-Yo, driving for the afternoon scuba class, and a Clearwater family meeting. This was supposed to be his summer break. He was going to give Paula a big kiss the next time he saw her for refusing his help with closing Luciana's.

Tutoring was over, and he didn't have to report for the first institute day for a while yet. He would continue to check on Luciana's and work his Sun Trips shifts, yet would still have a significant amount of time to do some calling around about any 18th century Cuban treasure that may have been anonymously donated to any museums within the last two years.

He dried his toothbrush, wiped down the sink, and turned off the light. When he stepped into the bedroom, the bed wasn't empty. He didn't understand.

Stepping forward, he noted her eyes were closed and her mouth open the slightest amount. No way was he sleeping in the shrimp's bed. That was three steps past creepy.

She'd specifically said she and Chloe were taking Chloe's room and that he was to sleep in here. And, that she wasn't going to have sex with him. That was not something a guy forgets. "Women," he mumbled.

Her eyes blinked open. Licking her lips, she whispered, "What about women?"

Had he said that last part out loud? "Nothing." He stood there, thoroughly confused.

"Are you coming to bed?" she grumbled.

"Yeah. Of course." He walked around to the empty side of the bed and sat. Since he had no instinct in this department, he laid on top of the comforter and crossed his fingers on his stomach like he was in a coffin.

"I'm going to drive alone to get Chloe tomorrow."

"I figured," he said.

"I don't want to sound irrational, but I honestly can't bend on this. Wait," she said and lifted to her good elbow. "What did you say, and why are you sleeping on top of my comforter?"

"I said I figured you would want to get her on your own." It was just like her. As far as the sleeping arrangements, he didn't know what to say. So, he stood and pulled the comforter back, sheets and all.

He tried to crawl in like it was expected. "You haven't taken pain meds since morning. You've done Pilates."

"Yoga," she said and lay back on her side.

Although he understood the need for sleeping together with no sex, he wasn't experienced in this area. So, he repeated his casket position. "How is there possibly a difference?"

She didn't answer but laughed harder than he'd heard in days, so that was something. She kept it up, sort of like an adolescent with drowsy laughter. It lasted so long, he rolled on his side to watch her. "The tape came off," he said, pointing to her forehead.

"It was loose," she said and sighed. "I pulled it the rest of the way. I think the air will be good for it anyway."

"It looks good," he said and circled the area with his thumb. "Very little pink around the edges."

She nodded and looked him in the eye. "Tell me about your first."

"Excuse me?"

"Oh. I guess I assumed, but maybe you've never, I'm sorry. Now, I don't know what to say."

"She had purple hair. She tricked me."

"Tricked you?"

"It's true. Mostly. I didn't know what was happening. Well, until I did."

The silence that followed wasn't even unsettling. "I, of course, fell hard after that fifteen minutes. Saw her the next day. She kissed me like a cousin and said she would call me."

"Ouch."

"Yeah," he said, then confessed, "I haven't been with anyone in a long time either."

"Oh. I heard that's not healthy."

"Just because I haven't been with anyone doesn't mean I'm not...healthy."

Her laugh was like a favorite song.

The drowsy laughter was slow to cease, but finally it did. "You know, I think we've been a couple for a while now," she said. "I'm sorry it took me so long to realize it. I wasn't ready."

"You've suffered a great loss." He traveled his hand over her cheek. "Five years doesn't seem like a long time to come out of something like that." Was that right? "Not that a person ever comes out of something like—"

"Liam."

"Yes?"

"This feels like forever."

"Oh." Oh! "Do you mean?"

"I do, I mean I want that, a lot, but—"

Everything raced south and his IQ dropped a few dozen points. It was like a fight between gravity and magnetism.

"I think I'm going to ask around at Show Me's tomorrow to see if I can get anyone to tell me if Blake Eaton suddenly bought a second home in the mountains around two years ago."

She smiled and rested the side of her head on his shoulder. "You're changing the subject."

"Of course, I am. You haven't even had your follow-up appointment yet. You are in more pain than you let anyone know." Lifting his arm, he was careful not to break her and wrapped it around her good shoulder.

She snuggled into him. It was a good thing he didn't have to lean over her to wash her hair or anything. The sweatpants did little to hide the gravity versus magnetism fight.

"I might do the same at Richard Beckett's office," he said, using his checklist of things to do much like the way he did the basic physics symbols. "And, I thought about checking around the net for museums with recent additions of anonymously donated Cuban treasure."

"I am completely—" She kissed his shoulder. "Hopelessly." She kissed it one more time. "In love with you." Then, she laid her head down and fell instantly asleep.

Liam couldn't quite put a finger on why he chose not to tell Matt what he was doing. Was it because he wanted Matt to spend every moment he could on his own leads? Because Liam was unsure of this direction he decided to take? Or, was it simply because Matt had been sort of an elusive jerk and wasn't sharing all he knew either?

Great, Liam thought as he pulled onto the pristine asphalt parking lot of Show Me's. Now, he'd resorted to passive aggressive behavior.

She'd left him sitting at the breakfast table. Willow made the best one-armed toasted English muffins and coffee he'd ever had. He might very well have been as excited to see Chloe as she was. But, that was later, and since he had the day off, the morning was meant for investigation.

He chose Blake Eaton first because Blake was a party boy. He and his big-haired trophy wife wouldn't be out of bed for hours yet. It gave Liam loads of time to browse around the place.

The only other three cars in the parking lot were lined up next to each other at the far end of the yellow-line asphalt. Liam recognized the dilapidated SUV that belonged to the live-with-mom-in-your-thirties, Wendell Hopp, as well as the Volkswagen bug that belonged to the gal who worked part time at the local florist shop. It was complete with flower and peace sign bumper stickers. Her name escaped Liam at that moment, but it would come to him.

The last vehicle was a sedan. Newer. He had no idea about that one. Pulling into the closet spot to the back door, he left the keys in the ignition and headed in.

Reggae played from a large silver boom box that perched high on top of a matching silver cabinet. Wendell and the girl wore white and worked furiously, heads down, chopping things of the green variety.

"Hello?" Liam called. "Howdy?" he said louder.

Wendell jumped. The girl simply craned her head and eyed him. Lisa Sampson. He wanted to fist pump the air for remembering but was there for more pertinent reasons. He pointed to the boom box with one hand and questioned a thumbs-up with the other.

Nodding, Wendell wiped his hands on the white apron that blended in with his white everything else and said, "Liam Morrison," when the music was lowered. "What brings you here at this ugly time of morning?"

It was 9 a.m. "Wendell Hopp." Liam held out his hand and smiled. "How are you doing these days?"

Wendell stuck out his chin and nodded several times. "Good, good. You?" Taking Liam's hand, he shook and shrugged at the same time.

Lisa had enough sense to still be staring at Liam like he had three eyes.

Liam scratched the side of his cheek. "Zoe Clearwater's getting married soon," he said and looked around. Everything was stainless steel, he noticed. Fridge, sinks, cabinets, counters. Everything except the concrete floor. "I'm a close friend of the family, you know. It's a small event, a few dozen people. Who's been here the longest and can give me some advice on if they wanted to kick up their heels a bit afterward?"

"Zoe's sister owns Luciana's," Lisa said.

Smart girl.

"Oh, I'm sure they'll end up there, but Show Me's is on the beach. It's a beach wedding and all. Do you know who's worked here the longest?"

She started to answer, but luckily, Wendell interrupted her. "That'd be Eli, but Corine, in the front there, does catering and event planning."

Eli Murphy. Of course. Bouncer and part-time Clearwater goat shelter builder. Worked nights. "Good to know. They aren't doing any catering, other than the cake, and I think I heard the words mints and nuts, but since it's not really an event type of thing, I might just ask Eli. He could tell me how busy early Friday evenings have been."

He waved and turned up the boom box on his way out. The looks on their faces were justified, but Liam was new at this and thought it wasn't too bad for his first time.

Eli could be mistaken for a brick wall. If Liam might have forgotten this, running right into him as he exited the building helped him remember.

"Liam Morrison?" Eli said as if he had been nearly plowed over. "What are you doing here?"

"So sorry, Eli. Wendell and Lisa said you wouldn't be in for a while yet."

There weren't many people on the island who Liam had to look up to. Eli was dark and thick and plenty tall.

He tilted his head. "You were talking to Wendell and Lisa?"

"Yes, right. I was wondering what Friday nights have been like around here." Liam reached under his chin and scratched his cheek. "Dane and Zoe are getting married, you know."

Eli waited for a long time before he answered. "You helping out Dane and Zoe with wedding plans?"

He was about to concede to his ignorance in this area, when a thought came to him. "Truth is, I'm thinking of asking Willow to marry me."

His face lit up enough to make Liam feel like a real ass. "That's great news, man. I always wondered."

"Keep that between you and me?"

"Yeah, yeah. Of course." Eli grabbed his hand and shook as he patted him on the shoulder hard enough to nearly knock him over.

"I'm thinking that either house we end up in, you know, if she says yes and all, will need some work. We all know you can make a killer goat habitat, but have you helped with any of Blake Eaton's renovations of his island or any of his vacation homes?"

Eli shook his head. "I don't know of any vacation homes. Regardless, I'm just the bouncer." He smacked Liam on the shoulder again. "You and Willow. Man, that's good news."

Liam considered bamboo shoots in his fingernails. Maybe going home and sticking his hand in nitro.

As Willow bumped over the end of the drive to her parents' home, she glanced in the child mirror that pointed to her little girl. Chloe's fingertips had been on the latch to her seat belt for the last two blocks.

How could one little girl cause Willow's heart so much warmth? "Look," Willow said. "Grandpa and Grandma are on the front porch." The color from the herbs and wildflowers surrounded them like a perfect day. Willow rolled down the window and waved.

Before she'd hardly had the chance to shift her smart car into park, Chloe released the belt and crawled out of her booster. She pulled the lock and tumbled out, then bolted to the front door.

"Grandma! Grandpa!" She ran and grabbed one in each little arm. Willow clasped the steering wheel, then leaned her chin on her hand and watched and listened.

"I missed you," Chloe squealed. "We had soooo much fun. Grandma and Grandpa...my other grandma and grandpa," she edited, "fed me waffles and chocolate milk. Look." She stepped back and cupped her stomach.

Willow's mother dropped to one knee. "Oh my goodness. That is a full tummy!"

Chloe wrapped her arms around her grandmother's neck and squeezed, the sight of it making everything right with the world.

She got out of the car in time to hear Chloe mention the constant topic of conversation on the hour ride back from the meeting place with the Martinez's.

"How's the egg? Liam said it hasn't hatched yet. Did you turn it? Mommy probably couldn't do it, because she has a hurt arm."

"But Mommy can drive," Willow said as she approached the reunion.

Ignoring her, Chloe continued with her inventory. "Is the light still on? Are the rags still cozy? Can we go see?"

"Come, child," her father said and took Chloe's hand.

"How did she take the sight of you?" her mother asked Willow as they followed them in.

THIRTY

"I'll try not to let that question break my confidence." Willow laughed. "And, I already told her about the accident the other day over the phone." She wrapped her arm around her mother's waist, resting the side of her head on her shoulder as they walked to the room with Seth's dresser and the egg. "A wise woman told me I needed to be transparent."

"Shrimp!" Raine came from the bathroom with a towel wrapped around her head. "How was the visit?"

Without letting go of Grandpa's hand, she grabbed Raine's with her other. "We had bubblegum ice cream. It didn't just taste like bubblegum, it had bubblegum in it! And, we went swimming." Chloe looked up to her and opened her eyes wide. "In a swimming pool!"

"That's some good news, little one." Raine followed their father and Chloe into the den. Willow and her mother caught up.

"Hello, little egg. Your mommy is home. Did Liam and Grandpa take good care of you?" She turned and her expression became deadly serious. "Is it time to turn her?"

Her father pretended to check his watch. "Right about now, yes."

As Chloe turned the egg, Raine whispered in Willow's ear, "You tell her about you and Liam?"

"No," Willow snapped back. "You're the only one who knows."

Raine crossed her arms. "Really," she said as a statement. "That could come in handy."

"Liam is looking into if any of the divers came into money about two years ago," Willow said.

"Which divers?" Raine asked.

Willow nodded. "Richard Beckett and Blake Eaton for now."

"Aunt Raine," Chloe asked as she tucked the rags around it. "When will we know if it's vibble?"

"I guess we could candle the thing," Raine said. "I mean, the egg."

Chloe's eyes grew into saucers, and she covered her mouth with her hand.

"No. Jeez." Raine stuck her hands out like she might need to break a fall. "It's only a term. You go in a dark place and shine a bright flashlight on it. You can see what's inside." She looked to the ceiling. "When did you find it?"

"Sixteen days ago," Willow said.

"Oh yeah. If it's vibble," Raine said and winked at Willow. "You'll be able to see the chick by now."

Chloe took a slow, deep breath, then nodded. "Let's call Liam. He should be here for this."

When Willow arrived back at her parents' home, Liam's Ranger was already parked next to Zoe's Jeep. She'd seen Liam's truck parked there dozens of times over the years. It made her heart flutter regardless.

The trip to Luciana's had proven both helpful and stressful. Paula was amazing. She'd done an incredible job with the books, and none of the newbies had quit, so there was that.

Willow had inventory and payroll and loads to rush order before Saturday, and if she was honest, her head and shoulder hurt more than any meditation was going to fix. Since no one would be waiting for her on the front patio in the midst of greens and vibrant color, she took the moment just to be.

Closing her eyes, she pulled her shoulders back and inhaled through her nose. Inventory, payroll, rush orders, grand opening.

Then, she exhaled slowly and completely through her mouth. Her baby sister's wedding, Chloe, she was alive, Liam. Her eyes flew open. Liam. It had always been him. His solid, unmoving security and consistency were sexy and thrilling, and he was hers.

Glancing around the yard she grew up in, flashes of memories sped through her mind. Thoughts of Seth and Jacob, the building of the goat shelter and Chloe as a toddler. And, Liam. He and Chloe were her future. She would see to it.

The front door opened. Chloe came running out to the edge of the top patio step, then lifted her foot and stomped it down. "Mom!"

Willow opened her car door and placed her foot on the crushed sea shell drive. Grandparents were wonderful and important, and they also spoiled little girls.

"Would you like to rephrase that?" Willow asked as she approached her. "Or sit in a time out?"

Chloe crossed her arms and dipped her chin.

"Don't you cross your arms at me, young lady."

"Mom, could you please hurry up? This is a matter of life and death," Chloe said as she straightened her arms and fisted her hands.

"Yes. The egg." Willow guided her through the front door. "How is it? I mean, how is she?"

"Liam is here. We are going to flashlight her."

Stepping through the front door, Willow laughed. "It's still called candling, even if you use a flashlight."

"Liam!" Chloe yelled at the top of her lungs. "Mommy finally got out of that pretend car she likes to drive."

Liam jutted his head out from the kitchen with eyes as big as saucers. "I don't know where she got that from."

Shaking her head, she followed them into the kitchen. In the middle of the tiny kitchen table was a pile of rags. On the rags was a single, white egg.

"Where is the light?" Zoe's voice called from the den.

"Under the drawer with the pile of rags," Willow said.

"Hello, Willow," Zoe yelled back.

Willow lifted her gaze to him. He'd been watching her over Chloe's head. He winked, and she dipped her head as the heat from her neck threatened to cover her cheeks.

"I'm looking under the rags," Zoe yelled from the other room. "There's nothing here but more rags."

"Not that drawer," Chloe yelled like Willow had. "It's in the under, under drawer."

The sound of running feet came from the den. Zoe halted to a stop in the threshold to the kitchen. Covering her mouth, she spoke through her hands. "I know," she said with her eyes watering. "I know where it is."

The muscles in Willow must have fallen, because Liam looked like he was bracing himself to catch her.

"How come you didn't get it, then?" Chloe asked.

Zoe said like a zombie, "Not the light, honey."

"Can I get it, then, Mommy?"

"I'll go with her," Liam offered and followed the short running legs to the den.

"Willow." Zoe grabbed her good arm. "We have to get to your boat." She craned her head toward the kitchen door Chloe and Liam had left through.

"What are you talking about, Zoe?" Willow squirmed away from Zoe's grip.

"I know where the under under is."

"What? Are you sure?"

"I am 110 percent sure," Zoe said. "Or, at least 90 percent."

Willow shook her head. "This is serious. Oh my gosh, Zoe." Willow's voice squeaked then. "Where?"

Liam came back with her father's shop light in one hand and a six-year-old wrapped around his thigh on the other side.

Her mother went back to drying dishes from the sink. "Sometimes what you're missing is right under your nose," she said as she set a plate on the rack next to the sink.

"Mommy?" Chloe stood, staring. "Are you okay?"

Zoe nodded to Willow as she pulled her cell from her back pocket and stepped out of the room.

Looking around, she noticed how everyone stared at her. Her father, mother, Liam. Nodding, she said, "Let's candle an egg."

"It's daylight," Henry said to Chloe as his gaze moved between Zoe and Willow. "I think we're going to need to do this in a closet."

Four adults and one child crammed into the pantry. Harmony plugged the shop light into the only outlet that was almost hidden under the shelf of green beans and above the one of canned peaches.

"Chloe has the egg," Willow said and hoped she didn't drop it. "Liam has the light. Mom, lights off."

Chloe's lip quivered in the eerie beam of light. Liam moved the light closer and all around, but there was nothing in there.

"I'm so sorry, honey," Willow said.

Her mother flipped the lights back on as her father grabbed the egg and Chloe began to sob. Willow stepped to Chloe, but her little girl turned to Liam and held her hands out wide. He lifted her as she wrapped her arms and legs around him like a vice. "I'm so sorry, Liam," Chloe bawled. "We worked so hard," she said like an adult.

"There, there," he said and rocked her back and forth. He glanced over to Willow and winked. That was it. The moment. It was as if her heart fell out of her chest and landed on the floor at his feet.

Driving to town, Liam had to admit leaving without finding out where Zoe thought this under under was located was harder than waiting to open gifts on Christmas morning. Dane was out on an eco tour. Liam was sure Zoe had known that, but neither of them had been apparently willing to break it to Willow. Wherever Zoe thought the under under was, she wasn't going to say it in front of

Chloe, and Chloe was in no condition to go off on her own while the grown-ups had a private conversation. It seemed as if he would have to wait for Dane as much as everyone else.

Liam decided to stop by one of Richard Beckett's offices. It so happened that the one he chose was next door to the bank branch that held Liam's safety deposit box.

His steering wheel almost turned itself.

What if he'd read what they had between them wrong? What if he was a high school teacher, and she was accustomed to a war hero? What if she wasn't ready? Didn't want Chloe to—

Without finishing the thought, he pulled into the parking spot six spots down from the front door and set his forehead on the steering wheel.

She'd said they were meant to be, even used the word forever.

She hadn't been under the influence, just said it. Twice.

Shifting into park, he got out and locked the door this time. His legs were like frigging molasses, and it made him want to kick himself.

One foot, then the other, he walked through the front door and up to reception. "Safety deposit box, please, Mary Ann."

Mary Ann was a pretty, middle-aged brunette with an overtly friendly demeanor. He was sure it was why she sat at reception for a living. "Opening or visiting?"

"Hmm?" he asked. Then, said, "Oh, right. Visiting." He rocked on the balls of his feet. "I have my key right here."

She marched around her desk like a pro in impossible heels. "Right this way, Liam."

His hands shook as he pulled out his driver's license.

"I'll need your— Oh, you're so good." She checked it and filled out a chart, then pushed it toward him.

He signed and followed her through the beeps and whistles into the safety deposit box room.

She tapped her chin as she searched through the numbers.

"Top, left," he said.

"Oh, yes. I see it." Scooting the stepping stool in front of the rows of metal boxes, she took his key and hers and opened the box.

"I won't need a room, Mary Ann." He knew right what he was getting.

"Yes, sir." She held the long box out with the opening toward him, then turned her head.

He lifted the lid and saw it right away. It rested on top of the title to his truck, his certified birth certificate, and the copy of his Will. The fuzz on the box had faded with time. It had belonged to his mother.

THIRTY-ONE

He reached in and picked it up. It only weighed ounces but felt like more. Stuffing his insecurities, he clasped his fingers around it and thanked Mary Ann.

"That's all I need," he said. "Thank you for your help."

"Anytime, now," she said.

Mary Ann would know what he took and why he would have taken it, but she was as professional as she was pleasant. Another reason he assumed she had that job.

At the other end of the strip mall, Beckett Realty was too close to warrant driving. So, he walked.

Since Beckett was gay, he'd been scratched from the suspect list when the suspect was thought to be Seth's mistress's husband. Now that Neil Roberts wasn't the killer, Beckett was fair game again.

Liam was covered in a layer of sweat by the time he reached the office, the midday sun beating down and drying up all of Ernest's puddles. The cool blast of air conditioning from the opening door was met with appreciation.

"Lou," he said to Beckett's oldest daughter. "How did I get so lucky?"

"Hey, Liam. I was just talking about you."

Lou had been a brunette the last time he saw her. That day, she had long dark hair and a dark tan. "I knew my ears were ringing from something," he said and helped himself to the guest chair in front of her desk.

"Simon Johnston was raving about all you did for his boy this summer."

Lifting his chin, he said, "Ah, Aiden. Yes. He was a prodigy for sure."

"What brings you by?"

"I'm thinking about buying a vacation home."

"On the island? Are you going to add landlord to your list of jobs?"

"No, actually one for me to actually vacation at. Not on the island, but maybe…I don't know. Didn't I remember that your dad had a vacation home somewhere? Where was that again?"

"Nope. Dad is obsessed with spending every penny he can on island property." She rolled her eyes, making her look younger than she was. "That, nice cars, clothes, and sunglasses, right?"

Liam laughed and hoped it sounded authentic. And, since that was the only line he had to find out if Beckett had come into obscene amounts of money two years prior, he said, "Do you have a business card? I'm going to do some searching and I want to have your recommendation if I find something."

She gave him that look as if he had three eyes in the middle of his head. He was getting used to it.

Liam leaned against the hallway wall with one ankle crossed over the other. Raine and Zoe sat on the couch and Henry on his recliner. Willow had refused a chair and sat on the floor with her legs crossed in something that reminded him of a pretzel. Harmony took Chloe on what she called a nature walk, which, in translation, was a way to get young ears away from their meeting.

Dane paced as if this were the most important hunt of his life.

That said a lot for someone who donated millions worth of treasure he'd discovered to the Smithsonian.

"This is delicate," Dane said as he wore a path in the carpet. "We're all being watched. I can't emphasize this enough."

It was like a tennis match. Five sets of eyes followed Dane as he walked and talked. Six, if Liam included himself.

"We can't all just get in a boat and go. They have people waiting for us to do that."

Zoe interrupted him. "You're scaring my family, Dane."

"Good." Dane stopped in his tracks.

In the eyes of most of the people in the room, Liam was still merely a close family friend. He folded his arms across his chest as Dane turned his back on him and faced the family, soon-to-be Dane's family.

Liam was going to fix that. He knew this wasn't nearly the time for it, but he was going to sink or swim, be part of the family or...or what? Walk away?

Shaking his head, he stuffed the thought and listened.

"I know these people. Treasure hunters. They may not look like Lucky by day, but in here—" Dane smacked his chest. "In here, they will be drunk with desire. It's not the money, although that can be a big part of it. It's the find, the win."

Liam doubted if Dane spoke of only the other hunters at this point.

"Okay, we get it," Raine said. "What do you suggest we do? They could be out there right now, loading up their boats with Seth's booty, as you put it."

"Luciana's," Willow corrected. "This belongs to Luciana. Seth would have wanted it that way."

"Whatever," Raine barked. "I don't want it to get into the hands of some self-seeking asshole treasure hunter—"

"Hey," Dane said.

"Sorry, man," Raine amended. "You know I don't mean you."

"Mostly."

"Or worse," Raine added. "In the hands of Seth's murderer."

Dane nodded and continued his pacing. "Yes. Yes, Raine is right. We're going out today, but we're going to be smart."

Like she was in school, Willow raised a hand for a turn to talk. "Maybe we should call Matt."

"No," so many said at the same time, Liam wasn't sure who all answered.

"He will take over," Henry said. "He'd have to. Send his own men down there. It would disrespect all that Seth wanted, all that he stood for."

"Is that what we need?" Willow added. "Credit for this?"

"Yes." Liam was pretty sure each of them answered that time.

"Okay. Agreed," Dane said. "We do this just us. Then, when we know what we know, we call Matt. Now, you—" He pointed to Zoe. "And." Dane turned in a circle. "What are you doing back there?" he said to Liam.

Liam shrugged and pushed away from the wall. "Simply taking it all in. What can I do?"

"You and Zoe are Sun Trips Touring employees. It will look natural for us to go out together," Dane said. "We have a scuba class going out at 5 o'clock."

"You're planning to search for Seth's treasure with a touring group?" Henry asked.

"They're our cover. They won't know," Dane reassured him. "We'll need someone in the boat, of course." He turned and faced Willow, then cocked his head. "If you and Liam would quit acting like you're not a couple, you could join us under the cover of a giddy couple who can't get enough of each other."

Liam stepped forward, set his open palm on Dane's chest, and pushed. "Where do you get off—" he said as Dane stumbled backward.

"You are proving my point," Dane barked. He righted himself and stuck out his chest.

Liam knew he should be scared, but fear escaped him.

A soft hand wrapped around his forearm.

"Liam."

He looked down. Willow was on one knee next to him. No. She

was not. His eyes grew as big as saucers, he couldn't stop them. He searched the room as if the answer of what he should do right then might be in the air.

"He's right," she whispered. "I love you. I want to be yours forever. You and me."

To add to the mess, the front door opened. Chloe barged in. She looked around the room at the people she loved and, even at six years old, knew enough from the expressions of her loved ones to be still and be quiet.

Harmony stepped around her.

"Will you marry me?" Willow said from the frigging floor next to him. This was not in his lesson plan.

Digging in his pocket, he pulled out the tiny ring that used to be his mother's. Taking the hand from his forearm, he guided her to a standing position and kneeled in front of her.

The first tear dripped over her lid as he put the ring to her third finger.

"I accept your proposal with a counter proposal." The mess was gone. The other people in the room invisible. "Be mine forever. Let's be a family. You and me and the most amazing little girl who ever walked the planet."

Together, they turned their heads to her.

Chloe's naturally brown cheeks each filled with a circle of red. Elbows locked, she lifted both her hands straight in the air, threw her head back, and yelled, "Yes!" With both feet, she hopped and stomped around the living room chanting, "Yes! Yes! Yes!" before she ended between him and Willow, giving them each a tight squeeze. She held on tighter and tighter, until she let go, then moved to hugging each of the other people in the room.

Liam slid the ring over her finger and lifted to his feet to stand with her. Her tears fell freely now. He took her face in his hands, swiped away the drops with his thumbs, and set his lips on hers. This moment belonged to them, and the world around them blurred.

Using a single arm for everything became tiresome. Standing alone behind the bar at Luciana's, Willow tried rolling her shoulder. The pain was instant but not nearly as intense. She used the rag in her left hand to wipe down the beer pulls.

The petite ring on her third finger caught the lights. White gold with a circular solitaire diamond centered between smaller ones cascading around her finger. How long had he carried it in his pocket?

She didn't remember ever seeing it on Liam's mother and wished she had that memory to keep with her. Liam Morrison. A smile warmed her face and caught her attention in the mirrors behind the bar.

The old school bell that hung over the front door rang. Expecting Paula, she continued wiping down the bar back and offered a greeting. "Good morning, Paula. I didn't expect you for another hour."

"I'm not nearly that short," Liam's voice said. "And I don't have—"

"Careful." Willow smiled as she made her way around the bar to greet him.

He laid his lips on hers and smiled through them. "I haven't seen you in two hours." Pulling back, he said, "Let me look at you." Lifting her left hand, he looked at his mother's ring. Her ring.

Kissing it once, he said, "Raine and your father have decided to serve as a diversion."

She pulled her head back and looked up to him. "A what?"

"A diversion," he said and took her hand. Pulling her around to behind the bar, he picked up her discarded rag and ran it under some water. "If you ask me, they can't stand the thought of staying at home while we're out diving for treasure."

She stood in front of the cash register and programmed it to print sales summaries from her missing days.

"Paula's done a great job keeping things going around here," he said as he rang out the rag. "Your father, too."

"Yes," she agreed as the report came out as a long receipt. "And, you. I am going to give Paula a raise after all of this. She deserves it."

"I've been thinking of Chloe," he said.

Forgetting the reports, she turned and lowered her brows at him.

"I support whatever you decide," he said as he picked up bottles and wiped beneath them. "But, I don't know that Chloe—"

He didn't finish his sentence, and that wasn't like him.

"Her name," he added.

What about Chloe? Oh. She was sure he wasn't referring to Chloe's first name. Willow had considered this as well. Should Willow take Liam's name? Was he wanting to adopt her?

THIRTY-TWO

Setting down the rag, he turned to face her. He stood tall and took a deep breath. "I don't think you should take my name."

She pulled her chin back. "I didn't see that one coming."

He reached her in two long strides. "It's not that I don't want you to. It's just that. Well, for now anyway."

"I've never heard you stutter so much," she said. "Or, ever."

"If you take my name—" He took both her hands and carefully held them in down by her sling. "—Chloe will be the only Martinez on Ibis Island. That doesn't seem right, but it also doesn't seem right to erase the name of her father. She already has no memory of him."

The backs of her eyes burned with emotion. He was doing that to her a lot lately. "Liam Morrison and Willow Martinez?"

His lungs expanded and released. He nodded once.

"People might talk," she said.

"Who cares if they do?"

Gripping his fingers, she pulled his arm around her and lifted to kiss him long and hard. She wasn't even sure if that was what she wanted, but for now, she was going to revel in the moment that she would spend the rest of her life with this man.

The bell rang again. Paula. She didn't know about their engagement or that they were even a couple. Pulling away, Willow straightened her apron, waiting for the chiding that would surely come from her but never did.

The earring on his one side dangled to his shoulder, and a row of leather bands lined his wrist and forearm. Lucky Nemo. He lifted a thigh to sit on the next to last stool.

She turned to face him as Liam snaked an arm around her and gripped her waist.

Liam spoke loudly. "We're not open."

Lucky paused his leg, but only for a moment, then sat. He lifted his arm and checked his wrist. There was no watch on his wrist. "I saw the back open and—" The walking cartoon character looked over his shoulder at the door before it opened.

Dane walked in out of breath. He must have been following Lucky.

"Lucky was just leaving," Liam said.

"I am?"

Willow didn't like the feel of this and texted Matt.

trouble at the lucianas. can you come

"What do you want, Lucky?" Dane stepped to him.

Liam let go of her and walked around the bar. His long legs had him standing on the other side of Lucky in seconds.

Lucky barely turned his chin toward him, then Dane. "A drink, son. I came for a drink."

"You came for that." Dane pointed to Seth's poem over the bar. "Let's get it out on the table, old friend." He said the last two words through his teeth. "I spotted him outside of the house this morning," Dane said to Liam and Willow.

Had he seen the proposal? No, the blinds were closed. She lifted to her feet. Chloe and her mother had been on a walk.

"You've been hanging around town for long enough. You got no job, and I'm not going on any hunts with you. Luciana Bezan's dowry is a myth. You wanna think otherwise, that's your business, but I find you around my family again—"

The bell. Matt walked in not at all out of breath.

"You call the cops on me, old friend?" Lucky asked.

Dane held up his hands.

Matt said, "Morning, Willow, boys. How's the grand opening plans?"

All three of them looked to her. "Oh. Good. Well. Good."

He walked with his hand resting on his holstered gun. "Been busy while you were out. Might wanna order a few extra kegs. I expect it's gonna be a big day." He stood behind the stool next to Lucky's.

Matt swung a leg around and sat as Lucky stood.

"Don't let me run you off—" Matt held out his hand.

"Lucky. Lucky Nemo. I was just leaving."

"Chief of Police Matt Osborne," he said, introducing himself. "Thank you for visiting Ibis Island." Smooth, Willow thought. One part greeting, one part order to leave.

"See you Saturday," Lucky said. Such a jab to Dane.

As soon as Lucky left, Matt asked, "Something you boys need to tell me about?"

Willow liked playing the giddy couple who couldn't get enough of each other, and the way PDA seemed to make Liam squirm. The ring on her finger made it all incredibly natural. There were six diving students on the boat, each of them tourists. It was painful to stay out of the water, but Zoe was the one who knew where the under under was—maybe—and Liam and Dane needed to be men and watch out for her.

And, there was the small issue of her shoulder. She sighed and settled for snuggling closer to Liam.

Dane whispered near her, "Don't forget the code if something happens up here."

"One long, two shorts. I've got it. I've got it."

Dane spoke up to the group. "Wait your turn for the ladder. Three minutes minimum. Enjoy the water, the wildlife and I recommend the crystal springs caverns. Now get off my boat!"

He directed each diver, one at a time, with his and her turn. When the last one was fully under water, he said, "Act casual. Don't rush." He pulled up his skins like a fireman in a drill.

"I texted Raine," she announced. "They're on their way south. Going out three miles from the abandoned piers. The ones the pelicans like so much."

"Good. That's good. Now, listen, Willow," Dane said. "I have these scooters."

Zoe stood. "We're using scooters?"

"These look ancient," Liam said. "They're huge. I'm not using this."

"No," Dane said and rolled his eyes. "Look." Tipping the blue one on its side on the boat floor, he flipped it open with a latch at the bottom. It was empty.

Liam lifted the red one and shook it twice. "Are they both like that?"

"Yep," Dane said. "They've come in handy more than once." He turned to Zoe. "In case you're right."

"Heh, heh. No pressure," she mumbled. "I'm hoping a good friend of mine with yellow eyes will show us Seth's under under. You must not be too confident. There are only two fake tanks."

"I tossed the first one over with the anchor. I'll get it when I jump."

"Stealthy," Willow said.

"Keep these low and out of sight," Dane said. "If Lucky is watching, he'll know what these are."

"Do you have a secret side door to the boat too?" Zoe asked. "Because, Willow has to get them in the water."

"Toss the first one with the hang bar, and the last with—"

"The poly line," Willow finished. "I can do that. This is fun."

"No," Liam said. "It's dangerous. We have to be smart."

"This is for Seth," Zoe said. "Do you think you fooled Matt? That feels so wrong."

"Yes," Willow said. "To both. He thinks we're still looking around under the water...something he's never done. And, this is wrong. He deserves to be included."

"His hands would be tied," Dane said. "He would have to trump us. No way."

Zoe nodded. "It's time," she said. "Now, get off my boat."

Dane kissed her long and hard. "Liam, you, me. In that order. Cheat on the spacing time."

Sitting on the side of the boat next to Willow, Liam set his lips on hers. He ran his hand down her side. Either the boat rocked and slid his thumb over the side of her breast, or he did it on purpose. Regardless, it sent waves of emotion and anticipation through her. Then, he tipped sideways and fell into the water.

"Wish me luck, big sister," Zoe said and walked off the swim step.

"It's down there, Willow." Dane held out a hand for a high five. "I can feel it."

And, she was alone.

She hadn't expected to be scared, but the fear was instant. Taking out her phone, she checked the battery life and made sure the ringer was on and turned up fully. Then, she took the fake scooter and tossed it with the hang bar.

Liam treaded water just under the surface and blew a kiss to her.

The water was crystal clear and as calm as a manatee strolling the shoreline. Liam held the fake scooter in front of him like it was real, except for the part where he wasn't moving fast and still pumping his fins. The blades turned as he swam, helping facilitate the façade.

Visibility was incredible. He wondered if it made the wildlife seem more plentiful, or if they truly were all out celebrating the end of Ernest. Did fish get cabin fever?

The only humans he spotted around him were Zoe and Dane. Even though he'd jumped first, he took caboose on the way to the under under.

A pod of devil rays swam close. A bull shark came at them. It was a nonaggressive swim and seemed not to notice the three humans carrying empty scooters.

The palm tree cavern came into view, and he'd be damned if he didn't see the resemblance to an actual palm tree at this angle. A small moray eel swam out of the base of it, reminding Liam the fate of this trip relied on a much larger and terrifying eel.

He spotted the cavern this time. Zoe was right. The absence of churning particles helped it appear like a magic trick.

The wet uncharted, maybe. The scene of a murder for sure.

His legs pumped faster to keep up with his friends, his someday sister and brother-in-law. His mind thrust back to Willow. Leaving her alone was one of the hardest things he'd done in a long time. Making faces to reassure her harder yet.

A handful of saucers above caught his eye. He crept up to Zoe and Dane and tapped them on the shoulder, one at a time. Pointing up, they all watched six tiny sea turtle hatchlings swim close to the surface, their little legs visible in the calm, clear waters.

Zoe held up the palm of her hand as a signal to wait, then pointed two fingers at her eyes for them to watch, before jutting a pointed finger toward the cavern where she'd found Seth's remains. He understood what he was to do.

Taking her fake tank for her, Liam held one tank in each hand. He and Dane waited as Zoe swam forward, painfully slow.

Was it going to come out? Did the moray eel still live in the wet uncharted? Is the cave even the wet uncharted?

He maneuvered to the side a few feet to see if he could get a better view. The teeth seemed to glow in the dark. They emerged fast and were the only things visible for the first few moments. Zoe held out a hand, and Liam thought she might lose some fingers. Maybe all of them.

Then, came the eyes. Large, yellow, and lifeless. Zoe never flinched. Not even when the slimy thing darted straight toward her. It slid underneath her outstretched hand and paused like it appreciated the human contact.

Crunch time. Would it show them the way?

THIRTY-THREE

As Zoe said it would, the eel took a nosedive downward and seemed to disappear into the sea wall. There. Liam saw it. He knew right where to go and assumed Zoe and Dane saw the same thing.

He was no treasure hunter, but the bug bit him. He didn't signal Dane or check what Zoe was doing. He wasn't even scared of what the eel might do from another invasion on its privacy this close to the first one.

With the two scooters dragging to his sides, Liam dove for the spot he refused to take eyes from. He anchored the tanks between rocks and watched.

It was as if the spot might disappear if he took his eyes from it. He saw nothing but wall. No opening, no shadow where a crevasse might be, but that eel went somewhere.

Rows of teeth and dead, yellow eyes be damned, he ran his fingers over the spot and found a void, an opening. His adrenaline pumped, causing him to consciously and forcibly regulate his breathing.

He had to lie sideways to get a look inside. It was pitch black. Of course, it was. He had to keep his head. He was smarter than this.

Releasing the flashlight from his belt, he noted movement from his side. Zoe and Dane held hands as they treaded water.

Smart. Flipping on the flashlight, he first pointed it next to the opening. The eyes and teeth seemed twice as large this close. He clasped his fingers around the flashlight, expecting the eel to rush him, but it didn't. It tucked back in the crevasse like a rock in a slingshot, waiting to spring.

Around the enormous slithering body, he saw green and red. Giant eel be damned. As if the colors might get away, Liam stuck his head in the opening. It was as if time slowed. He directed the beam of light over the surface.

Piles and piles of twisted jewel-covered metal were encased in black netting and tucked inside the crevasse. He didn't care if this was a wet uncharted or an under under. This was like a drug.

It wasn't what he saw in the pictures; this was more. So much more. Barnacles and encrusted silt couldn't hide the rubies that circled the gold plates or stems of the silver goblets that were circled with emeralds.

He turned to share his excitement with Dane and Zoe only to find a diver behind each with knives inches from their necks. The lack of sound when diving underwater had never been more unnerving. Clasping the flashlight, he instinctively held his arms out, palms down, as if he was in a high school hallway trying to calm a few volatile boys from losing their cool.

He had to rely on vision and touch. A stalemate ensued long enough for him to glance around for more divers, wondering how they were found, when they were found. Did Willow know? Was she safe?

He tried not to move as the divers slowly pumped their fins toward him, their bodies pressed against Zoe and Dane and the knives dangerously close to his friends' air hoses.

Their masks had some kind of reflective film keeping Liam from identifying them. One diver had to be male. He was tall and slender. Rain gear guy? The other curvy and small. Female.

Slowly, Liam lifted one hand as if in surrender as he lowered the other, then waved the flashlight around the opening of the under

under. The eel took the bait and jutted out, mouth open. Darting at the intruders, the female dropped her knife.

Zoe maneuvered away as the male punctured a hole in Dane's air hose.

A cloud of air bubbles caused everything to blur in a mass of confusion.

The bubbles turned pink, then red. A shape darted at Liam from the angry, red cloud. Zoe.

Two large bodies twisted and wrestled, making Zoe swim back toward the fight. Dropping the flashlight, Liam reached and grabbed one of her feet with both hands.

The woman floated away from the wrestling men, clasping her side as blood oozed between her fingers. She drifted closer, and Liam recognized her. He caught her with both arms as Zoe got away, and the male intruder darted for the surface. The bubbles from Dane's air tank slowed to a trickle.

Willow.

Liam handed the woman to Zoe and swam after the male.

His Willow. His life.

The male took to the surface too fast but, more importantly, away from the Sun Trips boat. Liam's autopilot halted him at the first safety stop. He checked his watch, spewing obscenities in his head at the wait. He would be no good to Willow with the bends.

Damn it, through the waves, he willed her to call Matt. The bottom of the boat was visible. He wanted her to look over the edge and feared she would all at the same time.

Would the man have someone to man his boat too? Of course, he would. Why did Liam leave Willow alone?

A trail of blood seeped from the diver's right thigh. The man was going to have the bends and stitches. Matt could watch for this in emergency rooms. Investigate the remaining original divers from Seth's last dive—

Zoe and Dane. Checking below, he spotted them as they came toward him, Dane sucking on his backup regulator and Zoe hanging onto Miriam. Movement from beyond them caught his eye. Men. Several of them. He recognized the gear. Coast Guard. How?

Beams from flashlights darted around the floor of the Gulf.

Frustrated beyond anything he could remember, he checked the time for this safety stop. Darting to the last stop, he could see the Sun Trips boat so clearly, it seemed like he could reach out and touch it.

———————

The splash and his voice seemed to happen at the same time.

"Willow, are you okay?"

The tone of Liam's voice sent pin needles through her. Pulling starboard, she spotted him but didn't understand. Where was the fake scooter? Why was there blood? "Yes, why?"

Keeping him in her sight, she craned her head all around. Boats dotted the Gulf. Some moving, some anchored. She saw them before she heard them.

Coast Guard boats, four of them, flew across the Gulf and all directed at her. Looking over the edge again, she noted Zoe and Dane had joined Liam. They didn't have their fake tanks, either. They did have a woman.

The woman may have used a reflective face mask, but Willow would recognize Miriam Roberts anywhere. She was bleeding.

The diving group. She knew the emergency code, but she was no instructor or captain or even assistant. The extinguisher had to be wrong, but it would have to do. She banged it against the swim step. One long and two shorts. She did it twice through, then waited and banged it out twice more.

The boats came close enough that she was able to make out Matt in the bow of the one in the lead.

She leaned over the edge again. "What happened down there?"

Matt made it to her before they could answer. "Willow," he called from the boat. "Are you okay?"

She nodded, although wanted to know why everyone was asking her that.

"Are you alone?"

She pointed down.

He looked over the bow as the Coast Guard boat headed around the stern.

"Did Raine call you?" Willow yelled to him before the four in the water would become visible.

He laughed. It wasn't the gentle laugh she was accustomed to. It was an angry laugh. Sarcastic, even.

Standing tall, she inhaled deeply and closed her eyes. She had to center herself and her spirit. As far as she knew, everyone she loved was okay. Anything else was water under the bridge.

"Willow," Matt barked.

Her eyes flew open.

"How many are down there?"

"Nine." Plus Miriam, apparently. "Ten."

He rolled his eyes. "Who?"

"Six divers, Dane, Zoe, Miriam, and Liam."

"You used divers as a cover?"

It sounded so much worse when he put it that way.

"Willow," Liam said. "Take my flippers."

The most inappropriate smile spread over her face.

That was, until she saw his expression.

"What happened?" she repeated.

He nodded as she took his fins. He eyed the Coast Guard as the boat approached.

"It's bad," she said.

He nodded again and climbed the ladder.

Liam didn't ask her why Matt was there. Not with words anyway. "Matt," she said loudly as a way to let him know she was as much in the dark as he was. "What brings you out here?" she yelled her crew would become visible.

"What brings me—?" he started, then stopped and ran his hand along the back of his neck.

She spotted the damage to Dane's air hose.

The Coast Guardsman jumped in after Miriam.

Dane and Liam looked at each other with a sadness that sent her back to panic.

"I've got men down there, so no more hiding your shit from me."

Liam hoisted into the boat and sat. Plopping his forearms on his knees, he took a deep breath. "Miriam Roberts, Chief. She was with one other diver that we know of, male. They attacked us. There was a fight. The man got away."

The Coast Guardsman in the water lifted Miriam as another pulled her onto the Coast Guard platform.

Liam seemed to look through Willow as he added, "There's also a ton of treasure your guys won't find, but the man with Miriam who attacked us will."

A ton of treasure? An instant war erupted in Willow's head. Another person she loved was stabbed for Luciana's treasure. But, treasure? Was this why Miriam was down there?

Matt turned and had a quiet conversation with the Coast Guardsman behind him.

Willow mouthed the word, 'Treasure,' to Liam. His eyes were bright as he nodded.

"Tell my man, here," Matt said. "Show him on the map. You three aren't going anywhere."

THIRTY-FOUR

L iam sat at the end of the long table. They were all there, everyone except Harmony since there was no one else to take care of Chloe on this short of notice. It was like waiting in the principal's office.

"You didn't get any pictures?" Henry asked.

"I didn't even have a camera," Liam confessed.

Henry nodded.

"Miriam Roberts," Liam said. "What was all that about?"

Henry said, "I'm sure Chief Osborne will get to the bottom of that."

"You sure you didn't recognize the dude?" Dane asked.

Liam shook his head. "No, but he sure looked a lot like the same build as the man in the rain gear who took my laptop."

"Do you think Matt has cameras or bugs in here?" Raine asked.

"I wouldn't put it past him," Liam said. "He knew we were out there somehow."

Dane asked, "Are you sure it wasn't the same treasure as in Seth's pictures?"

Liam took a deep breath and nodded. "Positive." He so understood the drug that was treasure hunting now. "Same kind of netting. Same kind of treasure, for that matter, but much, much more of it."

"And, it's all being hauled up by not Clearwaters," Willow said.

"But, Clearwaters are the ones who found it. Or at least a Corbin, a Clearwater, and a Morrison," Dane said. "And, a Martinez in the boat. No one can change that." He slid his hand over and laced fingers with Zoe on the table.

"Hey," Raine said. "We were the distraction, albeit a bad one. We didn't even fool the cop."

"Yeah, and how did he know—" Zoe began as Matt barged through the door.

"Because he's not stupid," he said and shut the door behind him. "You left a trail a mile wide."

He sat with them instead of at the head of the table or the dry erase board. Liam knew this tactic. Make the kids comfortably uncomfortable.

"Are you charging us with something?" Raine asked. "'Cause I really need a shower and have an island to check on."

Matt opened his mouth and shut it again. His brows lowered and he shook his head. "I'll need statements from each of you, even the distraction," he said, using quotations around the last word.

Maybe he did have hidden cameras.

"Dane?"

"Here." Dane raised his hand and smiled.

"Are you sure you're not hurt?"

"Very sure."

"I'd like you to get checked out anyway, and why are you smiling?"

"Miriam's okay?"

"She'll live."

"Then, I'm smiling because, ya know, treasure. We discovered where Seth Clearwater— Should we be writing this down? Where Seth Clearwater hid Luciana Bezan's legendary dowry. How is the excavation?"

Matt nodded. "They've got more boats and people and historians and appraisers, journalists and museum admins out there than I knew existed."

Dane rubbed his hands together. "This means—" He looked around and dropped his shoulders. "That we should finish up here as quickly as possible."

"Get comfortable, Mr. Corbin." Matt stood at that. Liam understood this tactic as well and did as he was told, got comfortable. "Your little stunt may have been deceptive, stupid, and frankly, rude, but it wasn't illegal. You were, however, a victim of an attempt on your life, the life of your fiancée and employee, as well as the person who sank a knife into both perpetrators."

Dane held up a finger. "Miriam was not me, I swear. That had to be the dude."

"We'll get through all of that, which is why you need to get comfortable. For now, I need each of you to know this." He stood tall at the end of the table. "You have a reception area full of people who want to interview and take your pictures. So, get your combs out."

Willow mouthed the word, 'Combs,' to Zoe.

Zoe shrugged.

"The doctor wants Miriam to rest for twenty-four hours before I question her. I told him he could have six to get her stitched up and settled. I'm—with an emphasis on the I'm—going to find out where this partner is, how steeped in all of this she is, and although my time here may be short, who killed your brother." He looked to Henry. "And son."

"And friend," Dane added.

"And friend," Liam agreed.

"What if she doesn't talk?" Raine asked. "What if—?"

"Don't let perfect be the enemy of good, because this is good. We caught her red-handed. I have guys searching her apartment as we speak."

Liam hadn't thought of that. Smart.

"Congratulations on the treasure. I've arranged for you to be there for the viewing or cleaning or acknowledgements or whatever that's all about."

Dane lifted a finger. "That'd be—"

Liam gave him a swift elbow to the ribs.

"Oww," Dane whined but lowered his finger.

"Mr. Clearwater—" Matt began to say.

"Henry," Henry corrected.

"Mr. Clearwater," Matt said louder. "Raine and Willow," he continued. "You are free to go deal with the mess in reception. I want you in here tomorrow at ten for your statements. Dane and Zoe, your statements are now."

"Each of you," he said and pointed a finger around the room. "Be warned—"

Raine yawned. Loudly.

Matt dropped his eyelids to half open and inhaled deeply. "I am in charge of this investigation. Interfere again and I'll have you arrested."

His face softened considerably before he said, "Now, go. You have a lot to celebrate. I'll have Dane and Zoe to you when I can."

Liam unlocked the front door for her. It was 4 a.m., almost time for the call from her section beach walker and she was just getting home.

Dragging her feet over the threshold, she grumbled, "We had double the number I had planned for. And, I planned for double what I thought."

"I'm not sure I followed all of that, but you definitely had a lot."

His long fingers rested on her lower back, making her forget what they were talking about.

"Finding Luciana's dowry the week before the grand opening to Luciana's probably helped those numbers," he said.

Oh right. Her pub. "Whether it's Luciana's dowry is still under investigation." That was what the Smithsonian people said anyway.

"A formality," he said, traveling his long fingers around her waist and holding her up. What were they talking about again?

"Chloe is gone for the night."

She knew he knew this. It was her grand opening night, so her parents had kept her for a sleepover. His feet stopped in their tracks regardless.

"Oh." His voice cracked at the single word.

She rotated around to face him fully. "We celebrated finding the treasure." She lifted on her toes to kiss him.

His eyes searched the room like he might find what to do out there.

Slipping her fingers inside the waist of his jeans, she said, "We haven't celebrated us."

"Because Chloe, but of course she's not, are you sure? I thought maybe——"

She ripped the Velcro from her sling.

"Oh. Wait. Should you——?"

His honesty was insanely sexy. She simply couldn't take it anymore. "I should," she said and lifted her shirt over her head. "We should."

His eyes dropped to her lips. His expression morphed into something she'd never seen in him before.

"Uh-oh——" she began to say, but he covered her mouth with his. His was needy and assertive. He took her face in his hands, tilted her head and pulled her in.

Their lips and tongues moved in a desperate dance as their feet turned and tripped on the way to the bedroom. Her bedroom. Their bedroom.

Her skin bubbled with anticipation like a turtle nest exploding after a hot summer. They stood next to the bed, and his lips moved from her mouth down her jaw and over her neck. "Will you say it?"

He pulled back and smiled at her. "My Willow," he said and lowered her to the bed. "My life."

He was careful, yet uninhibited; gentle, yet sexy. His long fingers seemed like they were everywhere, exploring, learning.

Her painfully honest and cautious Liam flipped hooks and buttons with ease, maneuvered clothing without ever risking her shoulder or head. When he reached for his own, she put a hand over his.

227

His brown eyes lifted to hers. She bit her bottom lip and said, "Let me."

His long arm drew lines from the back of her neck, down her spine, and over her backside before grabbing hold of her thigh. Just as he found her, she dug her fingertips into his shoulders.

This was her love, her forever. She was safe and adored. Her head spun over the first peak. Her body trembled, and she pressed her forehead into his shoulder. "Don't stop," she whispered as she fell down the other side of the mountain and time slowed.

With her good arm, she tugged his arm to crawl under him.

He shook his head and covered her mouth with his, burying her with everything that was him and taking her places she never thought she could go.

He seemed to sense when she was spent to the point of desperate and crawled into her. Her heart exploded with the rest of her as they joined. Two people joined in time who knew what their future held and that it was together.

The last push sent her over with him, their bodies draped in love and promises.

He fell back on the pillow as his chest heaved in and out. "I might have been," he said between gasps, "pent up."

She lifted her elbow to get a better look at his face. He seemed lighter, freer somehow. "I like pent up you."

Lifting a single brow, he turned his eyes to her.

"Not!" she said louder than she meant to. "That I am hoping you will be pent up again anytime soon." She kissed his shoulder, then rested her chin on his chest. "Or, ever."

Taking one last, deep breath, he blew it out as he ran his thumb over her scar. She could see the familiar war that went on in his head.

"You're here," she whispered.

The weight lifted, and he smiled her favorite smile. "Always."

THIRTY-FIVE

W illow stood next to Chloe at the end of the aisle. Her daughter's little fingers clasped the white wicker basket filled with yellow daisy petals.

Every chair was filled with friends and family and dozens more stood at the fringes. Knowing she had bucked tradition, Zoe planned on a few dozen. She hadn't offered a sit-down-dinner. No live band or dancing. A simple ceremony, a sacrament of commitment 'til death do them part.

Those few dozen folding chairs alone had bumped Zoe over her two thousand-dollar budget limit.

Death. Willow wondered if she'd feel sadness this day, but there was none. Jacob would forever be in her heart. Her love for him would not be matched or replaced. Liam stood on the other side of Chloe and waited for their turn to march down the aisle behind Raine and Matt. Without breaking her wedding procession smile, she reached behind Chloe and linked the ends of her fingers with him. It was hard to pose for the best photographer on the island instead of ogle at him in his beige slacks and short-sleeved, buttoned-down shirt and tie. Zoe had put some kind of product in his hair and his Florida August tan sent flutters through her heart.

His long fingers covered hers and squeezed. This new love would also never be matched or replaced. Completely different, yet just as wonderful.

The morning was warm and the Gulf breeze steady. She wanted to turn around and gawk at her stunning baby sister, but instead she maintained her poise and enjoyed the single guitar and the familiar faces.

Most bent their heads together in paired whispers. Some craned their heads around to admire the lineup.

Dane's parents went first. They strolled arm-in-arm over the sand. Coming from Alaska, Willow wondered what would be going through their minds at that moment.

Her mother and father were next. She in her billowy yellow dress and he as the most handsome grandpa on the planet.

It was the second time she had seen Raine in a dress, and since she was so much shorter than Zoe and Willow, the photographer made her wear heels. Dark, spiraling curls rested on her shoulders, random pieces tied high with baby's breath. The wide, lace-covered shoulder straps rested on her tan shoulders, making her look like an island goddess, yet neither of them could compare to Zoe.

Matt stepped next to Raine and held out his arm. She took it gracefully, and Willow gave her kudos for that. She didn't do too badly in her heels over the sand, and Willow gave her major kudos for it.

Whispering from the corner of her mouth, Willow said to Chloe, "Are you going to be okay?"

Chloe nodded several times, short and fast.

"You can walk with us, if you need to."

"Mom," Chloe whispered like an annoyed teenager.

Releasing their fingers, she and Liam left Chloe with Zoe. She slid her hand up Liam's arm and snaked it around his forearm. Walking like this with him stung the backs of her eyes and made everything right in the world. The unresolved murder of her brother. The fate of the Luciana Bezan treasure. Finding the rest of it. Walking with him down the aisle of a wedding ceremony was as natural as the rising sun.

Dane stood rocking on the balls of his feet. She'd never seen him dressed up. With slicked back hair, he stood with his hands folded in front of him. His smile was as big as Alaska.

She and Liam passed Dane's parents, with front row seats next to Zoe's mother and father. Each smiled while dabbing tissues to their cheeks.

Liam squeezed her fingers before letting go. She took her place next to Raine and turned. A chorus of "Awws" reacted to Willow's baby girl as she smiled and sprinkled flower petals like a pro.

Looking out over the crowd, she spotted the Sun Trips employees, possibly every single one of the eighty-eight Turtle Watch volunteers as well as what her mother referred to as her Stitch and Bitch sewing club.

Photographer or not, Willow took a moment to close her eyes tight. These people had been invited to share in fellowship and celebration at Luciana's. What if they all showed up? It did nothing to worry about it, so she opened her eyes and smiled over the crowd.

Zoe stood at the end. Her tea-length lace skirt brushed her ankles. The matching top was sleeveless and simple and Zoe. She stepped forward with the adorable flat white sandals she'd found in her closet. Ringlets of blonde curls danced around her face.

She stepped to the pastor and Dane took a step to her. Laughter covered the crowd as the pastor made a joke that it wasn't his turn yet.

The man in black offered some words of welcome before asking who gave this woman to be married to this man.

Their father answered and kissed her on the cheek before taking a seat as the guitarist sang, asking if loving is the answer, then who's the giving for.

Willow glanced over to who her giving was for. Liam was staring at her. His expression caused that familiar heat to start at her neck and threaten to cover her face. He winked and made her heart fall out of her chest.

Glancing from person to person in this group of people she dearly loved, she pulled Chloe closer and realized something. The turtle and the beach they came to nest their young may be her sanctuary, but not her peace. The peace was in her people, flaws and all.

And, although a killer may be standing somewhere among them, they may falter, but they would not fall.

"Dane and Zoe," the pastor began, "the promise you enter into today…"

ISLAND REVEAL

ISLAND ESCAPE SERIES, BOOK 3

Police Chief, Matt Osborne, stood with his mouth open. He watched as Ibis Island's lead sea turtle conservationist dove in the Gulf wearing her bridesmaid dress. On the bride's wedding day. Her arms broke through the waves. Damn, she was fast.

The only female in a group of four bystanders gawked, not at Raine as she swam out to the distressed sea turtle, but at him. "Aren't you going in after her?"

How to explain to her that he would be more trouble than help. Raine wasn't the dainty, organic conservationist type. She was introverted, bitchy, and might just be carrying. Nonetheless, he should have been keeping an eye on the lacey blue dress moving across the waves but instead found his interest in what was around the gawking woman's neck. "Nah. She's got this," he answered. It was a coin necklace encased in yellow gold. It seemed ancient.

A man with short, salt and pepper hair, who stood closest to the woman yelled, "Whoa! She got him! She's coming with the turtle!"

"Atocha," the woman said.

Looking up to her eyes, he lifted his brows.

"My necklace. At least I hope that's what you're staring at. It's booty from the famous Atocha Shipwreck. Surely, you've heard of it."

No time to explain his role as island chief was both interim and new, but he did have a murderous treasure hunter to find and had enough detective experience to understand that murderous thieves everywhere generally had a need to show off their 'booty' as the woman called it.

Slipping off his shoes, he spoke into his walkie. "Confirmed sea turtle, over."

Dispatch responded, "Ten-four."

Even though the body reported floating in the Gulf turned out to be of the sea turtle variety rather than the human kind, Matt decided to stick around. He stuffed his socks in his shoes and rolled up his dress pants. Something he noted the others on the beach did ahead of time. So much to learn.

"Ohs and ahs," resounded as Raine pushed the biggest sea creature he'd ever seen into shallow water.

When she stood, his breath caught. Her back was to him. The light blue dress clung to her. Not dainty at all. She was powerful and incredible.

The male in the group waded in.

Raine panted. "Take that side?"

Matt followed.

"Don't need you, Chief," she barked.

If he was going to be police chief, even in an interim role, he was going to have to work on their tumultuous relationship. Ignoring the jab, he stepped in front of her and grabbed the other side of the shell. The veins in his forehead almost exploded from the weight, but he and the man pulled it out of the water regardless.

Glancing over his shoulder, he found her collapsed, sitting on the backs of her heels, and clutching her thighs. Her chest heaved and her chin dug into her neck. The white flowers in her hair were gone and the dark, wet strands fell around and concealed her face.

He wasn't distracted by the wet dress anymore or her smartass dismissal. He wanted to pick her up and hold her. He knew better than to try.

An orange fishing line wrapped around the creature's front flipper and the head. Strangled? Drown? It was all senseless. "Thank you," he said to the man and held out his hand.

The man took it, shook, and nodded.

A solemn stretch of deafening silence was broken only by the steady crash of waves as they rushed in and sunk Raine's knees deeper in the sand.

She brushed the back of her forearm over her nose, sniffed loudly, then lifted her chin. One foot, then the other, she stood and rolled her shoulders as she marched with purpose to a cinch sac he hadn't noticed before.

Pulling it open, she shoved in her arm and came out holding a large tape measure. She seemed to try and stick it to her belt loop before noting she didn't have one and, instead, shoved it under an arm.

As she gathered the rest of whatever it was she was gathering, he looked over the turtle. The flippers were enormous, its head cocked unnaturally from the tightness of the fishing line. He didn't care if it was stupid, it bothered him. He took out the Swiss Army knife from his pocket and started working at it.

Raine pecked away at a tablet, then measured the beast from head to tail. It had to be at least a yard long. The handful of barnacles couldn't cover the incredible markings on the brown shell.

He asked, "What now?" as he cut piece after piece of the orange line.

"I measure, record, and report. Walter will come by and scoop him up."

He would find out who Walter was later. For now, he asked the more pertinent question. "Him?"

"Big tail."

It was enormous. Gross, really. "Scoop him up and put him where?"

Raine took a deep breath. "New construction hole, maybe. It's nature," she said matter-of-factly as if she hadn't just been close to losing it.

There was nothing natural about that fishing line. He didn't mention it, just kept cutting.

"Don't you need to do an autopsy or something?" asked the necklace woman.

"Laparoscopy, and no," she said as she did the same measuring for the width. "That will just piss me off."

"Piss you off?" Matt asked.

This time she stopped and tilted her neck until it cracked. "Eighty-five percent of sea turtles have plastic in their digestive tracts. I hate plastic. Why are you still here?" she growled and pecked at the tablet.

He knew she wasn't talking to the bystanders.

"My job?" he said as he sliced through the line.

"This," she said as she measured the gross tail. "Is my job. Finding out who killed my brother is yours."

Taking another glance at the necklace, he squinted and said, "Oh, I will all right." He sensed movement under his knife and brought his head closer to the beast. A flipper moved. "It moved," Matt yelled and jumped back, landing on his butt. "It moved. It moved."

Available in eBook and Paperback From Your Favorite Online Retailer or Bookstore

ALSO BY R.T. WOLFE

The Island Escape Series

Island Secrets

Island Pursuit

Island Reveal

The Nickie Savage Series

Savage Echoes

Savage Rendezvous

Savage Deception

Savage Disclosure

Savage Betrayal

Savage Alliance

The Black Creek Series

Black Creek Burning

Flying in Shadows

Dark Vengeance

ABOUT THE AUTHOR

R.T. was born and raised in the beautiful Midwest, the youngest of six ornery children. She married at a young age and began her family shortly after. With three amazing small boys, life was a whirlwind of flipping houses and working two jobs in between swim lessons and Candyland. Now that her boys are nearly grown, R.T. spends much of her time writing and on the road traveling from one sporting event to another serving as mom and cheerleader. She works to assist several non-profit organizations that have supported her books and to promote the work they do for those who cannot help themselves.

WWW.RTWOLFE.COM

facebook.com/rtwolfe2012

twitter.com/rt_wolfe